DR. PERFECT

LOUISE BAY

Published by Louise Bay 2023

ISBN – 978-1-910747-81-0

BOOKS BY LOUISE BAY

The Doctors Series

Dr. Off Limits

Dr. Perfect

Dr. CEO

Dr. Fake Fiancé

The Mister Series

Mr. Mayfair

Mr. Knightsbridge

Mr. Smithfield

Mr. Park Lane

Mr. Bloomsbury

Mr. Notting Hill

The Christmas Collection

The 14 Days of Christmas

The Player Series

International Player

Private Player

Dr. Off Limits

Standalones

Hollywood Scandal

Love Unexpected

Hopeful

The Empire State Series

Gentleman Series

The Wrong Gentleman

The Ruthless Gentleman

The Royals Series

The Earl of London

The British Knight

Duke of Manhattan

Park Avenue Prince

King of Wall Street

The Nights Series

Indigo Nights

Promised Nights

Parisian Nights

Faithful

Sign up to the Louise Bay mailing list at
www.louisebay/mailinglist

Read more at www.louisebay.com

ONE

Ellie

I pull my collar up, trying to keep the fog from curling down my neck, and step up to the large black door on Wimpole Street. It feels like I'm the first victim in a horror movie—the one that sets the scene for the real terror that's about to be unleashed on the female lead the audience actually cares about. Shivering, I make a mental note to watch something starring Reese Witherspoon or Sandra Bullock when I get home. I've got to stop with the Netflix Harlan Coben adaptations. I pull out my phone, scrolling to the last email I had from my new boss, Dr. Zachary Cove. As instructed, I press the buzzer for Dr. Williams.

The buzzer clicks but no one says anything.

"Hello?" I call.

The catch releases and my heart begins to race. I try and channel "Sandra Bullock in *The Proposal*" vibes and shrug off the "Sandra Bullock in *The Net*" vibes. I take a deep breath and push the door open.

It's just fog.

It's no more menacing than rain. It doesn't mean anything. Just my likely imminent murder—no biggie.

The hallway floor is beaten-up parquet, which probably looked beautiful at one point and could again if someone put in some effort. I step inside, letting the door close behind me, and don't try to muffle the clip-clop of my heels echoing up the stairs to the first floor. My new job is to sit behind a desk in a doctor's waiting room, answering the phone, arranging appointments, checking in new patients, typing dictation, and doing any other administrative tasks required to run a doctor's private practice who will be in the practice two days a week. It's the first position I've managed to get an interview for that wasn't minimum wage. With my experience limited to managing Shane's career, I'm grateful for any job at all. According to my meticulous calculations, this job pays me enough to reach my savings goals in just nineteen months—and that makes it a job I want to keep. Whatever they want me to do, I don't care. A couple of weeks ago, I saw a flyer attached to a lamppost offering part-time work. It said in big bold letters that it was excellent pay, so I called. Turns out, I do have my limitations and drug trafficking is where I draw the line. But if it's legal and pays well, I'll do it.

As the email promised, the second door off the hallway at the top of the stairs has a see-through acrylic sign that reads "Dr. Cove" in plain black font, and "Gastroenterologist" in smaller block capital letters below. I sigh with relief and my shoulders drop as I confirm I'm in the right place.

I've never met my boss. I've spoken to him over the phone, but the agency said it was normal to just turn up for a temporary position without any kind of in-person interview. Though Dr. Cove mentioned the position has the potential to turn permanent, I only need it to last nineteen months; twenty-one max, accounting for unforeseen expenses. If I've done my sums right—and I have, because that's all I've done since I got this job on Monday—nineteen months of this paycheck will mean I've saved enough money to get on with my life. Having made the terrible decision ten years ago to abandon university to manage my ex-boyfriend's burgeoning Speedway career full-time, I have no real qualifications, and my work experience apparently doesn't count for much. There's a lot of intangible, difficult-to-explain stuff that goes into "managing" someone, which I only discovered while trying to put together my resume for the first time. And then of course I don't have any references because my previous boss is also my ex-boyfriend, and I'd rather stand naked, astride a sandwich board, in the middle of Oxford Circus, than ask him for anything.

I push my past to the back of my mind and open the door to the office. In his last email, Dr. Cove said he would be in around ten and I should "settle in" beforehand.

The room is bright, which takes me by surprise. Maybe arriving in the fog meant I expected a windowless space, empty apart from a vintage operating table and a tray of knives. I seem to have emerged from my horror flick into an unremarkable waiting room. It's at the front of a Georgian townhouse, with three large sash windows looking over the street. It's not a big room. The floor has obviously been divided up between different doctors; a stud wall placed in the middle of this room means the eight chairs and desk make the space look a little cramped. I've never been to a private doctor before, but I expected it to be a bit...smarter and more glamorous. I shrug off my bag and put it on my desk, but I leave my coat on. It's cold. I root around by the Victorian-style radiator under the window and find a knob.

It starts to knock when I twist it. I take it as a sign it's heating up. I do the same with the radiator behind my desk.

Glancing around the room, it's clear the arrangement would be better with one less chair and my desk turned to face the window. I'll suggest it to Dr. Cove when he arrives.

There's a small table piled with magazines in the corner, with an overgrown palm plant next to it, which looks like it's providing shade to *Country Living* and—I start to flick through the magazines—*Vogue Australia*, November 2005. I think we can do better than that.

I take a seat at my desk chair and spin 360 degrees. As Shane's manager, I always worked out of our kitchen. I've never had a proper office chair. The desk drawers are empty apart from a one-pence piece and a paperclip. There's no computer, nothing. Not a notepad, pen, or sticky note. I have my usual notepad and pen in my bag, thank goodness. There's only one thing better than a freshly baked apple pie and that's good stationery.

I stand and take two steps to the door in the stud wall. This must be the room where Dr. Cove sees his patients. It's locked.

How am I going to "settle in"? There's really nothing to do. I wander over to the windows, which could stand a good clean. Maybe I can find some cleaning materials for communal use.

I head out of the office to explore. All the other doors on this floor are closed and I can't hear anything, even when I press my ear to the one directly opposite the stairs. Someone let me in. Surely they're still in the building.

I'm halfway up the second flight of stairs when someone shouts, "Hello?"

"Hi," I reply and then a woman with black hair and a very severe fringe peers over the banister. "Ellie Frost?"

I smile. Someone is expecting me. "Yes. I'm Dr. Cove's new assistant."

"Yes, Dr. Cove." She makes a sound like she's savoring a mouthful of chocolate. "It's his first day, but I've looked him up."

Why didn't I think of that? Probably because I was Googling, *what do doctor's assistants do?* The job description hadn't been very specific.

"Come up. The kitchen's up here."

She disappears and I head upstairs to find her.

As I reach the top of the stairs, a waving hand appears through the doorway farther up the landing. "In here."

I head towards the hand and find her in a tiny kitchen, just big enough for two. She's wearing bright red lipstick I could never pull off, which contrasts beautifully with her black hair and snow-white skin.

"I'm Jen. You're Ellie. I'll show you around—not that there's much to find. First stop, *this* is where it all happens. I know it's like a cupboard, but this place is pretty much soundproof if you close the door. Any time you need to blow off steam or vent, come in here. Don't, under any circumstances, use the loos. There are always patients in there. I don't know if they lie in wait, but I've been caught out so many times complaining about Dr. Newman." She sighs like she should be able to complain about her boss anywhere she likes. I instantly warm to her. "Here is the place to come. Plus, there's usually one of us girls to vent to. We basically tag team our meltdowns."

She's making it sound like we're working for Elon Musk or something. How bad could these doctors be?

"I'm hoping Dr. Cove will be nice to work for. I've not met him—"

She puts her palm up to face me, stopping me in my

tracks. "He's a doctor. Therefore he'll be difficult to work for. It's a given. At least he's only in two days a week. They all think they're God, and since you haven't got a medical degree, he'll assume you haven't got two brain cells to rub together. They're all the same in my experience."

"Have you worked here long?"

She shrugs. "Two years for Dr. Newman. Before that, I was with Dr. Scalding on Harley Street."

"And this is Dr. Cove's first private practice?" I ask.

"Yes, he's a newbie. Which means he's young." She winks at me like I'm in on her secret, but newsflash—I'm not. "Most of them start out at his age. They make consultant and then they start doing a couple of days in private practice."

"For the money?" I ask.

"Yeah, mainly, but some of them like the depth of patient contact they compared to being in a hospital where they're seeing loads more people, each for less time. And there's less admin involved, because we get paid to handle it."

"I'm only here as a temp," I offer. "Hoping to stay a while." Or at least as long as it takes to get my money together for Le Cordon Bleu.

She shrugs. "These doctors are so crap at their admin, they'll either forget to pay you or forget to fire you."

My heart settles in my stomach. Forget to pay me? "Can I skip the first option and take the second?"

"Absolutely."

I'm going to have to be such an incredible assistant, he's not going to be able to bear the thought of life without me. He'll be so terrified of me leaving, he'll be overpaying me, if anything. If I can manage Shane's Speedway career, I can manage the diary of a new consultant, who is only seeing patients two days a week, and encourage him to pay me on time. Anything has to be easier than trying to get Shane to do things he didn't want to do that were good for his career, like not calling all women he came across "sweetheart." And there was the Twitter incident where he retweeted a GIF from @womenshouldnotvote.

"Thanks for the heads-up. I'll have to make sure I'm unforgettable."

"That's the spirit," she says. "As long as you don't take their moods and bad manners personally, you're going to be great."

I smile. "Thanks. You said you looked up Dr. Cove. Anything I should know?"

"Nothing apart from the obvious. No scandals. No GMC investigations." She pulls open the door. "Come on, I'll show you where the loos are."

Apart from the obvious? I really should have looked him up myself.

"Actually, I'm going to take some kitchen roll, and—" I open the kitchen cupboards one after another until I come across some glass cleaner. "And this. The windows are a little mucky." I make a mental note to bring down some water for Pamela the Palm.

"We have a cleaning service."

"It's fine. It's not like I'm busy. And I need to make myself unforgettable. Remember?"

I follow Jen out of the tiny kitchen and up the corridor. "You have a water dispenser in there, don't you? But no coffee. It's not a huge deal, especially as Dr. Cove is just starting out, but at some point, he needs to invest in a coffee machine."

I nod, taking it in. Maybe I'll get a budget to manage eventually.

"It took Dr. Newman two years to get one of those little machines, but we got one a couple of months ago. Patients love it. It gives them something to focus on if he's running late."

"Do they run late a lot? Or wait for test results or..." I stop and realize I have no idea if patients will be waiting for test results. Did gastroenterologists use blood tests?

"All the time. Oh, and I set Dr. Cove up with TBTC, the bloods clinic further down Wimpole. Everyone uses it. If his patients need blood tests, that's where you'll send them."

"Thanks," I reply. "Anything else I should know? Even the obvious might not be so obvious to me." I'm desperate to know what's so *obvious* to her—both about the job, and Dr. Cove.

She points out the loos as we get to the bottom of the steps.

"I think that covers it, but I'm just here, next door to you if you need anything."

We stop outside the door.

"I don't suppose you know where I get a computer?"

She shakes her head. "Sorry, no. Maybe Dr. Cove will have you go and buy one. They're all pretty clueless when they start out. But we do have a number for computer support that all the doctors in the building can use."

That will be useful if and when I ever get a computer. Maybe Dr. Cove is one of those old-fashioned types who likes everything done on paper. God, I hope not.

"Okay, well, I'll get to cleaning windows and catch up later."

"Ciao." She blows me a kiss and I smile, like that's a normal thing for an almost-stranger to do.

I head back to the waiting room and begin to clean the

windows. I'm not going to start to rearrange things until I meet my new boss and establish what he's going to like and not like. I'm not upsetting the apple cart so early in the game. But no one can complain about clean windows.

I'm wearing a knee-length black skirt that's a little tight, but if I shimmy it up, I can take the large step onto one of the visitor chairs to reach the top of the windows. I'm seventy-eight percent sure that none of the pedestrians passing below can see my underwear—but it's mainly because seventy-eight percent of them won't be looking up.

The door to the waiting room bangs open and then, just like my brother did when my mum walked in on him going through the lingerie section of the Next website, I shriek and topple over.

The next thing I know, I open my eyes and stare up at a Greek god standing over me.

"What are you doing?" he asks.

I stare at the most perfect mouth I've ever seen. His lips are full and the color of ripe cherries, and his cupid's bow has peaks that would make Everest jealous. "I think I need mouth to mouth." The words are out before my brain can put all the pieces together and realize I'm probably talking to my boss.

"You were only out for a second. You need to sit up."

He's definitely not Prince Charming, because he doesn't even offer me a hand. I push myself up to a sitting position and reality hits me like a sledgehammer. My skirt is practically up around my ears. Great. I really hope this is Dr. Newman, come in to check on the palm plant, and not the new boss I'm trying to impress. Not only have I fallen on my head, I've also just shown Dr. Perfect Mouth my knickers. "I'm fine," I say.

"What were you doing up there?"

"Cleaning the windows. They were a bit grubby." I squint and try and figure out which part of my head is hurting.

He frowns. "Don't do it again. We have a cleaning service that does a lot of buildings around here. Get the number from Jen."

You're welcome, I don't say.

I scramble to my feet and he steps back as if he's expecting me to lunge at him. I've spent the last ten years in a relationship. If I'm ever ready to get back into dating, I probably will lunge inappropriately at men who I've just met—especially men as hot as this guy—but today's not that day. This is a guy I'm trying to impress. Not kiss. I think.

"You're Dr. Cove?" We're both assuming we know who each other is, but a formal introduction isn't a wild idea. "I'm Ellie."

"I bought you a laptop." He nods at a cellophaned box on my desk and I try and focus on what he's saying, rather than the scrape of stubble over his jaw. Once, after an argument with Shane, I spent an entire afternoon in a Google rabbit hole researching men's jaws. Apparently, a man's attractiveness has got a lot to do with his jaw. And what makes an attractive jaw is all in the length of the ramus and gonial angle. Dr. Cove has the longest ramus and most acute gonial angle I've ever seen—he's a walking textbook that proves the theory because *he's gorgeous.* So gorgeous that when he speaks, it's kind of annoying, because I just want to stare at his face. "Let's use Google calendars for appointments at the moment."

I swallow and look away, like his jaw is no big deal. "Okay."

I want to ask him if I should go to hospital, given that about nine seconds ago I was unconscious. Can I safely assume that because he's a doctor, he would say if I was in danger? How much do gastroenterologists know about head injuries?

"Oh, and don't go wandering off without telling me. I'll need to keep an eye on you for a few hours to make sure you're not concussed."

Before I have a chance to respond, he goes through the door in the partition wall and shuts it behind him.

Was that it? No setting out expectations for the role or even telling me what the week is likely to look like? I was so hypnotized by his jaw, I forgot to ask the most basic questions. I don't even know when the next patient is in.

Pulling my shoulders back, I shift my mindset. Willing myself to ignore Dr. Cove's looks and the fact that he's recently seen my knickers, and march across the room and knock on the door.

"Come in," he snaps.

The room is more barren than the waiting room with just a desk and a chair in front of an obscured Georgian window to the side and then an examination table, sink, and a couple of cupboards. He doesn't even have a palm plant.

"Could you tell me when you're expecting your next patient?" I ask, focusing on his eyes because they're not his hypnotizing jaw, but I'm caught off guard because his eyes are all blue, brooding intensity. Damn him and his gorgeousness. "Maybe we could have a sit-down to go through a few things?"

A tinny shriek echoes from his phone and I realize he's holding it in his hand. I've interrupted a call. I ball my hands into fists. I need to be killing it at this job—my entire future depends on it—and it's not going well.

"No patients booked in and I'll come out in due course. We can go through any questions."

I nod and back out of his office.

I need to regroup and get a strategy together for how to interact like a capable, proactive assistant, given I have a gorgeous boss with a snappish attitude.

Maybe he wouldn't mind wearing a paper bag over his head while I'm talking to him.

TWO

Zach

Something is off.

Even ignoring the fact that my only employee fell over and knocked herself out on her first day on the job, something's not right. Maybe it's just too quiet and I'm not used to it. An office on Wimpole Street is very different to a London hospital.

My phone buzzes and I pull it from my pocket.

I press accept and dump myself in the chair behind my new desk.

"How is it?" my mum asks.

"I just walked in," I reply.

"Are you excited?"

"I've only been here for five minutes." Fact is, I'm not excited. Maybe that's what's off. I'm starting my private practice, just like a lot of my colleagues who just became consultants. This is a chance for me to be out on my own, out from underneath all the paperwork and political bollocks of a hospital. It's a chance to make some real money and forge connections with my patients over the long term rather than seeing them for five minutes and then never again. I'm hoping this change will mean I can enjoy my job more.

But I'm not excited yet.

"How's your assistant? I can't believe you hired someone without meeting them."

"I spoke to her on the phone, and anyway, she's temporary." And available at short notice. Her CV was a little weird, but during the telephone conversation she'd seemed enthusiastic. One of us had to be.

My father bellows in the background.

"Okay, John," my mother says. "Your dad wants to know how you're marketing yourself. He saw an article about it in some magazine. I don't think you'll need it. People get to know who the good doctors are." There's a pause. "Have you done all the usual things though?"

She's presuming I know what the usual things are.

"You've let people know," she follows up. "Just colleagues at the hospital and friends from medical school. Those kinds of people."

That would be no.

"I'm in the midst of it." I swing my chair around and notice the whiteboard behind me. That might be useful. One by one, I open the three drawers in my desk. They're empty. We should get some stationery. "People at the hospital know. And some mates from med school."

"Have you got an email address and website?" she asks.

I suck in a breath. I haven't even thought about a website. "I'm going to have a meeting with my assistant when I get off the phone. I need her to do some research."

"Branding," my father shouts in the background. "He needs to brand himself."

"Don't listen to him," Mum says. "Just focus on getting

yourself settled. The work will come. You don't need to worry."

I'm not worried. That's part of the problem. Dad isn't wrong. I've seen other consultants launch themselves in the private sector with websites and logos and a pocket full of branded stress balls to give out. They'd all been more organized than me.

"Yeah. It's early days," I say.

"Have you gotten your insurer recognition through yet?"

I wince. I know enough to know that without the major medical insurers awarding you formal approval, their patients won't be allowed to see you. Without the insurer recognition, I have no practice. "Not yet. You know how these things take time." Given I've not yet sent off all the information to apply for recognition from the insurers, approval was unlikely to arrive. But that really should be top of the list, along with a website. And some whiteboard markers.

I can hear voices outside my office. I'm definitely not expecting patients. It's probably someone who's got the wrong office.

"Anyway, I'd better go," I say. "I'm meant to be having a meeting with my assistant."

"I'm proud of you, darling."

I nod. She says it all the time, to all of her sons. She wouldn't be half as proud if she knew how lax I've been about this new start.

I stand and move toward the door. The voices are getting louder. "Love you, Mum. I'll call you later if I can." I hang up and open the door. A clown carrying four helium balloons is demanding to see me.

Standard Thursday morning stuff.

"How can I help?" I ask, trying to stay neutral about the fact I'm addressing a *literal* clown.

"Are you Zach Cove?" He's got a broad cockney accent and I can't help but think that if this was a Harlan Coben thriller and I answered yes, he might pull out a gun and shoot me.

Here goes nothing. "Yes, I'm Dr. Cove."

"Finally," he says, exasperated.

"Congratulations. And celebrations." He starts to sing the Cliff Richard hit my grandmother sang at every opportunity and now my mother sings instead.

What did I do to deserve this?

He's holding four balloons. I hate all four of my brothers right now. I'm thinking this is Beau's idea, and that Nathan paid.

I stand there, allowing the clown-guy to do what he's been paid to do.

When he finishes, he looks at me and I look at him and then he hands me the four balloons—one for each of my siblings. They're star-shaped in different colors. "He said you'd know who it was from."

I nod and he shrugs before turning and leaving.

"Let's have that meeting," I say to Ellie, who's sitting behind her desk, staring at the door where the clown just exited. We might as well get some prep done. I head back into my office, the balloons bobbing and creaking behind me.

"Just so I can prepare myself, is that likely to happen again?" she asks as she comes in holding a pad and a pen. She's more attractive than I pictured her. She's got long brown hair tied up in a ponytail and bits at the side hanging loose. It's nice. Which is weird—not that her hair is weird. It's just been a while since I noticed a woman's hair.

"It's difficult to say." I've learned not to assume my brothers won't do something idiotic. It always comes back to bite me. I let go of the balloons and they pool on the ceiling.

"Is it?" she asks.

"Prepare for the unexpected," I say, like I'm some sort of sage Jedi master. I'm pretty sure there won't be much of anything unexpected in this job.

"Okay. Would you prefer me to wear a suit?" She takes a seat opposite my desk. "Or did you have a uniform in mind? I'm flexible."

I ignore the stirring in my trousers at the idea of her dressing as a French maid and doing flexible things in front of the window.

"Just dress smartly," I reply. Everywhere I turn, I realize not only have I not done the preparation I should have for this new chapter of my career, I've not even thought about what that preparation is. "At this stage, no uniform." Maybe further down the line, I would want my assistant in a uniform. Maybe not. I can't think.

"First thing, let's order some stationery." I lift my chin at the whiteboard. "Whiteboard pens would be good."

She draws her eyebrows together like she knows I clearly don't have a clue what I'm doing, but she notes it down anyway.

"And I need some business cards and letterhead." Anything else? "That kind of thing," I add in case I missed anything obvious.

"Yes. What would you like them to say? Is your clinic going to have a name or is it just you?"

"Just me," I say as if I'm sure. "Very simple branding."

"I notice you don't have a website. Is that something you're looking to get up and running?" she asks. "I could do some research and maybe get a few quotes."

"Yes. Good." She's one step ahead, which is reassuring and disconcerting at the same time.

"And you don't have any patients booked in yet?"

I shake my head. "Today's the first day. I need to get consultant recognition with the insurers. I won't get many patients before that."

She tilts her head to one side, revealing her long neck. "Hmmm, and you're super attractive. Have you thought about getting a public relations firm, or a manager? You could do television work. You know, be the in-house doctor on one of those morning shows."

She's running at a thousand miles an hour and I haven't even stood up yet. "I'm not interested in that kind of thing," I say.

Did I hear her say I'm super attractive?

"Or do you know any celebrities?" she asks. "I've done a bit of PR here and there and I could contact some people I know and get you some coverage if you're treating anyone famous."

"I'd have to check," I say, and I can't help the sarcastic tone in my voice. "But I'm pretty sure I owe my patients a duty of confidentiality—famous or not."

She laughs like I'm the one who's saying something idiotic. "I wouldn't give away names—just so we could tell people that you're a 'doctor to the stars.' You know, something like that. But then if you're not interested in the spotlight..."

"I'm not."

She nods and taps her pen against the notepad. "Have you started the consultant recognition stuff?" she asks. "I could help you with it."

"I'm—I think it's best if you get the computer set up. And if you're confident, maybe get some email addresses for each of us. Business cards and then a letter format that looks professional, I think that would be a good start." At least I should understand what consultant recognition involves before I delegate it.

"No problem," she says. "That will keep me busy for today. And of course I'll order some stationery."

I reach for my wallet. "You can take this credit card for expenses."

"Excellent," she says. "What about medical supplies. Do we need...gloves or anything?"

"The building supplies all that. Speak to Jen. I'm going to make some phone calls." I have no one to call. But I could research consultant recognition. And I want to scribble down some ideas that I've had about the cozy mystery I've been writing for the last decade. It's been a while since I've written anything substantial. I haven't even *tried* to write anything for a couple of months, but given I don't have any patients and I seem to have a competent assistant, for the first time in a long time, I have the opportunity to throw about some ideas. With or without whiteboard pens.

THREE

Ellie

I dust flour onto the work surface and set down my pastry.

"You really don't need to go to this much trouble," Cynthia says from where she's sitting on the barstool, glass of wine in hand, watching me and my pastry. "We could have had takeaway."

I roll my eyes. As if I'm going to order takeaway. Not when I can cook. Cheese and onion tart is one hundred percent pure comfort food, and therefore soothing to cook, because it comes with the anticipation of feeling wrapped in a warm blanket when it's ready. Not just any blanket, either—a blanket made of *cheese*.

"I want a chance to get used to the kitchen." Up until a month ago, I'd lived with Shane in a beautiful house in Buckinghamshire, which had a kitchen at least ten times the size of this one.

"Is it much more difficult to cook in a small kitchen?"

Before last month, Cynthia and I hadn't spoken for a couple of years. She'd been my closest friend since school, but as my relationship with Shane progressed, I seemed to lose touch with everyone in my world. Even my relationship with my parents—which had never fully recovered from me dropping out of university—was relegated to the occasional phone call. But Cynthia hadn't hesitated when I'd called her to tell her I needed help moving out of Shane's place and what I'd thought was my home. As fate would have it, her lease had been up just as I needed a place to live. Now I have my first flatmate. It's a new city and a fresh start after more than ten years with a man I thought I'd spend the rest of my life with. I'm unspeakably grateful to be facing it with a friend by my side.

"No," I reply, shaping the pastry with my palms. "It's good practice. At Le Cordon Bleu, you don't even have this much space. You get about a meter squared to do all your prep."

"So really it's a good thing you've moved out of that ginormous house." She smiles the same sympathetic smile I got when people learned I was Shane's manager.

"Exactly." I press the floured rolling pin into the pastry and start to flatten it. I'm trying to see all the bright sides of Shane and I splitting. I certainly have more time to cook. Cynthia is back in my life. My parents even dropped by the week Cynthia and I moved into this place. I worked out it was the first time I'd seen them in nearly two years. I gorged myself on crow pie and kept it down. Only a lifetime of hearty portions to go and they might start to forgive me, although my mother would never stop mentioning the career I could have had, *if only…*

My mother didn't need to keep reminding me. Like the smell of burnt onions, my terrible decision at eighteen would follow me around for the rest of my life.

"I was kidding," she says.

"I'm completely serious. It's not like I could afford to keep the place on my own, even if I had had that option."

"And he's not agreed to pay you any kind of settlement, even though you were together all those years?"

"I haven't asked him. I have some savings." I hadn't deliberately kept money from Shane, but I'd quietly been putting a tiny percentage of what we earned away in savings every month. I'd thought it was for us—for a rainy day or our retirement. When it became clear during the split that I was walking away from my job, my house, and any financial settlement, I didn't say a word about the savings. Shane always refused to pay me a salary—he said there was no point as we shared everything. Which we did. Until we didn't. Those savings would help with the tuition at Le Cordon Bleu. That, and nineteen months with Dr. Cove.

"But you lost your job, too."

"Like he said, I could have stayed if I'd wanted to. It was my choice to walk away."

"After he cheated on you. How could he expect you to stay?"

The short answer is, *because he's a self-centered twat.* I was bloody good at my job. He wouldn't find anyone better, and on some level, he must know it. But there was no way I was going to stay while he paraded his new girlfriend among the friends and fellow riders and WAGs I'd grown close to over the years. I'd lost my boyfriend, my home, my job, and my social circle in one fell swoop.

I focus on my pastry—its perfect consistency and even thickness. It took me a while to master the perfect pastry. But like most things, it just takes practice.

"Sorry," Cynthia says. "I'm still furious at him."

"I know," I reply. "He's not top of my Christmas card list either. But I'm trying to look at the bright side and not spend any more of my energy on him. I have a great flatmate who likes to drink wine, I get to cook more now, I even have a job." I couldn't think about Shane for long. It was still too fresh. Too painful. I was still holding the burn under cold water. I wasn't ready for the bandage just yet.

"Tell me more about your boss. Can I look him up? What's his full name?" I tell her and she shrieks as she Googles his name. "He's gorgeous. Is he single?"

"No idea." I pull my tart dish from the cupboard. I hadn't walked away with much from my relationship with Shane. I had no place to live, no furniture. When I talked to him about taking one of the cars, he'd lost it and told me his money had paid for it. So when it came to the contents of the kitchen, I'd not said a word. He was away the weekend I moved out and I took every single bit of kitchen equipment. I left him with a knife, fork, spoon, and plate. The rest— every glass, whisk, and tart dish—came with me.

"Did Dr. Gorgeous mention a wife or girlfriend? Did he have a picture on his desk or a ring on his finger?"

Okay, so I'd checked out his ring finger. I guess it was ovary-instinct or something. Shane and I had been together for so long, it had been a while since I'd even noticed how attractive other men were—but it was biologically impossible for Zach Cove to fly under my impervious radar. "I was focusing on the job. You know I need to impress this guy. I need this job for nineteen months."

She slumps back in her chair and makes a dismissive sound. "But you're so organized. You're used to problem solving. If Dr. Gorgeous has a temper, you're the impatient, spoiled-brat whisperer. Plus, you're the nicest person I know. You're going to kill it at this job."

"First off, you're a lawyer. It's not a high bar to be the nicest person you know." Cynthia's mum and my mum were friends. Cynthia was always used as an example of what I could have been, could have achieved, if only I'd stayed on at university.

"True," she says.

"Plus, Dr. Cove isn't my boyfriend, so I'm not sure I'll see the side of him that may or may not be a little spoiled." He didn't strike me as spoiled. More...moody and terse. Or maybe he just didn't like people very much.

"I'd like to see *every* side and *every* angle of Dr. Gorgeous."

Cynthia continues to salivate at images of my new boss while I finish off our tart and put it in the oven.

"Perhaps you'll have a wild office affair where he'll bend you over the examination table or do things to you with his stethoscope."

"I said I was trying to impress him, not scare him. I've not done my bikini line since I left Shane." Waxing habits aside, there is no way I'm getting naked with Dr. Cove. I can't risk jeopardizing this job before I've saved what I need for Le Cordon Bleu.

"While that cooks, I'm just going to do a bit of research." I'd brought my work laptop home because I wanted to research the insurer recognition process Dr. Cove had mentioned. For whatever reason, he didn't seem overly eager to get the wheels in motion, even though he won't get any patients until he does. The last thing I need is for him to decide against setting up a private practice and go back to the National Health Service full-time. I need to help him get patients through that door so I keep my job.

"Promise me something," Cynthia says.

I unknot my apron. "What?"

"Don't give yourself over to this job in the way you did to Shane."

I frown. "This is entirely different. Shane was my boyfriend."

"But you gave up everything for him, and I'm worried that's your default setting. You're in a brand-new job, why do you need to sit down and work at eight thirty on a Thursday? You've given up enough of yourself for a man who doesn't deserve you. Don't make the same mistake again."

"Working for Dr. Cove is a means to an end. Keeping this job means I can start the Grand Diplôme sooner. I'm not doing anything for him that doesn't benefit me." I've been through the calculations over and over. This job is the fastest route to Cordon Bleu. Nineteen months is completely survivable, even if Dr. Cove ends up being a total nightmare. In a minimum wage job, it would take thirty months—maybe more, depending on rent and bills in the meantime. No, I have to focus on making the job with Dr. Cove work. Whatever it takes.

I've learned my lesson. I thought Shane and I were unbreakable, yet here I am, at the end of our relationship, ten years older, without a career and with nothing much to show for the last decade other than a lot of kitchen equipment.

But maybe that's all I need.

FOUR

Ellie

I pull out a plastic container of cherry-almond squares I made last night. Since Shane and I split, I'm still having trouble sleeping—which gives me plenty of time to make sweet snacks. I'm not sure if it's my ex's betrayal that keeps me awake at night, or ruminating on everything I gave up. As Shane so helpfully pointed out during our last conversation, he never asked me to make him and his career my world. Not outright, anyway. I offered up every sacrifice on a plate. With a garnish.

I lift the squares to my nose and breathe in, letting the scent of fresh baking neutralize every bad thought forcing its way to the front of my mind. I need to focus on the future.

I took it as a good sign that when I arrived at eight this morning, Dr. Cove was already in his office. I assumed he must be expecting a busy day. I was excited, considering I've spent most of the week bored out of my head. Other than research and starting the insurer recognition process—

which Dr. Cove may or may not appreciate—I've done nothing but research recipes and give the windows another clean. The cleaning service for the building had been difficult to track down, and I wanted things as perfect as they could be.

I had eighteen and a half months of paycheck left before I could stop caring.

But two and a half hours after my arrival, my determination and excitement have wilted. Dr. Cove hasn't come out of his office at all. I'm running out of things to do.

Mutterings through the wall make me pause, still as a statue, so I try to make out what he's saying. Is he on the phone? Maybe to a patient who has his mobile? Unlikely, but I live in hope. Silence ticks by and I give up. If he doesn't come out in twenty minutes, I'll go in to him.

I pop a cherry-and-almond square into my mouth, closing my eyes as I enjoy the way it melts onto my tongue. It's the perfect ten-thirty snack.

"Are you asleep?" a voice asks.

I open my eyes and immediately want to die. He *would* pick the only ten seconds of bliss I've had today to come out of the office. "Dr. Cove!" I jump to my feet. "No! I was just snacking." I grab the plastic box full of treats and shove it forward, like a tin of cherry-almond squares is an explanation unto itself. "It's impossible to taste one of these without closing your eyes. It's like your taste buds are so overloaded that all other sensations have to shut down. I don't know if it's a medical thing or just instinct, but it's true nonetheless."

He looks at me like I'm a jabbering idiot, which may or may not be true.

"Try one," I urge him. "You'll see."

He winces. To be fair, his body looks like a temple. I'm sure he's one of those, just like Shane, who doesn't eat refined sugar, dairy, wheat, red meat, or alcohol, and snacks on broccoli. He probably thinks thirty minutes rowing every morning is the ideal way to wake up.

"Honestly, it's the closest you'll get to God today. I promise." I remember what Jen said about all doctors thinking they're God and internally cringe. I hope he doesn't think I'm insulting him.

"What are they?" he asks.

"Cherry-almond bites. Surely even you treat yourself occasionally?"

He frowns but reaches out, takes one and pops it in his mouth. I freeze, staring at him, trying to gauge his reaction.

He nods. "Tastes good. You made these?"

"Last night," I say. "Do you think they need a little more almond?" As soon as the words are out of my mouth, I regret it. He doesn't want to discuss my bakes. I'm here to assist him, not the other way around. "Never mind," I say. "But if you have five minutes, I'd love to go through a few things." With the help of my after-hours research, I figured out who the main health insurers are and filled out what I could on each of their consultant recognition forms. Most of it is online and fairly basic, but it isn't like I can actually submit the forms without Dr. Cove's approval. There must be a reason why he's dragging his feet over the entire thing. Or maybe he's already done it, and my efforts are totally in vain.

"Sure," he says. "Come through."

I wasn't expecting him just to say yes. For the last year of our relationship, Shane would avoid anything that resembled a meeting. In hindsight, he was avoiding any one-on-

one time with me at all—professional or personal. Like he said, I should have read the signs better.

I follow Dr. Cove through to his office, bringing my laptop with me. He's moved his desk out a little to give himself more room. It makes sense. He's very tall. And the scent in here is less "neglected office space" with the hint of expensive body wash in the air.

I shut the office door and he sits down, but he's distracted. And not by me.

I take a seat opposite him and wait. He's clearly thinking about something. His brows arch and lower. His perfect cupid's bow lifts and twitches. It's like he's having a silent conversation.

"Are you okay, Dr. Cove?" I ask.

He clears his throat and looks me dead in the eye. "Call me Zach. What do you need?"

I take a breath at the sudden change of pace, but I'm not going to waste this opportunity. "I wondered if I could change the waiting room around a little. I think if I move my desk opposite the window, it will free up some space."

He shrugs. I'm going to take it as a yes.

"And I noticed earlier that you've blocked out your diary from eight until ten every day you're in Wimpole Street. Is there anything I should be doing every Thursday and Friday to help?"

He glances sideways towards the door and I take the opportunity to fixate on his eyelashes. I wonder if he uses a serum. "Nothing for you to do. It's just until I get busier."

"So you'll be coming in late?"

He stands. "Nope. I'll be here. But please arrange any patient appointments for after ten."

"Okay," I say. Maybe he wants that time to do paper-work. I stand too, as if I'm going to throw myself in front of him to stop him from leaving his own office. "Before you go, I've been looking into the insurer recognition and have part filled what's needed for the top five. Do you want to check it over and we can submit it? Then things should start getting busier around here."

I just need it busy for eighteen and a half more months and then you can stay behind your desk doing...who-knows-what all you like.

I wait for him to exclaim in shock that I'm the greatest assistant who ever lived. Instead, he shoves his hands into his pockets. "What do I need to look at?"

I'm prepared with all the relevant tabs open on my computer. I place my laptop on his desk and twist it round so he can see. "I got most of the details from the GMC website." Cue his praise about how proactive I've been...but no, instead tumbleweeds bounce past the desk.

In a life radically different from my old one, at least being underappreciated is consistent.

I take him through the screens for the Bupa application, he says yes to everything, and when I ask him if I can finalize, he sighs like I've convinced him to adopt a cat he doesn't want. I press the submit button. "I imagine it will take a few weeks to get the approval through," I say.

"That's true," he says as if I've just given him the good news, rather than told him his practice is still going to be slow going for a while. Really, he should have done these applications way before employing an assistant or renting this place.

"Okay, so Cigna is really similar."

He glances at his watch like he's got something better to do. I shiver like someone has walked over my grave. Shane always had something better to do than be with me.

I shrug off the feeling and focus on Zach's long fingers as he trails one down my computer screen.

In just a few minutes we've submitted another application.

"We can do the rest later," he says, stepping away from his desk, like we're still talking about my cherry-and-almond bites and not the future of his career. I might be thrown off by his handsome face, but I swear there's something I'm not getting about this situation.

Clearly, filling out these forms is no big deal for him. I thought he'd be delighted and I'd have already earned my spot as assistant of the year. I'm going to need to try a different angle if I'm going to impress him. He's backing away towards his door. I think he's forgotten this is his office.

"Can I get you a coffee?" I ask. "Happy to pop to your favorite coffee shop if you want me to."

He shakes his head. "I'm fine." He reaches for the door handle but it's stuck.

He glances at me and I smile.

He turns back to the door and tries again, this time with more force.

"Did it lock by accident?" I ask.

"There's no lock on it."

I step forward. "Yes there is. It was locked the morning I arrived."

He steps back, giving me space and crosses his arms. "Well, unless it's an invisible lock, or maybe just a very, very tiny one that only *teensy* people can see, I can't see one."

My heart starts to rattle my ribs like it's trying to get out of jail. It's the same feeling I'd get when Shane lost a race. I knew he'd blame it on me or something I'd done or not done, and I'd try and prepare myself for his fury by figuring out what my crime might be.

"There must be." No lock? I could have sworn it was locked that first morning. But he's right, it's just a brushed metal internal door handle. My grandma used to have the exact same ones in her house. I grab the handle and pull.

I snap my head to him. "It's stuck."

He raises his eyebrows as if to say, *nice of you to catch up.*

I turn back to the door and try again. What am I doing? Zach has almost a foot on me and probably four stone. If he can't open it, how am I meant to?

"Try again," I say.

"I've tried," he replies.

I look him in the eye. "Try again. Maybe I loosened it for you."

He chuckles, but to my surprise, doesn't argue. He just steps forward anyway. I can tell by the way he braces his other hand on the doorframe and the tightening tendons in his neck that he gives it everything.

We're stuck.

"I'll call Jen," I say.

He sighs and I grab my phone from my pocket.

"You get on with your work and I'll figure this out," I say. The pounding in my chest is getting worse. I haven't had a panic attack since...since Shane and I split, but I can feel one threatening.

Zach goes back to behind his desk and I text Jen. But she's on her way to the blood lab and then has to pick up lunch for Dr. Newman. I fire off an email to the building maintenance emergency number and get a standard *we'll get back to you* reply.

There's nothing to do but wait.

"Help is on the way," I say, taking a seat. I keep my legs over to the side, so I'm facing the door and not his desk. It would be weird to sit here, staring at him. It's not weird to sit and stare at a door—no, not at all.

I glance around the room and realize that Dr. Cove—or Zach—has been using the whiteboard. He's rubbed off most of what he's put on there, but I can make out a couple of letters. There's a capital B and a "sec."

I narrow my eyes and lean forward. Is that the word *woman*?

He obviously sees me looking, and snaps his head around to follow my gaze. He jumps up and grabs the board rubber. "Just some research I'm doing," he explains.

Okay, so it's clearly *not* research. He's not a good liar. What's he so secretive about? Is he ranking his current bedmates in order?

I smile and nod at him.

He goes back to his computer and I gaze down at my phone, willing Jen to get herself back here ASAP or maintenance to arrive on the scene yesterday.

I can see Zach out of the corner of my eye. He's squinting at his computer. Then he's pouting. Then he fake smiles.

What the hell?

He meets my eye. "Research?" I suggest.

"For a friend," he says, completely unconvincingly. "He's a psych. A psychologist. He's sent out these questionnaires, and I'm filling one out. As a favor. Except... he's sent me the wrong one. He's sent me the one for women."

"Oh," I say like everything makes sense. But nothing makes sense, but I'm not sure it needs to. He's over-explaining.

"Yeah, it's all about male-female interaction in the work-place," he continues.

I glance at my phone to see if any of my lifelines have responded. No such luck.

"They're asking how women know a work colleague is interested in them in a romantic way. I was just trying to put myself in a woman's shoes and..." He trails off.

"You're asking me how I'd know if a work colleague was interested in me in a romantic way?" Nothing he's saying adds up. If I saw on paper what he's just asked me, I'd assume he was cack-handedly coming on to me, which would be super-flattering and also very awkward because he's my boss and I'm still...I'm still *post-Shane*. But there's no way he's this clumsy at making a pass at a woman. He's full-on movie-star gorgeous. Surely looks like his come with a degree of...game?

His eyes flash wide. "No!" He sounds horrified. "I'm just wondering, in the abstract—my friend doing his research paper," he corrects and his cheeks tinge pink with embarrassment. It's one hundred percent adorable. "He's interested in how a woman would know—never mind."

From that reaction, it's clear he's not making a move on me. Considering this is the first time Zach has asked for my help, I want to comply. If this is what it means to be a good assistant in this situation, I'm ready to prove my worth.

"Let me think," I say. This should be easy for me—I worked with my boyfriend for ten years. Surely, I'm the expert in this scenario. In the early days, Shane and I used to make out during the day, but that hadn't happened for years before I left. Most of the time, work bled into our social time together rather than the other way around. But that's not what Zach wants to hear. "I guess the guy would be very attentive. He'd probably seek out the woman's opinion a lot—you know, as an excuse to spend time with her."

"And because she's incredible at what she does—that's part of the attraction, right?" he asks. "She's brilliant."

He meets my gaze and my heart trips in my chest. He's looking at me with so much passion and fire—I've not seen him like this before. It's shot him way past adorable to sexy as hell.

Zach nods and types as if he's taking notes about what I'm saying.

I glance back down at my phone, silently hoping he can't read my thoughts. "And he'd probably smile at her more than...an ordinary work colleague," I suggest. I'm monumentally bad at this. How do I know what a guy in love looks like? Looking back, it's been years since I'd felt anything like that from Shane. I just hadn't noticed the way our relationship had drained away as the days and weeks and months all bled into each other. In the early years, every time I'd started to question whether I was happy, I'd get distracted by one of Shane's famous eruptions. That together with the fact that I was so desperate to prove to my parents that everything was great and that Shane wasn't the man they thought he was, meant I'd just focused on smoothing things over. I forgot to ask myself if I wanted what was left behind. By the end, I was so focused on keeping him happy, I totally forgot that I was supposed to be happy too.

Zach pauses his typing, but keeps his eyes on his screen. I'm grateful. I don't need another complicated working relationship. I have a plan and I need to stay focused. "But if he's not a smiler—you know, if smiling didn't come naturally to him—what else could indicate he was in love?"

Before I have a chance to ask what kind of research

project his "friend" is working on, something in the main office hits the door with a blow that makes the entire wall shake.

"Jen?" I call out.

"I'll have you out of there in a jiffy," she shouts like we're ten meters underground.

I glance back at Zach, who's oblivious. He's far too busy responding to his "friend."

FIVE

Zach

After a full day behind the desk at Wimpole Street, I started out walking because I thought a stroll through Regents Park would be a good time to have a think about exactly how to introduce my main character to the reader. I know Benjamin Butler, the head of hospital security, is an ex-professional football player, a lover of chess, and a man of extraordinary intelligence. And I also know he is still in love with his ex-wife and likes coaching the local football club. I just don't know how to introduce him to the reader—or, more accurately, I've written three opening scenes and can't decide which one would work best.

My mind shouldn't be occupied with Benjamin Butler when I'm trying to establish a business. It's just the first time in so long that I've had any substantial time outside of the hospital, and it happens to coincide with a break from my family trying to set me up with various women. Having two days a week when I'm not at the hospital, exhausted from work, or being berated by my brothers is a breath of fresh air, and what's filled that fresh air are ideas. Not ideas for my new private practice, but ideas for books I want to write.

Benjamin Butler is the main character in a cozy mystery set in a London hospital—an idea I've been playing with for years. The last few weeks have breathed fresh life into him, and it feels like an old friend has come to stay. I also had the idea for a series about a primary school teacher who spends her evenings and weekends tracking down stolen goods and reuniting people with objects that were sentimentally valuable to them in various ways. I've even had an idea for an ex-Met police officer who retires in Norfolk and finds mystery and murder on his doorstep. The ideas are spilling out of me like pus out of a boil, completely preoccupying my thoughts on Thursdays and Fridays—and increasingly on my days off.

Walking helps me sort through them. I thought I'd get through Regents Park, then pick up a cab before Primrose Hill. But I ended up just walking the whole way, and all of a sudden I'm on Hampstead Heath. The ideas are flowing so thick and fast I'm voice-noting myself so I don't forget anything.

I check the clock on my phone. I'm going to be about fifteen minutes late getting to Nathan's for dinner. Given his four brothers and his parents are doctors, he's no doubt used to it. But not from me. I end my voice note about Benjamin Butler being called to the morgue to discuss another body that's appeared out of nowhere and message the group chat among the five of us brothers to say I'm going to be fifteen minutes late. It always depends on shifts which brother will be able to make the dinners we arrange together, but all logistics are on the chat together so if anyone can make it last minute, everything is there for everyone to see.

Baby brother Dax is the first to respond with the inevitable retort. I don't even need to read his message to know what it says: *Perfect Zach is late. Is Mercury in retrograde?*

For some reason my brothers think I lead a charmed life. I do in many ways, of course. I enjoy a lot of privileges. But no more than any of them do. They've tricked themselves into believing that life comes easy and that nothing bad ever happens to me.

My flow of ideas is interrupted by thoughts of my siblings. I shove my phone into my coat, keeping my hand in my pocket, feeling the buzz of the jokes about me in the palm of my hand.

Before long, I'm in Highgate, standing in front of Nathan's grand house. He's the only one of us who isn't a doctor, and part of me hopes my other three brothers can't make it tonight, or at least run later than me. I like to hear about his life outside of a hospital. I've never told him, but I've always admired how he dropped out of medical school. He plowed his own path.

"How's perfect Zach?" Madison, Nathan's wife, says as she opens the door.

I don't respond and she stands aside to let me in. "Is everyone here?" I ask. I haven't even kept up with who is meant to be coming tonight.

"Just you so far. Jacob and Sutton are due any minute. Nathan's back in the kitchen."

Nathan's picking out wine when I appear. "How's my perfect brother?" He doesn't look at me as he continues to focus on the bottles in front of him.

I don't respond. What's the point? They'll think what they think, no matter what I say.

"Shall I get something from the cellar?" he bellows. Presumably at Madison.

"It's a Friday night. Go wild." Madison's good for my brother. I never thought I'd see him settle down. But then again, I didn't think I'd be a doctor for as long as I have been.

"This will do." He pulls two bottles of red from the fridge. "It's only you and Jacob and Sutton tonight."

I follow him over to the counter where he sets about opening one of the bottles.

"So how is life in the private sector?" he asks.

"Good," I reply. When what I really mean is, *I've really enjoyed the time to myself so far. I'm in the final act of the first Benjamin Butler book. It's the most fun I've had in a while.*

"Of course it is. No doubt patients are battering down your front door, trying to get an appointment with you."

If only he knew. I'm sure Ellie wonders if she's working for the worst doctor alive, given she's not seen a single patient enter our office. But they'll come. Especially now she's filled out my recognition forms. I'll get insurer referrals any day now. The insurers don't seem to care who you are as long as you've got practicing privileges at an NHS hospital.

"I guess."

Nathan looks at me for the first time since I arrived. "You sound your usual enthusiastic self." He holds my gaze and for a split second I'm tempted to tell him that I don't want any patients. Not in the private sector, not even in the NHS. I don't want to be a doctor. I want to spend all my days how I've spent today: thinking about stories and characters and plot and writing, writing, writing.

Of course I don't.

"What are you enjoying about it so far?" he asks.

The best thing about private practice is Ellie. She's competent and capable and—an image of her bending over my desk flashes into my mind, her legs parted, her hands gripping the edge as I slide up her skirt—I need to change the subject.

Luckily Jacob appears with Sutton and the sight of them together almost makes me smile. She's so good for him. She brings out the best in him. "What going on?" he asks.

"Nathan's opening wine," I reply. We are not talking about my private practice, and I'm not thinking about my assistant. On my desk. Naked.

"Sounds good."

"Is it just the five of us tonight?" Sutton asks. "You haven't brought anyone, have you, Zach?"

I groan. I really like Sutton and I really like Madison, but when they're together, they spend far too much energy trying to identify a perfect woman for me.

"Angelina Jolie's single," Madison says. "Is she your type?"

I shake my head and I see another flash of Ellie, this time her eyes are closed, and she has a look of ecstasy on her face. I wouldn't say Ellie's my type exactly, but apparently she's taken up residence in my brain.

"Zachy's perfect. He doesn't need a woman with a vial of blood around her neck."

A vial of blood around her neck isn't the reason Angelina Jolie isn't my type. It's much more about the fact that I don't know Angelina Jolie—and it's only when I get to know a woman that I can find her properly attractive. It's probably why I've been single for so long—the only women I meet are my brothers' girlfriends and work colleagues, and both are strictly no-go zones.

"Anyone at the new job?" Nathan asks.

Since when has he become invested? I pull my eyebrows together, confused as to how Nathan got recruited into Sutton and Madison's mission to get me married off. "No."

"Don't worry, mate, it will happen for you when you're least expecting it."

"Jesus, you lot, leave me alone. Getting laid isn't my first priority."

"That's right," Jacob says. "How's the new practice? If you let me have some business cards, I can hand them out."

"Thanks," I reply. "I'm actually having a sandwich board made up. I thought maybe you could do a few hours in the cafeteria a couple of times a week?"

"Your mood is particularly pleasant today," Jacob says.

"All the better for seeing you," I reply.

"Knock it off, you lot," Sutton says. "Leave Zach alone. He can't help it if he's perfect and you're jealous."

I knew there was a reason why I liked Sutton. "I'm not perfect."

She pats me on the arm. "Of course you are. We all know it. Your brothers are just angry they're not just like you."

"I'm. Not. Perfect."

Nathan starts handing out wineglasses, and for some reason, I can't just accept the glass and take a sip. It's like I've been set at a simmer for years and all of a sudden I'm boiling over left and right. "No," I say.

Nathan pauses and then hands the glass to Jacob. "Would you prefer white?"

"No," I repeat. I don't know what I'm saying no to. Nathan always has great wine. It's like my feelings about the job are just seeping out all over the place—

No, I don't like my new private practice.

No, I don't have any patients.

No, I don't want to be a doctor.

No. No. No.

"Are you okay?" Jacob asks as he sets his wineglass down.

I shake my head. "No. I just—no." I turn toward the door. I need some air. I need to get away from people, my family, all the questions.

"Hey," Nathan calls after me down the hallway and I stop, turn, and wait for him to catch up to me. "What's going on? You can talk to us. I know it's stressful starting up a new business and everything, but you're going to be fine."

I shake my head. "I don't think so." I glance over his shoulder. Everyone's continuing as usual in the kitchen. I lower my voice. "I know all the things I should have done by now to get the new practice going. I haven't done any of them. I haven't got a website, or systems in place. I certainly don't have any patients. And you know what, Nathan? It feels fucking fantastic. I don't want any patients. I like the peace and quiet." I push my hands through my hair. It feels like I'm freewheeling downhill and there's no stopping what I'm going to say next. "I hate being a doctor. I've never liked it. I've put up with it. I'm good at it. It comes easy to me, but I don't enjoy it."

He leans against the wall like his legs are too weak to hold him upright.

"I'm sorry," I say.

"Sorry? What are you sorry for? I'm sorry you've been faking it all this time and I never realized?"

"Is everything okay?" Madison calls down the hallway.

Nathan nods. "Fine." He lifts his chin. "We won't be long."

He peels into his study and I follow and he shuts the door behind us. "Have you always hated medicine?"

I sigh. I feel bad that of all the people I finally boil over on, it's Nathan. He was forced out of medicine, and has always felt like the black sheep of the family as a result. He would love to be in my shoes now, and I feel selfish for unloading on him. "I shouldn't have said all that."

"Of course you should, if it's how you feel. I can't believe you haven't said anything before. Has the private practice made things worse?"

I collapse in one of his bottle-green velvet chairs by the desk. "It's just given me a bit more time to think. Usually, I'm so busy, I don't really realize that I don't like it. I just get on with it. But now I've had some time to myself—time when I should be thinking about how to build my practice and what I want out of the next ten years—all I can think about is how I don't want to be practicing medicine anymore."

Nathan pulls in a breath like I've just told him I'm cheating on my wife. "Do you know what you do want to do?"

I'm not sure I'm ready to tell him what I really want to do. The problem is, I'm not sure I can keep it in. "I want to write."

He frowns. "Write what?"

"Books. Cozy mysteries. Thrillers. That kind of thing."

"Wow. Okay. So, you want to go back to university and study?"

I hadn't even thought about that. "I don't think so. I just have all these ideas that I want to put down on paper. The last few weeks I've read a few books on story structure and I've been reading more." I scratch the back of my head. "That's the other thing. The last decade I've spent in medicine, I haven't had space in my head to think about all this stuff. Yes, I've written here and there, but only when I feel like if I don't, I'll end up in an asylum. I've never had any real time. It's like when you're a doctor, it's impossible to *be* anything other than a doctor, do you know what I mean?"

A flash of disappointment crosses Nathan's face. Guilt floods my gut and I groan.

"I'm sorry," I say. "I'm being an insensitive arsehole."

He shakes his head. "Really, I'm over it. I'm richer than all of you anyway." He flashes me a grin. "I'm just fucking sad for you, mate. I had no idea you felt like this."

"You see? Not so perfect, am I? I've been sleepwalking through a career I don't want for the last decade."

"I agree. That's far too long to be spending your life doing something you don't want to do. You need to start putting things right."

I roll my eyes. Easier said than done. "What, you want me to pretend I'm going full-time private practice and resign from the hospital?"

Nathan looks at me like I've got the brain the size of a cotton swab. "No, I think you should write a book."

"I just told you, medicine requires every part of you. I don't have—"

"So give medicine up." He says it like he's handing me a gold medal and I should be grateful.

"Just like that," I challenge.

"Yes, Zach. Just like that. You're clearly not happy and it's not like you'd be resigning just to lie on the sofa and listen to Coldplay while wanking off ten times a day. You have a plan. You know what you want to do."

Before I get to ask him where the Coldplay-and-wanking thing came from, I'm aware of the voices in the kitchen and the clip-clop of heels on the hallway floor. Madison sticks her head around the door.

"Is everything okay?" she asks.

"Give us a minute, will you?" Nathan asks. "Make an excuse. We need a chat."

I sigh. We needed more than a minute.

"I don't have a plan," I say as Madison turns around. "I have some ideas and I'm sort of halfway through something. The last few Thursdays and Fridays, I've reserved my mornings to write, and I can't get the words down fast enough. And I love it."

"That's enough of a plan. Resign from your job. Give notice on your lease on Wimpole Street. Give writing a try."

"And then what? I figure out I can't write and I go back to work with my tail between my legs."

"Absolutely not. You shouldn't ever go back to medicine if it's making you as miserable as it sounds. You'll just have to think of something else if writing doesn't work out—but it will. You've never been bad at anything in your life." Nathan pauses and tilts his head like he's thinking. "Apart from maybe squash."

"I lost one game," I reply. I know the day he's thinking about.

"You didn't just lose the game. You lost control of your arms and legs." Nathan has a smirk, an expression he's had since birth that can cut your confidence in half in a second, and he's using it now.

"I was a junior doctor and I'd been on shift for thirty-six hours." I groan at the memory. The hours aren't as long now, but the way medicine demands your soul hasn't changed.

"If you want to be a writer, you'll make it happen. It's who you are. But you've got to take this opportunity. If you continue the way you have been, you won't ever come up for air again. Take this chance before it's too late."

"But what if I hate writing when I get the chance to do it every day?" So far, I love it, but if I had to make a living out of it, that might change. "Worse, what happens if no one likes what I write?"

"Let that be tomorrow's problem. Worst-case scenario, we're pregnant. You can be the kid's manny."

A surge of energy spreads through my body. "Madison's pregnant?"

Nathan tries and fails to cover the grin. "We're going to tell you lot tonight. We called Mum and Dad earlier."

I pull my brother into a hug. "This is amazing. I'm going to be an uncle."

"Don't let on I told you. Pretend you're surprised when we tell you later."

"Of course. I can't believe you're the first of us that's going to be a dad. Mum and Dad are going to love this. Might go halfway to making up for their disappointment about me if they find out."

Nathan fixes me with a serious look. "You know they're going to support you no matter what. They always did with me."

I pull in a breath. I know my parents want me to be happy. And I know on the outside they will support every decision I make. But I want every inch of them to be proud of me, and if I gave up medicine, I just don't know if that would be possible.

"Yeah." It's all I can manage to say. My parents' approval is another obstacle on the course out in front of me if I'm really considering writing full-time. But Nathan's right—if I'm ever going to try to be a writer, it's now. It just seems like an impossible mountain to climb. "I'll have a think about stuff this coming week." I'd booked the week off from the hospital with the intention of focusing on the private practice. Maybe I need to be making bigger decisions.

"Whatever you do, I'm here for you," Nathan says.

"Just don't tell anyone. Not even Madison. I don't want it getting out and everyone weighing in on what I should or shouldn't be doing. I need a clear head."

"You have my word, except I have to tell Madison."

I groan. "I don't want this getting out. Not yet."

"I'll make her swear a blood oath. It won't get out." Nathan is an excellent secret keeper. Keeping his best friend's secrets had nearly ruined his life in the past. I know mine is safe with him. And if he trusts Madison wouldn't say anything, I do too.

Whatever happens, I can't carry on like I have been doing and living in limbo. I need to commit to medicine and set my desire to write aside, or I need to give writing a go.

By the end of next week, I'll make a decision—once and for all.

SIX

Ellie

I've spent the first thirty minutes of Monday morning sitting behind my desk, researching doctor's waiting rooms online to see if I can come up with ideas on how to improve this place. I've talked to Jen and the other two assistants about their roles and responsibilities, to make sure I haven't missed anything. The issue is, ninety-five percent of their jobs involve patients: booking them in, cancelling them, moving them around, organizing scans and blood tests and booking in endoscopies and fitting in emergencies. I don't need to do any of that, because we still haven't had any patients through the door.

Jen assures me that as soon as the insurer recognition comes through, things will change. But what if they don't? What can I do to make sure I keep this job for the next seventeen months?

I've calculated what I need to save each month so I can apply for the June intake of Le Cordon Bleu in just over a year and a half, and I've created a spreadsheet to keep track of every pound standing between me and my future life.

The life where Shane is just a bad memory. The life that's about me. Every month, I fill in the spreadsheet, noting what I've saved. I watch the *outstanding amount required* box ratchet down. It's far more satisfying than it should be, even with the small amounts I've managed to set aside with the minimum wage temp jobs I've had up until now. My spreadsheet also has the date I have to submit the application highlighted. I've noted down the list of equipment I'm going to need to buy before I start. I've even noted down the skills I'd like to practice before I get there. There's no harm in a head start.

Except that whatever I do now, it won't be a head start. I'm going to be forever playing catch-up because I wasted ten years of my life on Shane. We'd started out as a partnership, a power couple. Somewhere along the way, I'd become just a woman who managed his business, cooked his meals for him, was his emotional punching bag. A woman who was never quite good enough at any of it for him.

I'm not sure when things changed, or maybe things were never how I'd seen them in the first place. Cynthia never said anything, but I could tell by the way she wasn't surprised when I told her the way Shane treated me that she'd either known or suspected all along that he wasn't good for me.

I just wish it hadn't taken him cheating on me and throwing me out of my home for me to see it for myself.

There's no point in dwelling on the past. I need to focus on my spreadsheet.

Everything's in place. I just need Zach to go get us some patients.

Just as I start to spiral over our barren waiting room, Zach arrives. What is he doing here?

The best way I can describe his expression is troubled.

He's still hot as hell, but he has a definite uneasy look about him.

"Hi," I say as he trudges across the waiting room towards his office door.

He stops and looks at me like he wasn't expecting to see me. Because I'm invisible to him, apparently. He probably forgot he recruited me to sit here all week and do precisely nothing. Now he's remembered, I'm probably going to get the sack.

"I wasn't expecting to see you until Thursday," I say, because he still hasn't said anything.

"Yes. Well, I'm going to be here all week."

I can feel my entire body start to perk up. He's committing. Really committing to his practice. This is great news.

"We won't have any patients," he says, and he must see the way my shoulders droop. "If any try and book in, put them in for next week." Then he heads into his office and closes the door.

I lean forward and literally bang my head on the desk and then just stay there, because I have nothing better to do. I can't bear just sitting here and not being productive. I'm in an anxiety spiral. I need to be busy and useful and I want to put everything into this job so I can keep it. If my current situation had been designed especially for me, it couldn't be more tortuous.

I recognize the creak of the doorknob too late.

When I upright myself, I come face to face with Zach, who's looking at me with a quizzical expression.

"Could you get me a coffee, please?" he asks, and my insides start to melt a little at his lovely manners. I mentally chastise myself—he's a human being displaying basic manners. The bar I've set myself has been far too low for far too long.

I jump to my feet. "Of course. What would you like?" Now I wish I'd memorized the entire Starbucks menu so I'm prepared.

"Just an Americano. With an extra shot."

"Of course. Starbucks? Or Costa?"

He shrugs. "Whatever. Put it on the credit card." Then he turns to disappear back inside his office.

"Have you thought about advertising?" I blurt. I have no idea if doctors advertise or if it's even allowed.

"Advertising what?" He scowls at me.

I take a beat, wondering how to answer. What does he think I mean he should advertise? "Your new practice. Maybe in some specialist pharmacies?" I was clutching at straws and I knew it.

"Just the coffee, please." He goes back into his office and shuts the door.

I take a deep breath. I need to trust him. This business is his livelihood. His future. It's only my next year-and-a-little-bit. He needs this to work more than I do. I'm determined to convince myself that him being here and wanting coffee is good news. Great, in fact. He's taken the week off his NHS job and is coming in every day. If he didn't want this private practice to work, he'd have gone away somewhere to get some sun. So what if he doesn't have any patients at the moment? He *will* do, won't he? Still, my coffee run is a perfect time to put a call into the recruiter to see if anything else has come up.

I slip on my coat, scarf, and hat and shoot down the stairs, at the same time as I'm putting on my gloves. Getting coffee is pretty much the first thing I've been tasked with. I'm going to make it good.

Ribbons of breath appear as soon as I'm on the steps down to Wimpole Street. It's so cold, I almost need the air warmed before I breathe it in. It's a shock to the system. The nearest coffee shop is Costa, just on the corner of Wigmore Street. It will take about five minutes to reach it. But I'm going to make it count. I pull out my phone and catch the wool of my gloves between my teeth and pull them off. I'm going to call the recruitment agency to see if Zach has called them or if they have any other jobs coming up that I might be better suited for.

"Hey, Debbie," I say when she answers. "It's Ellie. I was just wondering if you've heard from Zach at all?"

"I spoke to him about a week ago. He said things hadn't really got started yet but that he's pleased to have you in place so when they do, you'll be ready."

"I'm ready," I say.

"You've got to be patient. This is a great role for you. You know how tight the market is and with your CV—it's tricky. This is a great opportunity. You've got to hang tight. You haven't even been there a month yet."

"I just get the feeling something's off."

"He's just starting out. Things are bound to be slow. I bet you in a month's time, you're going to be calling me to complain you're overworked."

The idea is like pulling a hot water bottle to my chest, and for at least five seconds, I feel better. But how would she know what's going to happen in a month's time? I couldn't even tell my boyfriend of ten years was sleeping with someone else. Debbie doesn't have a crystal ball. "But just in case this doesn't work out, have you got anything else you think I'd be suited to?" I'd rather jump ship now to something else, rather than be pushed in a week when I've got nothing to go to.

"Not at the moment," Debbie says. "Like I said, your job history makes it tricky. And you've got no references.

Working for friends and family always makes things more difficult."

"But I'm organized and proactive and I've got a lot of common sense. That's got to be in short supply."

"You need to try and make it work where you are. Going into a permanent position from a temporary job is the best you're going to do at the moment. The last thing you need to do is get a reputation as an employee who can't stick around. You said it yourself. You're proactive and have a can-do attitude. You've got to make yourself indispensable."

My heart is slipping into my shoes. She doesn't realize that my current situation is unsustainable—she doesn't know that we have no patients. But her tone of voice tells me she's done talking to me about this.

"Okay, thanks, Debbie." I try and sound upbeat, but I'm having a hard time stopping the gongs of doom from echoing all around me. I cancel the call and burrow into my scarf.

Even though it's only just into November, Costa has the Christmas decorations in the window. I place the coffee order and look at what they've got on offer as a snack. Maybe I should get Zach something. It's the usual croissants and pain au chocolat alongside jaunty gingerbread men who I hope aren't left over from last Christmas. Then there are those weird, disgusting waffles that taste like sugar had a baby with sugar and called it sugar. And some cupcakes. Nothing particularly inspirational and nothing as good as the fudge brownies I made last night and brought in for my morning snack today. I don't think Zach's rock-hard bod is going to want any of this. He asked for coffee, and that and only that is what I'm going to get him. He's my boss, not my boyfriend.

SEVEN

Zach

I try and fake a smile when I pass the head of gastroen-
terology before putting my lunch tray into the stand.

Things must be bad. I never fake a smile. I'm trying to
cover up the discomfort I feel about being back here after a
week off writing. The days went by so quickly, I resent
being back. Having such a great week has watered and fed
my general displeasure with my job and it has grown into
something much darker.

Not only do I not want to be here, I actively want to be
somewhere else.

I check my watch. I'm going to chat to the patient who
was admitted yesterday and who I'm going to do a biopsy on
this afternoon, then head to my office to do some paperwork. I've had two appointments cancelled this afternoon
because the patient tested positive for E. coli. It's a fuckup,
but I'm grateful. I'm not in the right frame of mind to be
diagnosing people.

I glance to the floor so I don't catch anyone's eye and
head to the ward.

My patient is a woman in her early sixties. I'm pretty sure she's celiac from her blood test results, but she needs the biopsy to be sure.

As I reach the entrance to the ward, I bring up her notes on my iPad and remind myself of her case before I enter. That way, I don't have to pause at the nurses' station and risk anyone trying to strike up a conversation.

When I'm done, I stride over to the nurses' station. "Which bay is Mrs. Fletcher in, please?"

"Four," one of the nurses I don't recognize says. She mumbles after me but I don't stop. I can't do chitchat this morning.

"Mrs. Fletcher," I say as I approach her bed. "How are you this morning?"

"Fine, Dr. Cove, if you ignore the vomiting and stomach cramps." Mrs. Fletcher is clever, feisty, and strikes me as the kind of person who doesn't like chitchat either.

"Your blood work is showing a substantial possibility of celiac. The results of the biopsy will confirm things. Now that you're not eating gluten, things should start to settle down for you."

"I know, I know. I just want to get the results and figure out how to live with this blasted disease. I have two months left until I retire and I want to be ready to travel. I want to make plans."

"You like your job that much?" I know that feeling.

"I've loved my career. I've read some of the best books ever written. And in my own way, I've made sure those books have been read by more than just me and the writer. I'm proud of what I've achieved. It's just time to move to the next phase of my life."

Suddenly she has my interest. "Books? Can I ask what you do?"

"I'm a literary agent. Have been for the last forty years."

My stomach swoops and I take a seat on the visitors' chair next to the bed. "You know, I'm writing a book."

She starts to cackle. "Of course you are. Everyone is, my dear. Starting to write is the easy thing. Only a very few people actually *finish* a book."

"People have jobs. And families—"

"Oh there are myriad reasons. And no one wants a book from everyone who starts writing one. Frankly, most publishers don't want a book from most people who finish them. But if it's your medicine, so to speak, then that's fine. Write for your own reasons."

"I really want to finish it. I took last week off and got to the second plot point. I could barely keep up with how fast the words were coming out."

I glance up at her and she's staring back at me. "What are you writing?"

"A cozy mystery. Set in a hospital. The protagonist is the security guard who's a former professional footballer. He's spent his life underrated, but the police find themselves relying on him to solve murders and mysteries in the hospital."

She nods. "I don't hate the concept."

I let out a half laugh. "I'll take that as a compliment."

"I rep some of the best thriller writers in the genre. If I say I don't hate it, you should take that as the best compliment you ever received." She narrows her eyes at me. "I tell you what, if you manage to finish it in the next two weeks, I'll read it. After that, I'm not doing anything but handing stuff to other agents. Already they're acting like sharks around chum."

"You will?" My heart lifts in my chest and I stand. "I can give you what I've got so far, if you want?"

"No. I want a completed manuscript. Like I said, starting a book is the easy bit. It's the finishing that's hard."

"I'm going to finish mine," I reply. I know I can't remain as a doctor. It's like the last week I made my way through a series of one-way turnstiles and now I can never go back to where I was. I have to make a change, and it feels like Mrs. Fletcher might be my exit strategy. Even if she doesn't like my work, the chance to have a literary agent read my work is an opportunity I can't pass up.

She shrugs. "Sure. It's good to write what you know, and you know hospitals. I'm not promising I'll get to the end of it, but I'll make it to the first plot point."

"Fair," I say. "And I'll get you a diagnosis—one way or the other."

"Sounds like a good deal," she says.

For the first time since I stepped back onto hospital grounds, I feel enthusiastic about my day. I've got two weeks to finish a book that makes Mrs. Fletcher want to read to the end. Challenge accepted.

EIGHT

Ellie

I've created a smorgasbord of deliciousness, even if I do say so myself. I step back and admire last night's cooking portioned into plastic boxes. If I don't have a full day today, at least I'll have a full stomach.

First up—breakfast burrito.

I remove the box and set it aside, then put everything else back in a paper bag so no one can see what it is. I tuck the bag into the back corner of the communal fridge and hope labeling it with my name is enough to keep anyone from snooping—or stealing—what's inside.

I take the plastic container, along with the fork I brought in, and head downstairs. I'm just back in my chair when Zach comes through the door.

"Good morning, Dr. Cove," I sing. I feel really good about today. I've been tracking the insurer recognition applications and two have come through this week. I even had someone book in for an appointment tomorrow. Things are on the up.

"Morning," he grumps.

"Can I run out and get you a coffee?" I ask.

"Maybe in about an hour," he replies.

"Certainly."

His gaze falls on my breakfast burrito. I want to keep my cooking for myself, but the way Zach is looking at my burrito makes me want to feed him. "It's a burrito. Would you like some? I brought way too much with me."

He freezes and meets my eye for the first time this morning. My heart hitches and my stomach swirls at the unexpected eye contact. "You made it?" He says it like he's hoping I'll say yes—like if I made it, it must be good. It's ridiculous that such a small indication of flattery and appreciation can make me feel so good, and I'm embarrassed at the pride that floods my veins.

My parents thought it was just a career I gave up at eighteen. It was so much more.

I pull back my shoulders. "I did. It's pretty good, actually."

"I'll take some." His voice sounds like the chocolate-and-coffee sauce I made once to go with Shane's steak. It's rich and lush and gives me goose bumps.

"Certainly." I grab a plate. "I have some great news for you," I say, following him into his office. "You have a patient consultation tomorrow morning. All booked in for eleven thirty. We haven't really gone through prices for self-pay patients, so I said I would call her back to confirm. I've done a little research and I think three hundred pounds would be acceptable for a first consultation. Two fifty for follow-ups. You don't want to under-sell yourself but at the same time you're new and you don't have that many patients." Or any, I don't say.

"Tomorrow?" He shrugs off his coat. He's in jeans that hug his thighs like jam on a scone, and a blue shirt that makes his eyes look bluer than usual. And usually they're bluer than blue. "A patient's booked in?"

He doesn't look as happy as I expected him to look. Running his hands through his hair, I try not to stare at the way the fabric of his shirt grows taut over his arms. In another life, I could imagine having a serious crush on Zachary Cove, if that life was one where he smiled a little more often and gave his assistant something to do.

"Yes, that insurer recognition is kicking in," I say. "It's only a matter of time before they're queuing out the door." I hand him the burrito. As he takes the plate, his fingers scrape mine and it's what I imagine it's like to receive an electrical shock straight to the heart. I feel an almost physical *jolt*. He meets my eyes, his brows pulled together as if he's confused, and I wonder whether he just felt the same thing I did.

He looks away and sits, taking a forkful of burrito before he's fully in his chair. I might be imagining things, but it sounds like he lets out a small moan of pleasure at the first bite. I have to look away before I start mentally undressing him. "This is so good."

If I ever give him food again, I'll need to make sure I don't have to touch him when I hand it to him or listen to him eat it. There's no telling what I might do.

He swallows and digs in for another forkful. "But the appointment? You're going to have to cancel it."

My face heats like I'm standing too close to a fire. He can't be serious. It's the first glimmer of a future that I've had in nearly five weeks.

"Why?" I ask.

"Because I'm busy."

"Doing what?" I blurt and instantly regret it. It's none of my business what he does in his office all day every day.

For the last couple of weeks he's in the office before I arrive and leaves after me. Maybe he set up Minecraft on his computer or something. Shane's addiction to video games was a source of tension between us. He insisted it was the best way for him to cool off before a race. And after a race. And between races. It drove me mad. Pun intended.

I just wanted us to make the most of our time together between races. Looking back it should have been a sign, but I was in so deep, I didn't see. Dr. Cove doesn't strike me as a Minecraft kind of guy. Then again, I don't know him that well.

Dr. Cove clears his throat as if to say *none of your fucking business.* "I need to get on. Please shut the door." He doesn't even look at me.

Shit. Far from making myself unsackable, I'm practically writing my own letter of dismissal.

"I'm sorry. I'll get you coffee in an hour." I leave him, being careful to shut the door as quietly as possible on the way out so I don't escalate anything. Shane always slammed doors, and I hated it, even though it was never intentional— so he said. Looking back, he knew it made me anxious, yet he never seemed to make any effort not to do it. Was he deliberately trying to make me anxious? Was it his way of showing his displeasure or trying to make me feel bad—a form of punishment for not giving in to him right away?

Dr. Cove isn't Shane. My logical brain knows this. But another part of me can't help making connections between the only two workplaces I've ever known.

Back on my own, I sigh. The one patient we've had in nearly seven weeks and he's turning it down.

I pull out my notebook. I need distraction. If this place had a fully functioning kitchen, I'd be able to manage my stress better. I'd just cook myself calm. But no such luck.

Creating recipes is the next best thing. I'm working on a new marinade for a chicken dish, but I can't get the ginger amount right. Or maybe it's the citrus throwing things off? I could try blood oranges instead of regular oranges. One of each? Maybe I'll abandon it and attempt another fruit soufflé.

I go through my notes and then research ingredients online for the next forty-five minutes. Then I put on my coat and head out to get coffee. I might have one myself this morning.

"You want an Americano?" the girl behind the counter says.

I sigh. "Yes, please."

"Anything else?"

A place at Le Cordon Bleu and the money to pay for it, I don't say. "I'll have a medium cappuccino, please."

"You look miserable," she says. "Want to talk about it?"

I think I've misheard her. She's a perfect stranger. She can't possibly be asking me to share my innermost thoughts with her while she makes my cappuccino, can she?

"I'm a writer," she says. "I like listening to people's stories."

I'm going to have to find a new coffee shop.

I force a smile.

"Honestly, a problem solved is a problem shared," she says.

"A problem shared is a problem halved," I correct her.

She shrugs like she was almost right rather than completely wrong. "Is it a breakup?" she guesses. "Or an unrequited crush on your boss?"

I open my mouth to speak but find I don't know what to say. Dr. Cove is attractive but I don't have a crush on him exactly. Well, I guess it depends on how you define "crush."

If we were at a bar and he asked to buy me a drink, I'd let him. I'd be a fool not to. But it's not like I'm behind my desk imagining him naked—well, apart from when he started to eat my burrito—not a euphemism.

"Or maybe you're already sleeping with your boss and he's just called it off."

"I'm not sleeping with my boss." I glance over my shoulder to make sure no one I know has joined the queue. "Can I get my coffee?"

Coffee shop girl smiles. "It's coming. I figure I've either got to have the life experience to write about things or I've got to listen to other people's life experiences."

"Ever thought about using your imagination?" I ask.

She laughs. "You're funny."

"I wasn't trying to be."

She slides two cups across the counter. "Good luck with your boss. I hope he's not married."

Okay, I'm definitely finding a new coffee shop. I take the two cups and head out. Hopefully, the mid-morning snack I have in my bag will restore Dr. Cove's faith in me after my outburst.

NINE

Zach

I've written a book. The words ring in my ears as I head to the wards for rounds.

I've written a book.

Okay, so no one but me has read it, but it doesn't mean I didn't type "The End" on my manuscript last night—one day before my two-week deadline. Mrs. Fletcher told me that finishing a book was hard, but it wasn't for me. I couldn't have stopped the words from hitting the paper, even if I'd tried.

Being back in the hospital after a week off writing doesn't seem so bad today, because I've *written a book*. The high is better than any drug ever invented.

"Hey, Dr. Cove. Nice to see you," Nicola, the A&E nurse in charge, says as I get to the nurses' station. I don't often get called down to A&E, but whenever I do, Nicola is on shift. "You seem...happy."

I exhale, thinking about what she said. I am happy. Really happy. I have a sense of achievement I haven't experienced in—maybe ever. Not when I graduated medical school or saved my first patient.

I feel free.

"I'm always happy, Nicola," I say in a flat tone. "Why am I here?"

"A patient of yours, Mrs. Fletcher, was admitted in the early hours. She's demanding to see you. If you can discharge her, we'll all be happy."

Guilt slices through me. I wouldn't have sent Mrs. Fletcher my manuscript last night if I'd known she was feeling poorly. I may not like being a doctor, but that's no excuse for letting my patient care lapse. Before I can spiral too far down this mental rabbit hole, I grab her chart. Apparently, Mrs. Fletcher was readmitted last night for severe dehydration. "I'll go and see her now."

I round the curtain of her bay and Mrs. Fletcher looks up from her iPad, beaming at me like I'm a long-lost friend. "Dr. Cove, you're back. And you used your time off wisely, I see. Thank you for your email."

My stomach lifts and dives. She's the only person to have sight of my book, and for some reason, it makes me a little unsure of myself. "You should be resting," I reply. "I never expected you back here, or I wouldn't have sent it through to you."

"Well, I'm hoping I'll be gone now I've seen you, so I can go back to my life. It was my daughter-in-law's pizza that I ate. She said it was gluten-free, but let me tell you, it wasn't. I need to get out of here. I can't very well call publishers to try to sell your book while I'm in here, can I?"

My heart tightens in my chest like every part of my body has to be as still as possible in case the slightest movement changes what Mrs. Fletcher just said.

"You have to read it first." My words are cautious. She's

joking, right? She's not seriously saying she's going to take me on as a client. A little online research revealed that Mrs. Fletcher is a rock-star agent—a legend of the literary world who's repped every one of my favorite thriller writers other than Harlan Coben and Stephen King. News of her impending retirement was announced in every industry news outlet I came across, and it's fair to say publishing is devastated by the loss.

"You sent me the manuscript last night. It's nearly midday. Of course I've finished it. I've got nothing else to do, have I?"

Staring into my iPad, I try to block out her words. I can't think about her reading my manuscript until I've discharged her. I need to separate being a doctor from escaping being a doctor.

"Well, you can send me my rejection email after I'm done discharging you. Tell me how your pain is."

"I'm fine." She waves her hands in the air. "I just need to be more vigilant about what I'm eating. Sign on the dotted line and get me out of here. We need to discuss what's next for your book."

"Very well. The nurses will manage your discharge. But your reaction to gluten will be worse if you have it by accident now that you're not eating it. You need to be careful."

"Yes, yes. Just tell me I can go home," she says, throwing her arms in the air.

"It will take some time to get all the paperwork done, but the nurses will tell you when you can leave."

"I'll try and be as patient as I can."

"Good," I say.

"So when can we talk about your book?"

I pull my mouth into a smile, trying to cover the instinct to say *now, now, now*. "I have other patients."

"When do you get off shift?" she pushes.

"Eight."

"Then I'll call you at half past eight. Does that suit?"

I've waited a decade, but waiting six more hours seems impossible. But that's how it has to be. I'm committed to medicine for now, which means it has to come first.

"That suits just fine," I tell Mrs. Fletcher, then push all thoughts of her and my book to the back of my mind as I head to the ward for rounds.

I GET HOME JUST before my phone rings.

"I want to work with you," Mrs. Fletcher says before I've even managed a hello. She pauses like she's waiting for me to say something.

"Work with me?" I didn't mis-hear—I just want time to let the words sink in. "You want to represent my book?"

"I loved it. The detail is fantastic—it feels so real. The hero is likeable despite his flaws. And I like the way you write women. I think it has mass appeal. I really do."

"This is my first book," I say.

"I know. And I have notes. I want you to ramp up the love story between Ben and Madeline. There's definite chemistry there, and I get he still bears the scars over his divorce, but I think his wife should die. It will make it more compelling that he shuts down. I want Maddie to awaken something in him."

"I'm not writing romance. The book is a mystery."

"You ever watch *Moonlighting*?" She scoffs. "Probably not, you're far too young. But do yourself a favor and watch the first series. I'm sure you can get it on YouTube or something. I don't want you to watch it for the quirkiness or the atmosphere—your book is more serious. Watch it for the chemistry between Cybil Shepherd and Bruce Willis. They're *electric*. And it feels like your hero and heroine here could have the same thing going on. I guess it helps that her name is Madeline, but I immediately thought of *Moonlighting*. She's a bit prissy and does things by the book. She comes from money—I love that. And the will-they-won't-they thing is guaranteed to get people hooked."

Nowhere in my manuscript does it say Madeline comes from money—but in my head, she absolutely does. It feels kind of weird that Mrs. Fletcher gets that vibe, like she can see into my head.

"That's my main note. It will take a lot of work to do it well, but I believe you can. If you want to work together, I'm going to annotate the manuscript in hard copy—I'm old fashioned, shoot me—and highlight areas I think are ripe for some of the chemistry to explode. Along with a few other notes I have."

"Sounds great," I say.

"But I have two issues. First is, because of my A and E visit, I'm behind at work. So, I'm not going to be able to let you have my detailed notes for a week or so."

"That's no problem."

"Well, it might be. Usually, I'd give authors a month—maybe more—to let me have a revised manuscript. But I don't have that long. You know I'm due to retire and I want to get this book sold before I do. I want your career to be the last I help launch. You're a talented writer and I want to see you at the right publisher, with an editor who's going to look after you. I want to look after you just like you looked after me."

It's like someone just put the emergency brake on my feelings of complete and utter joy.

I take a moment to collect my thoughts before I say, "Mrs. Fletcher, you don't owe me anything. I don't feel comfortable working with you if you feel an obligation because I treated—"

"Absolutely not. I never feel any obligation to anyone. Like I said, you're a talented writer. You know, some writers..." She pauses like she's trying to figure out the words she needs. "You can tell when you're reading an author who loves to write. I can tell you do. More than that, you're good at it. I don't like talent to go to waste. It's as simple as that. If you're committed, you can have a very successful career. But maybe you love practicing medicine more than you love writing, and writing is just a hobby for you...?"

I hear the question she isn't asking, and it feels like when I answer, the words will be a binding contract. When I voice them, there'll be no going back.

"I don't love medicine." I exhale. "I love to write." The confession feels reverent. Yes, I told Nathan, but he's my brother. It's the first time I've spoken the truth to anyone who matters.

"I can tell." I can almost hear her smile on the end of the phone. "I want to help you because you have talent. And because you're a jolly nice chap. If you don't love being a doctor, you have a real alternative. And I want to make that happen for you."

"Where do we start?" I ask. I'm ready for this. Finally. For years I've tried to fight against it, but now I'm ready to fight for a future I actually want.

"Well, that's the other problem. My retirement date is set in stone because I have a ninety-day cruise booked the week after my leaving date. I have three months left. With Christmas coming up, realistically, I need to be able to shop your book before people break for the festive period. And no publisher buys anything past the first week in December. I need a revised manuscript two weeks after I send you my notes. That's three weeks from now."

Two weeks. Unless I call in sick, there's no way I'll be able to get it done.

Shit. I want to do this. I really want to. I just need to find a way.

"Okay. I'm in."

"You think you can fit it into your schedule?"

The truth is, I'm not sure. But I'm not willing to let this opportunity pass me by. Not when I'm so close to a dream I've been too scared to admit means the world to me. "Absolutely," I tell Mrs. Fletcher. "I'll make it work."

TEN

Ellie

The dream about Zach Cove I had last night is playing on a loop in my head. In it, I walked into his office to find him inexplicably naked, baring the most beautiful bottom I've ever seen. Not to mention his muscular thighs, hard abs, and arms that looked like they could lift Big Ben. And when he turned around —I'm not generally a penis person. I think they're ugly, weird things. Don't get me wrong, used in the right way, they can be magical, but the look of them just bouncing about in the shower or jiggling while getting changed—well, I always look away.

Last night, Zach's penis was downright *bewitching*. Dream me couldn't keep my eyes off it—like I understood what it was capable of and therefore had nothing but the deepest respect and veneration for what *stood* in front of me.

Unlucky for dream me, that's when I woke up. A little sweaty. As if Dr. Cove and I had both been in bed and very busy all night long.

I know it's stupid, but this morning when he came in

and seemed to have a spring in his step, I couldn't help but wonder if he'd had the same dream I had.

I hang up my coat and pick up the coffee I've just brought in, along with the container of snacks I made last night. I have a feeling this week is going to be good. Dr. Cove is definitely in the best mood I've ever seen him in. I'm sure this is the week he'll be throwing himself into his new practice.

I knock on the door and he calls for me to come in. I plaster on a grin and try to tamp down the feelings of embarrassment I feel oozing from my every pore.

"Your coffee," I say.

He's not sitting, tapping away at his laptop as usual. He's standing and seems to be...packing up his bag.

"Thanks." He looks up. "I'm leaving."

My heart sinks into my stomach. "Oh, right. Will you be gone for the rest of the day?" I ask, trying to sound like it doesn't matter to me either way. But if he's leaving, he won't be here if any patients call and want to see him for an emergency appointment. Unlikely, but I live in hope.

"Yes." He freezes, lets go of his bag, and turns to face me head-on. "Actually, I'm to be gone now for two weeks." He must see the shock and disappointment in my eyes, because he instantly tries to reassure me. "You don't need to worry. You still have a job. I'd like you to stay and deal with phone calls and correspondence."

What phone calls? I want to scream at him.

"What shall I tell people?" *If anyone calls, which they won't,* I don't add.

"I'm taking a sabbatical from work," he says. "I'm still working on that..."

"The research project?" I say.

"Exactly. And...it's gotten to an exciting stage." He pulls the drawstring of his backpack, then snaps the top shut.

Wasn't it his friend's research project? "Do you think it will lead to a lot of work?" I ask.

A grin curls around the corners of his mouth like he's trying not to smile. Real Dr. Cove is even better looking than dream Dr. Cove. His jaw, the way his nose juts out and his chin is so proud—he's all angles in so many ways. But the softness of his smile? The way he keeps his hair a little long, like he's just forgotten to get it cut, and his blue eyes, whenever they meet mine—it's like an invitation to dive into Maldivian waters. I've never thought it before about a man, but he's beautiful.

"I think so. Yes."

"Well, that's good. Anything I should prepare for?"

He shakes his head and flips the rucksack onto his back. He steps around his desk and puts his hands on my shoulders. A zap of electricity sparks like the first time we touched and our eyes meet. He drops his hands and my gaze follows, tracking his fingers to see if actual sparks fly off.

"You're doing everything you need to be doing."

It's infuriating, but I can't say anything. It's like his touch has activated some kind of sedation button in me. Maybe his scent—all rainstorms and fresh pine needles—has me mildly chloroformed or something.

"Okay." I manage to squeak out a pathetic response, when really, what I should be doing is asking him to tell me straight out if I have a job when he comes back. Does he really want to make a go of this private practice?

Instead, I ask, "Shall I book in any patients from the second week in December?"

The lightness in him dims for a second, like a flickering table lamp with a bulb about to go. I only just manage to override my instinct to reach out and soothe him. "Call me if anyone wants an appointment."

"You'll have your mobile?"

He nods and hands me a piece of paper. "This is where I'll be if you need to know for any reason." I'm careful not to touch his hand when I take the slip.

He passes me and I spin to watch him leave.

For far too long, I waited around for things to get better with Shane. I kept believing that if I did everything I could and we held on, everything would be okay.

And look how that turned out.

It's time to get honest with myself about whether I'm repeating the same old mistakes.

LINKEDIN IS MY PERSONAL NEMESIS. That and the word *market* when describing salary. They should just be honest and say, *we plan to pay you as little as we can get away with.* I reckon in the last hour and a half, I've applied for twenty jobs and left messages at three recruiters to call me back.

I'm scanning Le Cordon Bleu website when the door buzzer sounds and I nearly hit my head on the ceiling, I jump so high in the air.

The buzzer has never sounded.

I've never had a patient to let in. It must be someone who's pressed the wrong button on the intercom at the door.

"Dr. Cove's office," I respond.

"Package for Dr. Cove," someone replies. Sounds like bullshit to me. Dr. Cove never gets deliveries.

"Who is it?" I call.

"Rapid Couriers. Can you let me in?"

I wish we had a camera system.

"I'll come down now. I can't unlock the door from here." It's a lie, but something's off. I scramble downstairs just as another patient's leaving, and when the door swings open, a guy in a bicycle helmet, holding a brown package, is standing on the doorstep.

"Package for Dr. Cove?" I ask as I get to the door. The courier hands me the large brown envelope without saying another word. It's heavier than it looks, and just says DR. COVE in flowery writing on the front.

It's the size and weight of a chunk of paper. Weird. Zach didn't say he was expecting anything.

He's only been gone for a couple of hours, but I need to call him. This package could be important.

I race upstairs and dial his mobile.

"Ellie," he says when he answers, and my knees fizz at the gravel in his voice. I have to sit.

"A package just arrived."

"Shit," he says. "I thought she was sending it straight to Scotland." He sighs into the phone. "Can you get it couriered to the address I gave you? I'm about to get on a plane."

A plane? Where the hell is he going? He didn't sound like he was off on holiday. I grab the yellow Post-it that he gave me this morning and take a proper look at the address. Scotland.

"Of course," I say.

"I need it as soon as possible. Today. Or tomorrow at the latest."

"Leave it to me," I say. Arranging a courier isn't hard. And it's not like he's asking me to get it to a remote Polynesian island. It's Scotland.

"I can scan it in and send it over if you want?" I suggest.

"I won't have a printer up there and I need the original. I don't want to miss anything."

"No problem."

We hang up and I Google couriers. I'm about to hand over credit card details to the woman on the phone when she says, "Hang on. We can't guarantee tomorrow. It's a three-day minimum to the address you've given me."

"Are you sure?" I ask.

"Yep. That's what the computer's telling me."

"But it's Scotland."

"Don't know what to tell you. Three-day minimum."

"Okay, I'm going to have to leave it."

I hang up and phone another courier company. They tell me the same thing—it's going to take three days. The next one is worse. It will take them five days. I bring up Google and put in the address. Where could Zach be going that will take a courier three days to get to? I could probably *walk* to most places in the UK in less than three days.

The map zooms in on a small island off the west coast of Scotland.

Yikes. It's about as remote as it gets. What's taken Zach there? Does he have family in the area? A girlfriend? Is he just trying to finish off his research project in peace?

I try a couple more courier companies and no one can help, so I text Zach. I just want to make sure this package is as urgent as he says it is.

Most couriers are saying it will take at least three days. Does that work?

If he turns around and says no, I'm not sure what our options are, but at least I'll know what they aren't.

As I wait for a reply, I explore his location a little more closely on the map. It's just southwest of Skye, a small island called Rum. The only way to get there is by ferry. Why on earth would Zach want to go there of all places?

My phone beeps on my desk and I know it's Zach even before I look. I sweep my thumb up to reveal his response.

No, that doesn't work. I need that package tomorrow at the latest. Make it happen.

My heart sinks. This job isn't anything like I expected, but it's still the shortest route between where I am now and where I want to be, at Le Cordon Bleu. My course is clear: if I can't get a courier to deliver this package on time, I'm going to have to take it there myself.

ELEVEN

Ellie

My body sags with relief at finally being on the ferry to Rum. We might still be in the UK, but I could have left my flat at the same time and made it to Mexico by now. I'm a step away from renaming myself Frodo, except I don't have a ring, just a slightly battered brown envelope I managed to leave at the check-in desk of the Glasgow hotel I had to sleep in last night. Thankfully, they delivered it to the room, just in time to stop my minor heart attack when I realized I didn't have it. Despite not having touched a drop of alcohol, I went to bed, head dizzy and body aching with the need to lie down. I'd woken up much the same way, and the four-hour drive from Glasgow to Mallaig hasn't helped much. At least I made the ferry.

It's my first trip to Scotland, but there's not much to see. We are floating in a blanket of grey cloud, a fog that hampers sights and sounds. What I can see of the sea crashing against the boat looks cold, dark, and uninviting. Not that I was planning a dip. There are no soft sounds of bagpipes. No rugged views of the mountains. No sexy men in kilts with legs that look like they could kill a man. I wish I was at home.

It's worth it, I tell myself. *He's really going to appreciate what you've done for him.*

It's an odd mix of quiet and loud on the boat. I can't hear voices or traffic or other familiar noises, but at the same time, it's anything but silent. The wind whistles and howls like a petulant teenager, and the waves boom and crash like the snores of a sleeping giant.

Then the sound of the tannoy cuts through the racket as it crackles, hisses, and comes to life. "This is a safety announcement. All passengers, please make your way inside the boat immediately."

My heart clenches in my chest. Safety announcement? I glance around. There's only a few of us standing on the deck. Everyone else that boarded the ferry is already sheltering from the elements. I'm closest to the door to the inside, so I turn and bend to pick up my case when the boat rears up like a spooked horse. The movement tips me over and I land against the side of the ferry, my shoulder taking the brunt of my fall.

Before I work out which way is up, two men appear and lift me from under my arms. I yelp in pain as they pull me to my feet. "Get inside," one of them cries.

I look around for my case, but it's gone. No! I can't have lost that bloody parcel. "My case!"

The man who yelled at me points toward the other guy who's heading inside, pulling my luggage with him.

Thank God. I make my way toward the door, the ferry lifting and falling in a way it hadn't been up until now. I step into the interior of the ferry and the door slams violently behind me, as if to say, *you bloody idiot, don't come back out until you're told.*

The room I find myself in is painted white in that shiny outdoor paint and there are windows, waist height, on three walls. It's actually brighter in here than it is outdoors. There's a door through to another room, but about eight people are sitting on the three benches that line the walls of this room. I grab my case and slide onto the end of the wooden bench facing forward. To the side of me, a woman fiddles with a rosary. To be fair, if I was Catholic, I'd be making the sign of the cross and saying some Hail Marys right now. I know it's Scotland, but this sea is rough. The only ferries I've ever been on are the huge car-transport types we used to go on when I was a kid to cross the English Channel to France. None of them were ever quite this...bouncy.

I glance around at people's expressions, trying to figure out if they're scared. If people aren't allowed out on deck, maybe the conditions have changed since we set sail. Maybe the crew isn't prepared for seas this rough.

I turn to the woman next to me, my fear surpassing my embarrassment at talking to a complete stranger. "Is that normal for them to ban people from the deck?" I ask.

She doesn't turn to look at me as she taps at her mobile phone. "I've never known people to be out on deck in the winter."

I'm clearly not a local. But given that I'm not even allowed to take the rental car across on the ferry, because all cars on Rum require a permit, are there any locals on Rum? And how on earth did Zach end up here of all places?

It's none of my business, I tell myself. I'm just here to deliver a package and I'll be off the island and back to Glasgow by the end of the day.

A very long hour and forty-five minutes after we set sail, we dock at Rum harbor. Alive.

"Thank you," I call out as I come down the metal walkway onto solid ground. I'm not sure if I'm talking to the captain, the crew, or the woman with the rosary beads—any and all who kept us safe, I suppose.

Now, I just have to find Kinloch Cottage. That's all the address I have. Kinloch Cottage, Rum. I glance around, trying to get my bearings, but don't have to work out which direction to go. There's only one. I follow the rest of the ferry passengers up the road. Most of them are being picked up in cars at the small car park about fifty meters from the harbor. But two continue up the road and I follow them. They must be heading into town. Or the village, or wherever there's life on this tiny island. When the two people I'm trailing get into a car farther up the road, I realize I have no idea where I'm heading or how long it will take me to walk there. I guess part of me just supposed there'd be a taxi stand off the ferry? No such luck. To make matters worse, the fog that engulfed us on the ferry seems to have followed me on land, and I can't see more than ten meters ahead.

Fuck fog.

Fuck Scotland.

Fuck Zach Cove.

I stop, wondering whether I should go back to the ferry terminal to see if anyone there knows how to get to Kinloch Cottage. The beep of a car horn makes me jump, but the couple in the car I followed off the ferry pull up beside me.

"You want a lift?" the woman, wearing a brown bobble hat, says. She looks as confused as I do.

"I'm looking for Kinloch Cottage. Do you know it?" I bend down, not wanting to miss what she says.

"Kinloch Castle?" she asks.

I pull out my phone to check the address Zach wrote

out for me. "I don't think so. He definitely said Kinloch Cottage."

"She wants the English guy," the man in the passenger seat says. "In the Cove house."

The Cove house? Does Zach own this place? It's hardly a handy holiday home you can pop to at the weekend.

"Ahh," the woman says, "the English one. Of course. I can drive you. Hop in."

On any normal day, when a stranger tells me to hop into the back of their car, I'd run a mile and probably call the police to report an attempted kidnapping. But at this point in my journey, a little bit of kidnapping would be a welcome break from reality. I'm here for it.

"That would be great," I reply. "Thanks so much."

"You need a hand with your case?" the man says.

"No, thanks, I'm good." I stick my case on the floor and then round the boot and get in the other side. I didn't realize how cold I was until I'm in the car. "Thank you so much."

"No problem. It would have been quite a walk. And our place isn't far from Kinloch Cottage." She smiles at me. "You recovered from that ferry ride?" she asks on a laugh. "Not sure if they'll get off the dock. I'm surprised it ran."

"Thank God it did," the man says. "Don't want to get stuck in Mallaig." They both laugh like getting stuck in Mallaig is like being trapped in a theme park after all the rides are closed for the night.

"Down there you'll find the post office and general store." The woman points to a road that leads down to the coast.

"I'm not staying," I say. "I'm just here to deliver a package for my boss. Then I need to head back."

The man starts to say something but the woman taps him on the knee and he decides against it. Hopefully he wasn't about to confess my fate and say, "You're not going anywhere. We're going to kill you, roast you, and have you for dinner."

"It's just up here," the woman says in a singsong voice. "Not long now. Kinloch Cottage is the farthest out of all the homes up here. The rest of us like to be within walking distance of the shop. And we run the post office, so we have to be close. No matter the weather, we're always open, aren't we, Charlie?" She doesn't wait for a response. "When the weather gets bad, there's no driving anywhere."

"Makes sense," I say. "I'm sure it's beautiful in the—"

"It's always beautiful," she says. "You just can't see it today. Fog is a funny beast. Here one minute. Disappeared the next."

"Better than the snow," he says.

"Here we are." We pull off the main road, down a dirt track. "I'll leave you here and turn if that's okay."

A small, one-story, white-washed house is just visible through the soup of the fog. It's probably only thirty meters away. "Perfect. Thank you so much."

"Our pleasure. Welcome to Rum. See you again."

Not likely, I don't say. I'll be on that ferry, back to Mallaig before the end of the day, and I won't have any reason to stop at the post office between now and then. I climb out, pulling my case behind me. "Thank you again." I wave and close the car door. My stomach churns with anticipation as I straighten and head toward the house.

I'm excited to see Zach's face when he realizes I've come all this way to deliver his package by hand.

TWELVE

Ellie

I lift the circular door knocker on the white paneled door and it lands with a clunk. I do it again and wait. He's going to be so grateful. I can't wait to see his face.

Zach opens the door and my stomach flips. It's only been a day, but I'd forgotten how attractive he is. His blond hair looks more unruly than it usually does and he's in dark grey joggers and a grandad t-shirt, the first few buttons undone, that reveals a little bit of chest hair I've never seen before.

"Ellie?" he says as if he's just woken up. "What? How?"

"I brought the package," I announce and can't help but beam at him. I'm so pleased with myself. "I couldn't find a courier who would get it here in less than three to five days. You were adamant you needed it before the end of today, so I brought it myself."

His eyes widen and he pushes his hand into his hair, his t-shirt lifting to reveal ten centimeters of muscled torso. "Wow." The *wow* isn't delivered the way I would if someone had moved heaven and earth to give me what I needed. I get the same pit in my stomach I used to get when Shane would complain over the lack of mainstream media coverage I was able to secure for him after a race. Fact was, the mainstream media didn't give two shits about Speedway. Frankly, not many people gave a shit about Speedway other than the riders and their families. Even the die-hard fans seemed to dwindle over the ten years I was Shane's girl-friend-slash-manager.

"I don't want to interrupt," I say. "I just want to drop this and go. I'll get the next ferry back to Mallaig."

He frowns, then steps aside and opens the small door as wide as it will go. "Come in."

"Honestly, it's a long journey back, I shouldn't stay." I'm exhausted. The prospect of a four-hour drive back to Glasgow after another two-hour ferry journey doesn't fill me with glee, but sitting around making small talk with someone I barely know—even if he is hot as hell and has seen my knickers—isn't going to make the idea any more appealing.

"Come in, Ellie." His forceful tone catches me off guard. "There are no more ferries today."

I shiver and my ribs ache with cold. What does he mean *no more ferries today*? "I took the first one over. I'll get the afternoon one back."

There are two ferries a day. I checked.

"There isn't an afternoon one. Not in November. You must have looked at the summer timetable." He shuts the door and passes by me.

A ball of anxiety sticks in my throat. I'm the assistant. I'm meant to be organized and proactive. I'm meant to be able to read a ferry timetable. "I'm sure there's another," I mumble.

"Do you want a tea or coffee?" he calls from wherever he's disappeared to.

I glance up. The cottage is tiny. The front door leads straight into the living room, where on the left there's a red brick inglenook fireplace at one end, with a large sofa opposite. Other than a basket filled with logs, that's all that will fit. Beside the fireplace there's another small door, where Zach's voice is coming from. I put my case down and go through. The kitchen is larger than I expected but still small, and looks even smaller because Zach is so big.

"I don't want to put you to any trouble. I'm fine, I just need to find a hotel and I'll go back on the morning ferry."

"There are no hotels on the island. You'll stay here tonight..." His voice fades out as I realize I'm stranded and the boss, who I'm supposed to be helping, is making me a coffee.

This is ridiculous. I'm hopeless. No wonder this is the only job I could get that paid more than minimum wage. I've got no skills or qualifications. I'm no good at doing anything other than planning my boyfriend's calendar.

Buried tears push to the surface and threaten to spill over. "Excuse me," I blurt out before fleeing the kitchen and out the front door. What am I doing here? What was I thinking? I lean against the house and then sink to my knees and cover my face with my hands.

I'm useless. Shane was right. How am I going to handle a year at Le Cordon Bleu when I can't even travel to Scotland without fucking it up?

My parents were right, too. Ditching university for my boyfriend was the worst decision of my life. The people I've managed to keep as friends are busy climbing their career ladders and here I am in the middle of nowhere, not even able to deliver post properly. I've spent the last six weeks doing nothing. That's all I'm good for. If Zach actually ever gets patients, he's going to fire me because there's no way I'll be able to handle it.

"Ellie?" Zach's come outside and is standing over me.

"Can you give me a minute?" I ask, not taking my hands from my face.

"It's cold out here. Come in."

"I'm fine. I just need a minute."

I'm not fine and it's going to take a hell of a lot longer than a minute to recover, but I can't cope with my boss witnessing my going under.

I hear the door close and I exhale, thankful that at least now I can melt down without an audience.

Deep breath in. Long breath out.

Realistically, I messed up. But at least Zach has his mysterious package. If he could have waited three to five days, he should have said. The only way to get this package to him today was to bring it myself, so that's what I did.

He's going to have to put up with an overnight guest, but at least he got his package. I stand up. Worst-case scenario, he'll fire me. I've been fully expecting that for a few weeks now, so I'm no worse off now than I was before I left London this morning. Well, I'm close to five hundred pounds worse off, but at least I've got an example of my proactive nature.

I take a deep breath and turn back to face the house. Zach's looking back at me through the glazed door. He looks concerned. Or irritated. I don't know him well enough to know the difference.

I need to deal with what I've got, not what I'd like. I step forward and he opens the door almost immediately.

"I should have said thank you," he says. "For bringing

the package. It means a lot. I should have realized couriers would take ages to deliver it here."

"I just want to be the best assistant I can be for you. If I'd have known there were no ferries and no hotels..." My stomach swims with shame and anxiety. Hot tears prick at my eyes but I blink them back. My reaction isn't about Zach Cove and his package, and he doesn't need to get the brunt of my frustration over the last decade of wasted career options.

He reaches out his hand like he's going to pat me on the arm and I brace myself for the crackle of electricity I've felt whenever he's touched me. His hand hovers and he pulls it away. "Take your coat off and get warm in front of the fire."

I have nowhere to go, so I've just got to swallow this awkward situation down and make the best of it. I shrug off my coat and hang it on the rack by the door.

"You go back to doing whatever you're doing. You don't need to entertain me."

"I can spare ten minutes," he says. "I've made coffee." He nods toward a small table at the end of the sofa.

"Thanks." I take a seat and wrap my hands around the mug, warming my palms.

"So, did you fly up here this morning?" he asks.

I groan inwardly. "Last flight last night, or I wouldn't have made the ferry."

"Wow." He's perched on the arm of the green tartan sofa and he looks about as comfortable as I feel. But he makes uncomfortable look good. His trousers hug in all the right places and the grandad t-shirt clings to him, revealing his triangular torso and thick arms. Maybe he has free weights hidden in his drawers at work and spends the entire time he's in his office doing reps. Or something. "Like I said, I'm grateful. I should have had the...the package should have been sent straight here. There was obviously a mix-up."

I nod as if I understand, but I don't. I want him to tell me what's so important. "Yeah. They must have been confused when you were leaving or something." It's not 1999. What can't be emailed? "Do you have internet here?"

"It's patchy. There's good reception in the post office. They only charge a pound an hour."

I pause, hoping he's going to fill in the blanks. Like, why in the hell he didn't get the thing emailed. But he doesn't make the connection between what I'm saying and his mysterious package. "Honestly, I can take care of myself. You go ahead and...do whatever it was you were doing before I arrived."

I'm not sure what I'm going to do, but I'm sure I'll find something. "Actually, why don't I cook us dinner. Do you have anything planned?" I jump to my feet. That's how I can make myself useful. I can cook. We both need to eat, and getting in the kitchen is the only thing to hand that will get me out of my head—the very last place I want to be.

THIRTEEN

Zach

I link my hands behind my head and blow out a breath, staring at my laptop, which is set up on the dressing table in the only bedroom in the cottage. Thank God for Ellie. Having Mrs. Fletcher's notes has unlocked something in me; I get what she wants me to do and why. It helps that she's highlighted places in the manuscript where she thinks I can add some low-key flirting and connection.

It's mainly the love story Mrs. Fletcher has focused on in her comments, too. Areas where she thinks there's chemistry that could be ramped up and gaps where she thinks more of it should shine through. Now that I'm going through the pages, it's clear there's chemistry between these characters. It just hadn't occurred to me that it could be... developed. Or that it *should* be developed. She's right though—it works. It adds more to Benjamin's back story. It adds a heart to his sharp mind and gruff exterior. It's not that he's dead inside—he's just exacting and demanding, and for a woman to get his attention, well, she has to be extraordinary.

Mrs. Fletcher is officially a genius.

But my fingers feel like they're going to fall off. I need a break. I stand and lean forward, careful to save the changes I've made so far today.

It's just gone four, but I have another two or three hours in me if I have a break now.

I turn over the annotated manuscript, just in case Ellie needs to come in the bedroom for any reason. Mrs. Fletcher's scribbled comments are *everywhere*, and they certainly don't look medicine-related.

I head out to find a cup of coffee.

Of all the things I expected today, an overnight guest was not one of them. I'm grateful Ellie brought up the manuscript, but it would have been easier if the courier had brought it. I just don't like the idea of anyone knowing what I'm doing here. It needs to be private. Separate.

And Ellie's...not *distracting*, exactly, because the writing is all-consuming, but being with her in this small space, no bigger than my office and waiting room combined, is intense. Back in London, for the first hour or so in the mornings I'm in the office, I'm very aware of her, just the other side of the wall.

If Mrs. Fletcher manages to sell my book, everything changes. That's what I need to keep focused on. Yes, I'll have my family and their ideas about what kind of career I should have, but if I went to them with the news that a publisher had actually bought my book, they might not be quite so upset about me wanting to leave medicine. Dad might still feel proud.

I open the bedroom door and the gentle scent of lilac winds around me like I'm walking among wildflowers. It's the same in the office. The smell is summery and pretty and it announces Ellie's presence instantly. I try and bite back a grin. Maybe it will be nice to have some company —someone to pull me out of the fictional world that I live in during the day. Maybe it will make me fresher tomorrow.

"Hey," I say, leaning on the kitchen doorframe as Ellie washes something in the sink. "You okay?" She was so upset earlier and I'm not quite sure why. I get that she wanted to get home, but I'm surprised she took being stranded here overnight so badly.

She turns and smiles and it's like someone's turned up the dimmer switch on my day. "Hey. Can I get you a snack?"

I laugh. She's forever offering me something to eat. "I just came to grab a coffee."

"Let me do that. Is there a cafetiere?" She turns and starts to open cupboards and I try not to notice the way her hair falls to about halfway down her back, just above the waist that sharply curves in and then out again, like a fifties movie star wearing a corset.

"I'm all about the instant," I say, nodding towards the jar by the kettle.

She turns, her eyebrows pulled together. "Really?"

"Hard to believe because I'm a man of such great taste?"

She blushes and I can feel the heat of her cheeks in my chest. She's beautiful. "I assumed that..." She shakes her head. "Ignore me. I'll put the kettle on."

Ignore her? I'm not sure that's possible.

There's not loads of room in the kitchen and so I let her fill the kettle with water and switch it on. Better that than I accidently knock her. Every time I've laid a hand on her, I've felt a buzz of electricity. I can't quite make up my mind why.

"How's work going?" she asks.

I nod. "Good. The stuff you brought up has been really helpful."

The love story element has been more difficult to write than I expected without the notes. When I discussed it with Mrs. Fletcher on the phone, it seemed straightforward enough. I'm not used to thinking so deeply about what women are thinking or how they're likely to react to something a guy says. But like Mrs. Fletcher says, I'm just laying down touch paper. It doesn't need to be lit. At least she's given me clear signposts where I should write, so I just have to figure out the what and not the where.

"That's good," she says. "I'm sorry if me being here has disrupted things."

"The very opposite," I say. Without her, I would have been stumbling around in the fog, not quite knowing what to do.

Her blush deepens and desire presses against my chest.

Maybe it's Madeline's blush that Benjamin first notices about her. Or the slightly worried look that underpins her smile, just like Ellie has. Maybe he wants to know what has her so concerned.

"You want a snack?" Ellie asks again as she pours the freshly boiled water into the mug she's set out.

Instinctively my hand goes to my stomach and Ellie's gaze flickers to my hand and then sharply back to the kettle as if she's been caught with her hand in the cookie jar. I bite back a grin. "I'm good with coffee," I say.

She picks up the mug and, instead of handing it to me, slides it onto the counter next to me. I can't help but wonder if she's trying to avoid touching me. Has she felt what I did each time we've touched?

I take the mug. "I should get back to it."

"Let me know if you need anything to eat," she says. "You know I love to cook."

I can't help but wonder if she spends all her free time in the kitchen and why, if she loves to cook so much, she's not doing it for a living.

I raise my mug and head back to the bedroom and Benjamin Butler.

The way I see my hero is, he's content to be by himself until Madeline crosses his path and something inside him is awoken. Slowly. And I can see him fighting to put it back to sleep—to *not* like her. But I think he can't help being first of all intrigued by her and then impressed by her. Yes, that's the way a hero like Benjamin would fall in love. His head would have to be won over first. They need to have a mental connection before they have a physical one. Maybe they think similarly. Or they work in the same methodical way. Perhaps he thinks she's too focused on technology and new methods, yet they both like to carry notebook and pens rather than keeping notes electronically. Maybe she pushes him a little more than most people do. A bit like Ellie did with the insurer recognition. Yes, Benjamin tries to resist Madeline, but even if he doesn't know it, she's what he needs. Fate has them in her crosshairs.

FOURTEEN

Ellie

I've done the best I can with what was in the fridge and cupboards. I don't know exactly what Zach was planning to eat tonight, but I'm guessing it involved baked beans given the eight cans on the windowsill.

Luckily, he had some kind of welcome box of provisions that hadn't even been opened, and I've managed to put together toad in the hole with cabbage, mash potato, and gravy. A favorite of mine I haven't made for years, since Shane hated it.

I assume Zach will emerge from his bedroom at some point, but dinner will be ready at eight—any minute now. Surely he won't work past then. There's a small table in the kitchen just big enough for two. Just. I've set it with place-mats and cutlery. Dinner has got a few minutes and I've washed everything up—by hand, since there's no dishwasher.

I lean against the kitchen counter. How can I make this better? Mustard, obviously, but I don't have any. I've emptied every cupboard, trying to discover a hidden jar, but there isn't one. My gaze catches on an empty cup on the windowsill with the word *Rum* printed in blue, cursive font. I glance out the window. There's not much growing outside the cottage. It's a pretty unforgiving landscape. But there is plenty of heather. I grab my trainers from the mat and shove them on. I'll need to be quick because the timer is about to go off on the oven.

I don't bother with a coat, and as soon as I step outside, I regret it. It's the kind of biting cold that only happens every couple of years down south, plus it's eerily dark. The lights of the cottage coming through the windows is the only way I can see, and I can't make out anything in the distance at all. I pull the door nearly all the way closed to keep the cold air out without locking myself outside in the process. The cottage is amazingly well insulated. The fact that I've been cooking and the fire is burning helps. There's a bush of heather in bloom right by the front door. I bend, taking in the reddish-purple flowers. They look much more vibrant the more I focus on them. I pick a few stalks, and as I stand, a gust of wind nearly blows me off my feet. I grab the door-knob to keep my balance and inadvertently pull it shut.

Shit.

I try and open it but the catch is on.

If Zach didn't think I was a complete disaster before, he will do now.

I'm starting to become aware of the joints in my fingers and my teeth start to chatter. I'm going to have to knock on that door. I lift the door knocker and wait. But there's no answer. I lift it again and it clunks on the rest just as the door is tugged open.

Zach scowls at me. "What are you doing?"

"Sorry," I reply. "The door blew closed." I sneak past him and go and stand in front of the fire, clutching the stalks of heather. They definitely weren't worth it, but I'm not letting them go now.

"You okay?" he asks. "You should wear a coat if you're going outside."

A curl of dread rises in me. Shane never let me forget a mistake.

I nod, bracing myself for the impending shaming bound to come next.

But Zach doesn't say anything, just heads back into the bedroom.

I let out a breath and try and figure out what just happened. He was right, I really should be wearing a coat if I'm going outside—except, I only expected to be out a few seconds and I hadn't realized it was going to be so cold. Maybe he'll bring it up again later.

I realize I should have mentioned that dinner's ready. "I've made dinner," I call out. "It's ready when you are."

Zach's head appears from around the door.

"You have?" His hand goes to his stomach again and I very definitely do not let my eyes follow. I saw enough earlier to know he's got washboard abs.

"Toad in the hole."

He nods. "Okay. I'll be right there." No mention of me locking myself out in the freezing cold. Almost like he's already forgotten.

The buzzer on the oven sounds and I head back into the kitchen and set about dishing up what I've prepared. I put the plates on the table, put the water in the cup and shove the heather in just as Zach appears in the kitchen.

"You've set the table."

"Yes, would you prefer to take your plate and carry on working?"

He hesitates, thinking about it. "No, this is fine."

I realize I'm about to have dinner with a virtual stranger. A handsome virtual stranger. Another day, different circumstances, and this could be a date.

It has been a very long time since I've had a date—if dating in your teens even counts. More like a trip to the cinema, a sloppy over-enthusiastic kiss, and awkward conversation—at least that's all I can remember pre-Shane.

"Thanks for this," Zach says as he takes a seat.

His words warm me. It's nice to be appreciated. "No problem," I reply. "I hope I didn't tear you away from your research."

"I need to pace myself. And it's late." He picks up his knife and fork and I do the same. "I love cabbage," he says.

I can't help but laugh. It seems such a boyish, sweet thing to say. "Good."

We eat in silence for a few minutes, but it's not awkward. He's got nice table manners. Shane always ate like there was a sand timer on the table, and when all the grains had run through, a hatch would open on the table and swallow his plate.

"It's delicious," he says. "All of it. My mother makes this for me and my brothers. It's just as good as hers."

I try and swallow a grin—as good as his mum makes? I'll take it. "How many brothers do you have?"

"Four. I'm the second oldest."

"There are five of you?" I can't help but wonder if they're all as good looking as Zach.

One side of Zach's mouth rises in a lopsided grin. "Yeah. Looking back, I don't know how my parents coped with us when we were younger. They both had really demanding hospital jobs."

"They're doctors?"

He laughs. "I can tell you're not in medicine. Dad is. Mum's a surgeon. And so are three of my brothers."

"Wow. I bet that leads to a lot of shop talk around the kitchen table."

His smile dims and he nods. "All the time. It's good and it's sometimes not so good. What about you. Do you have any brothers or sisters?"

"A younger sister. She's still at home."

"Oh wow. Much younger, then."

I tilt my head and shoot him a *really? I'm-not-that-old* look.

"What?" he asks. "Did I get it wrong?"

I shrug. "She's ten years younger than me."

"So much younger. I'm not saying you're old. How old are you anyway? Thirty?"

"Twenty-eight. But thanks."

"So I was right."

"No," I reply. "You thought I was two years older than I am. Not the best compliment I've had today." I'm smiling as I speak. I don't know why, but it makes me feel a bit better that he's not smoother. Maybe because I've made mistake after mistake in front of him. I'm not perfect and neither is he.

He rolls his eyes. "It's two years. I'm thirty-two. I assumed we were about the same age."

I laugh. "Stop digging that hole you're in. I'll take thirty if your more accurate guess is thirty-two."

"If you're pretty at twenty-five, you're pretty at thirty-five," he says matter-of-factly, and the word *pretty* echoes in my brain like the sonorous chime of a church bell. "Women don't age between twenty-five and thirty-five."

"Is that your medical opinion?" I don't fish for compliments or ask him to clarify whether he's calling me pretty. If he did, it was inadvertent, and I don't want to embarrass him.

"Just my male opinion."

"Men don't age between thirty and forty-five," I say. "And a lot of men get better looking in that time period. They grow into their bodies and their faces or something."

"I look forward to it." He takes a forkful of food and chews.

"Not likely. You've hit the ceiling." I wince, regretting the words the moment they leave my mouth. I've got to learn to keep my inside voice, inside.

He frowns. "The ceiling?"

I shrug. It's not like he doesn't know he's good looking. "You're not going to get better looking," I say.

He chuckles but doesn't say anything and the fact that he doesn't unleashes something in me. He has a weird kind of confidence that's like an ovary magnet. It's either he's had compliments about his looks so often over the course of his life that it barely registers, or he doesn't care that he's gorgeous. Either way, it's like suddenly, I can't stop noticing how handsome he is. He's got broad, solid shoulders, and long legs that are poking sideways under the table in a seemingly deliberate attempt not to encroach on my space. He's got the kind of body that could stand between you and a hurricane—like a superhero who uses his body to shield innocent civilians. He should put a call in to Marvel.

He glances up and I look away. I've been caught staring. I just can't not. I need to snap out of it.

"So, you're going to be up here two weeks?" I ask.

"Maybe a little more," he replies. "Depends how things go with my...you know, the research."

I want to ask him why on earth he took on the expenses of an assistant and an office on Wimpole Street when he's doing research. But I don't want to talk myself out of a job. He's a clever guy. I'm sure he knows what he's doing.

"Let me know if there's anything I can help with. Data entry. Proofreading. Anything. I like to be busy."

"Thanks." He doesn't seem enthusiastic. And then he breaks out into a smile so wide it makes me ache. "Your snacks are good."

"You think?" I grin. "I love to cook."

Our eyes meet and it's like a physical touch, sparking the same electricity I felt the previous times he's touched me.

He clears his throat and looks back down at his plate, like he feels it too and is just as confused.

He finishes his meal, and there's not a morsel of food left on the plate.

"You want some more? I have plenty of—"

He shakes his head and I stop. "The only thing that could have made that better would have been a glass of red wine," he says. He nods at the heather-filled cup. "We even had table decorations."

I feel a bit stupid, but I like people to enjoy eating my food. "A glass of wine would have been—maybe not such a good idea." I wouldn't trust myself a glass of wine down in front of Zach. I've already told him he's good looking and I'm completely sober. Lubricated by alcohol, there's no telling what I might do or say. I'd probably lick that completely lickable neck. Or tell him I think he might be the best-looking man I've ever laid eyes on. I dodged that bullet. Thank God tomorrow, I'm on the ferry out of here.

"There's something I have to tell you," he says and I put down my knife and fork.

I knew it. He's terminating my contract. My horrendous journey up here has been for nothing. I take a steadying breath, ready to accept my fate. "Don't worry, I know what you're going to say."

"You do?" he asks with a frown. "So you knew you were looking at the summer timetable?"

He's making no sense. "What?"

"You know there are only three ferries a week to Rum from Mallaig?"

A ball of fire ignites in my stomach and I have to stand. "What? But there's a ferry tomorrow, right?"

"No, not until Sunday. Depending on the weather."

The fire fizzles out and I slump into my chair, putting my head in my hands. "I'm so sorry. I thought I was doing the right thing. I'm so fucking desperate not to get fired—I wanted you to think I was terrific at my job. I'm such an idiot." It's not just the ferry that's completely humiliating. It's the feeling that I can't ever get any traction on my life after Shane. He's moved on, and nothing much will have changed for him, other than he's fucking a different woman. No doubt she's probably already moved into his house. But for me, my life still lies in ruins. And whenever I try to rebuild my foundations, they dissolve or decay as soon as I turn around.

I need to catch a break.

"Shit, Ellie." The scrape of Zach's chair stops my tears from falling. I can't take any more humiliations today. He won't see his assistant cry.

"I'm fine." I look up to find him standing over me, clearly not having a clue what to do. I want to run away or at least go into another room, but the cottage is tiny and it's not like I even have a bedroom I can run to. "I'm completely fine. I'm sorry, I'm going to have to stay another night and then I'll be out of your hair. I promise I won't impose on you any more than I have to." I stand, trying to show that I am fine, but he doesn't move. Instead he bends, trying to catch my eye.

He puts his hand on my shoulder and the electricity is back, but this time he doesn't flinch away. "It's okay, Ellie. It's amazing you brought me the letter. The package. I'm really grateful and it's made a tremendous difference to how much I can get done over the next few days. You being here isn't a problem. For me anyway."

I don't know if it's his touch, the tone of his voice, or that I'm breathing in his scent of pine trees and campfires, but my body begins to melt. "I'll cook for you." My voice is weak.

"You don't need to." He smooths his hand down my arm, setting off a crackle of sparks across my skin. "But I'll eat it if you do." He laughs and it's the most genuine, warm, comforting sound I've ever heard. I can't help smiling up at him.

We stare at each other a beat too long, our smiles mirroring each other, and then he looks away.

"I should organize sleeping arrangements. I have to work in the bedroom tomorrow. That's where my desk is. But tonight I'll take the sofa and—"

"No," I say. "Absolutely not. I'm completely fine on the sofa. There's no way I'm going to come up here, have to stay because I can't read a ferry timetable, and then kick you out of your bed. Not ever going to happen."

There's a count of silence and then he looks me dead in the eye. "I'm sleeping on the sofa." His voice is deep and serious and full of concentrated masculinity. It's so intense I have to look away and place my hand on the table to stop myself from toppling over.

I know there's no point in arguing.

FIFTEEN

Zach

My mind drifts back to the first thought I had this morning when I woke up. It's the same thought that has come back to me at various points in the day today: I'm fucked.

Because...Ellie.

I can hear her move between the kitchen and the living room. I saw her this morning but we had something to discuss and focus on. She wanted to use the car to go down into the village to buy more supplies. I gave her tips for getting down there without getting stuck, and which shops she could get what in. Then around midday, she asked if I would like some lunch, and delivered me the best chicken sandwich I've ever eaten.

Today's been fine. But it's tonight I'm worried about. Tonight as we sit across from each other at dinner and I try not to notice the outline of her chest, or how her eyes seem to look bluer in this northern light. As I try not to be amused by the way she's incapable of hiding what she's thinking but still has a layer of mystery I'm almost desperate to uncover.

Most of the time she just says what's on her mind and the rest of the time it's written on her face. And it's because of that, I know she's also feeling this...*energy* between us.

I check the time on my laptop. It's nearly eight and I catch the smell of...is it bread? Or cinnamon? The aroma of something fucking delicious is drifting through to the bedroom.

I wish it was only the food I'm looking forward to this evening.

Opening the bedroom door, I find Ellie leaning over the sofa, rearranging the cushions. I can see down her shirt.

Fuck. I close my eyes, the image of white lace and milky-white skin is scorched onto the back of my eyelids.

"Hey," she says and I open my eyes. "I was wondering when you would appear. Dinner is about ten minutes out. Can I get you a glass of wine?"

I should say no. "You're not my servant, Ellie. I don't expect you to—"

She grins. "I know. You know I love to cook."

Silence twists between us.

"Okay, you get the wine," she says, "and I'll finish off here."

Honestly, a glass of wine right now is exactly what I want, even though I'm a little concerned it might loosen the already shaky boundaries between Ellie and me that come with sharing such a small space.

I head into the kitchen and find a bottle of red on the kitchen counter. I take the corkscrew from the drawer just as Ellie comes in.

"Chicken piccata with lemon garlic rice and green beans tonight," she says as she bends over to look through the oven window.

She's wearing jeans that look like she poured herself

into them and I don't hate it. Her arse isn't chasing Kim Kardashian for attention but there's a good handful there and—

I need to get a grip. "Sounds great, although I don't know what piccata is."

She stands and beams at me. "Great! You'll love it." She's radiating something I haven't seen before. Or maybe I've caught glimpses of it. Whenever she talks about food, she lights up.

"I'm sure I will." I take two glasses and the bottle over to the table to get out of the way. "Anything I can do other than pour the wine?"

"I'm just plating up and then that's it. Oh and I baked some bread, so we have that as well if we want to get good and carbed. I don't know about you, but first of November kicks in and I just want to eat one hundred percent carbs. I guess our basic human instincts never leave us." She catches my eye, and I swear to God, I think I'm blushing. The basic instinct I'm having right now has nothing to do with carbs and everything to do with unpeeling her jeans from her and kissing her between her thighs.

My expression must be giving me away because she looks away, a little flushed.

"Here." She sets the food on the table and smiles at me. "Bon app."

I place her wine down on the table and she raises her glass.

"Thank you," I blurt. "For cooking," I clarify, although I'm not sure that's what I'm thanking her for. "It looks delicious." It's like something I'd expect to see in a restaurant and smells better.

"It's my total pleasure. I love cooking, but what's even better is cooking for someone other than myself."

"Does it matter who it is?"

She tilts her head like she's really thinking about the question. "Yes."

I hold her gaze and after a beat she looks away.

"Well, I hope I'll do until you can get back home to..."

She lets out a dull laugh. "My flatmate. She'll eat anything, which is great. Oh, I forgot the bread." She comes back with two side plates with half a slice of doorstop-thick bread that I might actually want to marry. I take the plate from her and tear off a chunk. It's still warm and I can't help but groan as I chew.

I open my eyes and catch her watching me, her teeth sunken into her lip. I shift in my seat and unfold my legs, not pulling away as I slide mine against hers. The electricity sparks between us, just like it always does when we touch. I leave my leg against hers and she doesn't pull away.

We lock eyes and an understanding passes between us —a threshold has been crossed.

She looks away. "I hope you like it."

"I will," I say and start to eat.

"Did you get everything done that you wanted to?"

Maybe she's just chitchatting.

Maybe she's trying to figure out more about the "research" I'm doing.

Maybe she's trying to rebalance the dynamic between us to work colleagues.

But that ship has sailed.

"For today." I take a bite of the chicken and it's the best thing I've ever tasted. "Jesus, Ellie. This is delicious. Where did you learn to cook like this?"

She blushes slightly and my dick stirs. She's gorgeous. If she's wearing makeup, I can't tell. Her skin is glowing, her eyes are bright and wide and her dark hair is piled on her head like she's completely comfortable. She looks happier than I think I've ever seen her. I guess this is at-home Ellie as opposed to work Ellie. I like it. A lot.

"I'm self-taught—" She stops herself even though she was clearly going to say more.

"But..." I prompt.

"I'd like to...learn more."

She's hiding something and she's terrible at it. It's both hilarious and utterly charming. "So, what's your plan, because I can tell you have one."

She sighs. "I do, but...you're my boss."

I shake my head because thoughts like that are entirely unacceptable. If I start thinking about her as an employee? My brain can't reconcile the soft press of her leg against mine with the idea that I have any kind of power over her career. "Not tonight. Not while you're here."

She narrows her eyes as she considers what I've said. "Promise? Can you wipe clean your mind if I tell you?"

"I promise."

"I want to go to Le Cordon Bleu. I'm saving. It's why I need this job so badly."

Guilt stabs me in the gut at hearing how much she wants the job. I've practically ignored her since she started. I've not even considered that she's worried she's going to be fired. "Okay," I manage to choke out.

"I don't mean to be disloyal. It's going to take me a while to save. I won't leave you high and dry, when the time comes."

Here she is worried about being disloyal to me, when if my plans come off, I'm not going to need an assistant. "You don't need to worry about being disloyal. No one commits to a job for life anymore."

"Right," she says and sadness flickers across her eyes. "Wish I'd figured that out a little bit sooner."

I try to think back to what her CV said about her previous job, but I barely took much notice. I just needed an assistant and she'd seemed more enthusiastic than I was over the phone, so I hired her. "Were you cooking before this job?"

She shakes her head. "No, I was managing my boyfriend—my ex-boyfriend's Speedway career."

"Speedway? What's that?"

She groans like she wishes we weren't having this conversation, or maybe at the thought of her ex-boyfriend. "A bunch of men who never grew up racing around dirt tracks on motorcycles that don't have any brakes."

"I've never heard of it. Didn't realize it was a thing. And you were his manager?"

She shrugs. "The sport isn't as popular as it was, but they have hardcore fans and the riders are celebrities in their own corner of the world."

I can't help but laugh. The picture she paints isn't flattering. "I get that. Being famous in your corner of the world. It can be...a pain in the neck for people around them."

She swallows and holds my gaze. "You're not getting away with stopping there. Please elaborate." She says it with a smile, but in a tone like she fully expects me to comply.

I laugh—she's so completely transparent and that's so refreshing. "My parents. Both are phenomenal in their fields. Everyone in medicine knows about *the Coves*. And despite it being my name, when people talk about 'the Coves,' they mean my mum and dad." A couple of times, I'd overheard people talking about "the Cove brothers." But I got the distinct impression it had little to do with our medical expertise. "I'm proud of them. Don't get me wrong. But it's weird."

"Because of people's expectations?" she asks.

I pause. "Yes. And...also, because they're so brilliant...so objectively successful, it's hard to question them—professionally, I mean."

I glance at her and she's frowning. I'm probably not making much sense to her.

"They're wonderful people though. Both retired now." I laugh again and it's not at all bitter—more resigned and incredulous. "Their legacy lives on. I think because they were both brilliant in their own right but they were married, so they became this power couple. It's never really happened in medicine before."

"So you feel like you're in their shadow? Is that why you don't seem to want any patients?"

I blow out a breath. I'm on dangerous ground. She's confessed personal stuff to me and I don't want to tell her a series of lies or half-truths to cover up what I'm really doing here—it would feel like a betrayal. "Let's not talk about work."

"Sorry if I overstepped."

I shake my head, sliding my other leg against hers, trying to reassure her that I'm not upset. I just don't want to lie to her. It seems I've spent the last decade of my life lying to myself and I'm running out of road. The more I write, the more I *want* to write, and the more I can't picture myself doing anything else. There's no going back after this trip, but I want to enjoy this calm before I have to reenter reality and figure out how to move forward.

We finish dinner and set about clearing the table, piling plates up on the kitchen counters, ready to wash.

"Wash or dry?" she asks.

"Don't mind."

"Well, yellow is my color," she says, reaching for the rubber gloves. "So I'll wash."

She snaps the gloves on with a ping that I feel in my balls and turns to the sink. We work as a team, washing and drying until the kitchen looks back to normal.

"Anything else before I take these bad boys off?" she asks, holding up her gloved hands and glancing around the kitchen.

I didn't realize I could find lack of vanity such a turn-on.

"Just one thing." I throw the tea towel I'm holding onto the counter and take a step towards her, closing the gap between us.

I cup the back of her head and hold her gaze. "This is long overdue, don't you think?"

She swallows and nods, and I grin before I press my lips against hers.

She tastes sweet and fresh like oranges with a hint of cinnamon, and I can tell by her short breaths and the trip of her pulse under my fingers that she wants this. But she's nervous. She's a delicious juxtaposition of unflinchingly capable and entirely innocent. I want to know her better, unwind her defenses, peel back her layers.

She discards her rubber gloves and her hands smooth up my chest. I shiver and deepen our kiss. I don't know if it's because I'm here—in Scotland, being who I want to be—but I feel a freedom I haven't felt in a long time. Maybe ever. And somehow Ellie feels like part of that freedom.

I shift, pushing my thigh between her legs and she moans into my mouth. The sound vibrates through my body, making every cell stand to attention.

Instinctively, I break away and take a step back, wiping

my mouth with the back of my hand, waiting for my pulse to stop thumping in my ears.

Her mouth is reddened from my stubble and strands of her hair have fallen around her face. She looks fucking incredible, but if I don't get a grip now, I will push further than I should.

And *when* I fuck her, I don't want her to feel pushed.

"Okay," she says.

"I hope that's not your grade for that kiss." I lean back on the counter and can't help but grin. "Because, it was at least an *excellent*."

She tilts her head and hums. "Nope. For it to qualify for excellent, it would not have ended so...abruptly."

"I'll work on that for next time."

"Maybe," she says, pulling the yellow gloves from where they lie discarded on the counter and arranging them neatly at the sink.

Definitely.

SIXTEEN

Ellie

I wake up with a start. I swear I just heard a bomb go off.

A bang echoes throughout the house again and I leap out of bed, throw on some clothes and go and investigate.

As I'm entering the sitting room, Zach is coming into the cottage, an armful of wood in his arms. I've never been a girl who's into woodchopping lumberjack types, but I'll make an exception for the Zach that just came through the door. His stubble is longer than I've ever seen it and it suits him. He's got a look of determination in his eye that I saw just before he kissed me last night.

He meets my gaze and I feel our kiss buzz between my legs.

If he hadn't broken it off, I would have climbed him like a tree and begged him to take me to bed. If his tongue is as skilled as I think it is, I wouldn't have gotten much sleep last night.

But he did break it off. It was probably the smart thing to do. He's my boss, after all, and I'm going home today.

"Amber weather warning," he says. His voice is deep and authoritative.

"Amber what?"

"It's going to snow later. I'm getting wood in. We're pretty cut off here and this place can get snowed in apparently. We need to get prepared and make sure we've got plenty of wood from the storage barn."

I need a lift to the ferry. Is he saying he doesn't have time to take me? "Shall I try calling a cab to get a lift?"

"There are no ferries today, Ellie."

His words hit me with a force and I step back into the arm of the sofa and sit. "No ferries. Shit." I should never have come here. What was I thinking? "I'm so sorry. This is such a shit show."

He dumps the wood by the fire, turns, and leans over me, one hand either side of my thighs. "Listen to me. I'm grateful you brought the package. I like having you here." He pauses, eyes dipping to my mouth and then back to meet my gaze. "We need to prepare." He presses a kiss to my lips like it's nothing and then stands. "Let's go get some food. There's a chance the warning will turn red and there's no telling when we'll next be able to get out to buy supplies."

I can still feel the press of his kiss, but I stand and pull my boots on.

"It's already windy," he warns as he hands me a hat. "Hence the door slamming shut. I've been trying not to wake you."

"I want you to wake me," I say and feel my cheeks redden. I know I'm responding to an emergency, but even if there wasn't a weather warning, I'd still want him to wake me. "You want to stay here and get the wood in and I can go to get supplies?"

"No," he says. "We'll do it together. I don't want us splitting up."

I don't know if it's his tone or the authority in his voice, but there's something about him that makes me feel safe. I never realized it was missing, but I never felt that with Shane. Not once.

"I need to get a list together."

"I'll give you ten minutes. I'll set up my work stuff in the bedroom for when we're back."

"Let's go, then."

We drive slowly into the small village and park right outside the main general shop. It is in no way a *super*market. It's tiny. But it's a shop and they have food. "How long is this weather going to last? How much do we need to buy?" I ask as I step out of the car.

"No idea. A few days?" he suggests.

"A few?" I try and control the hysteria rising in my stomach. "I didn't bring enough knickers."

He shoots me a grin but doesn't say anything.

"Do you have a freezer?"

"Yeah, there's a freezer."

"I can make soup and curry..." I mumble to myself. If I'd had more time, I could have planned out some menus.

"Can we get some stuff so you can make that bread again? It was incredible."

I press my palm against my reddened cheek. If someone calls my food incredible, there's not much I wouldn't do for them.

The door to the shop opens inward and he holds it open as I pass by, our bodies brushing against each other. I glance up at him. He feels that buzz when we touch, I can tell he does. We're going to be stuck in the same house together for days? The energy between us is already simmering, but I'm not sure I know how to turn down the heat.

"Okay, so let's get some flour," I say. "I might even do some socca." I remember from last time where the baking ingredients are, so I grab a basket and head left.

As I stop in front of the flour selection, Zach takes the basket from me. "Load me up." He grins at me like we're in the middle of some kind of supermarket sweep gameshow. He always seems so...unhappy in London.

Gorgeous, but glum.

This playful side of him is much better and sexy as hell.

The shop is small but its shelves are packed floor to ceiling with provisions. There are various sets of step ladders that have rails either side and wheels one end that can be moved about so people can reach the stuff near the ceiling. I spot some oats and go grab a set of ladders.

"Wait," Zach says.

"I'm good," I say as I start to climb.

"You sure? I can—"

"I'm sure."

He doesn't make a fuss about my refusal and it's clear his offer is about helping me and not protecting his delicate ego by having a woman climb a set of ladders in front of him. It's refreshing. And more than a little sexy.

I pull the bag of oats from the shelf and scan what else I can reach. Ahh, yes, chickpea flour. The bell over the door rings and catches Zach's attention. I use the opportunity to take him in from this angle. His hair is all mussed and somehow his arms look even more muscular from up here. They're not cover-yourself-in-fake-tan-and-flex-for-the-cameras big, but they're I'm-just-a-guy-who-can-chop-wood-and-throw-you-over-my-shoulder big. And I'm here for it.

"You having fun up there?" he asks, lifting his chin. It's

clear by the amusement in his eyes that he knows that I've been checking him out.

I laugh. There's no point in denying it. "Just appreciating the view."

"Oh, you're going to see plenty of it over the next few days."

A heavy ache throbs between my thighs. I'm not sure if his comment was meant to come across as loaded as it does, but either way, I'm happy to take as much as I can get.

"What about apple pie?" he suggests as I get down from the ladder. "As long as the pastry is premade, it's something I can actually make."

"You can?" I ask. "They teach that at medical school?"

He lets out a half laugh on his exhale. "Cove family med school. My mum is an excellent cook and there's always an apple pie in the process of being made."

"There's nothing better than homemade apple pie. Let's see if they have any cooking apples. I can always make the pastry." Fuses of excitement light in my chest. Snowed in with a whole lot of cooking ingredients might be one of the best things that has ever happened to me.

"This is better than Christmas for you, isn't it?" he asks as he follows me farther down the small aisle. "I've never seen you this excited."

"If I'm going to be finicky, I would have liked time to prepare some menus and maybe access to some—oh, here's the herbs and spices." Despite its small size, this shop has a remarkable range of ingredients.

"You know what I like with my apple pie?" He steps closer, snaking his arm around me, pulling me to him and closing the gap between us. "Cinnamon." He presses a kiss to my cheekbone and then releases me, but my legs have turned to jelly and I stumble back a few steps.

"Cinnamon," I say, trying to regain my balance. "Cinnamon." I trail my fingers over the jars of spices until I find what he wants. Apparently cinnamon does it for Zach. I drop the jar into the basket he's holding and move on, trying to ignore the way it feels when he looks at me. It's like I can feel his stare—like his gaze has mass and weight and meaning.

We work our way around the shop, making sure we have enough of what we'll need. Pasta, rice, couscous, flour of all kinds, beans, and lentils. Fish, veal, and chicken. Then we get to the vegetable section.

"People fall into two distinct categories for me," I say. "Lovers of aubergine, or idiots. Which are you?"

When he doesn't respond, I turn and he's smirking at me. "Aubergine? Like the emoji that represents...a penis?"

I sigh over-dramatically. "Are you a fourteen-year-old boy trapped in a—" I look him up and down. He didn't get any less hot in the ten minutes since I last ogled him. "A man's body?"

"Oh Christ, you gotta strap in. When you meet my brothers, you're not going to know what hit you. There's at least one dick joke per hour or their oxygen starts to wear thin." He presses a kiss to my head like it's no big deal that he just mentioned me meeting his family. I mean, we've kissed once. Even though I feel like we're going to combust every time we're near each other, he needn't get ahead of himself. He reaches over me and grabs an aubergine. "But for the record, I love me some aubergine. Any chance of some moussaka?"

"One of my specialties," I say, instantly distracted by the idea of cooking that tonight. "And we already have the cinnamon. Is there any lamb mince?"

"I might never want the weather to clear," Zach says as he lifts up the first of two baskets he's been carrying.

On the counter are various items for sale, including a carousel of tourist keyrings. This place is pretty remote, and it's difficult to imagine them selling many of them. Particularly in winter. Gently, to stop anything falling, I turn the carousel, wondering if I should get one as a souvenir of one of the most memorable trips I've ever taken.

The guy behind the counter looks like he's around twenty. He's sporting facial hair like it's a science experiment and has round, Harry-Potter-like glasses. "It's just turned to red," he says to no one in particular.

"Is that right?" another voice from behind the counter replies, and then a short woman in a dark green wool jumper and jeans springs up next to him like she's been waiting to pounce.

"Jim just said."

I pick a keyring off the carousel. It's just a smooth, grey stone, with two white veins of quartz running through it, but there's beauty in its simplicity.

She turns to us. "You're at the Kinloch Cottage, right?"

"Yes, my cousin's place," Zach replies.

She lets out a disapproving snort and shakes her head. "Never seen him. Just make sure you've got the generator filled up. Don't want any unnecessary SOS calls. In a red weather warning we only get SOS calls around here if some tourist has been stupid enough to leave the house, or some tourist has been stupid enough not to prepare."

"There's a generator?" Zach says. "Vincent never said anything."

"How would he know?" she asks. "He's never been to the place. Disgusting if you ask me. Anyway, you seem like a nice couple. Do yourself a favor and pick up some petrol for the generator."

"How do I even know if the generator is working?" Zach asks.

"Angus checks it regularly just like he's paid to." Her tone is like she's talking to a five-year-old. "But of course he doesn't keep petrol in it because—" She pauses like she's just realized she doesn't know why.

Harry Potter fills the gap. "The ethanol evaporates. Petrol needs to be fresh."

The disapproving woman nods. "Exactly. Generator's in the outbuilding but you can go through the shed so you don't have to go outside. Key's hanging on the door by the downstairs loo."

I wondered what that other door by the loo was for. She seems to know an awful lot about Zach's cousin's house.

"Thanks for the tip," I say.

"But get the wood you've got in your shed in. Kinloch Cottage can get completely covered in snow because of the drifts. You might not be out for a few days."

I glance up at Zach but he doesn't look concerned. "Yeah, we're going to head to the petrol station and then back to the cottage to get the rest of the wood in."

I'm so used to being the one who has to come up with a solution for every problem, that it takes me a little off guard that Zach seems to know exactly what's happening next. We're dealing with life-or-death situations and he's...on it. It feels good.

"Does this kind of weather happen a lot around here?" I ask.

"A few times a year. You get used to it. Have to say, wasn't expecting it to turn red so early in winter." She shakes her head and her face softens. "You'll be grand.

You've got all your shopping. Your wood. Go get the petrol and it'll be fine. I'll send Angus up there when it's safe, just to check on you. And you have the emergency kit as well." She glances between Zach and me and we must both be wearing the same *what-emergency-kit?* expression.

"In the box under your stairs. Really, if he's your cousin, he should be telling you this stuff. You've got a torch and a radio and some foil blankets in there."

Foil blankets? The seriousness of the situation starts to trickle in. This isn't just me not being able to get the ferry home and having to stay inside a pretty stone cottage with a hot guy and plenty of ingredients to cook my days away. It suddenly feels more serious than that.

SEVENTEEN

Zach

If nothing else we'll be warm, because we have enough logs in this cottage to last at least ten days. Thankfully, Ellie didn't shy away from helping to bring them all inside and we were done before eleven. Even though it's nearly the middle of the day, it still feels a little like evening time. It's not far off being completely dark and it suddenly feels very cold. Ellie comes out of the bathroom, wrapped in a towel, and pads across the sitting room towards the bedroom.

I have to hold myself back from taking hold of one end of her towel and watching her unwrap herself as she heads to the door.

I offer a half smile.

"I feel a thousand times better. I recommend it," she says.

"Showering with you?" I clarify.

She tilts her head in an almost chastising way and scurries past to get to the bedroom. She's right. I feel sweaty and cold at the same time. A shower is just what I need.

I'm pulling off my final layer of a long-sleeved t-shirt

when Ellie reappears. "Oh, sorry, I didn't realize you were—"

I push my fingers through my hair as we stand opposite each other—her in just a towel, me in just my jeans. It would be so easy to close the gap between us and spend the rest of tonight...

"Just wanted to know if you wanted anything from the bedroom before I...you know."

Get naked? I don't suggest. She's practically naked now. I guess she has to towel herself dry. Maybe she's got lotion to apply all over her soft, pale skin. Is she the kind of woman who likes to get dressed right away, or does she put her makeup on and style her hair in her bra and knickers the way teenage boys assume all women do?

The images my mind is creating are making me unsteady on my feet as all the blood rushes to my cock. "You take your time. I think you had the right idea. I'm going to take a shower while we still have hot water."

She transfers her weight from foot to foot, and somewhere in my imagination, I like to think she's wondering whether she should suggest she joins me.

I'm not going to need that hot water. I need to cool down.

"Okay," she squeaks out and I turn and watch as she heads back into the bedroom.

I stand rooted to the spot, unable to move because I'm concerned my dick might break off, I'm so hard.

And then I realize, I've left my laptop open and my book, annotated with Mrs. Fletcher's comments, on the desk in the bedroom.

Shit.

The blood drains from my dick and I sprint to the bedroom. I don't even think to knock before I open the bedroom door and Ellie jumps at my intrusion. She's standing over my laptop, running her finger on the open page of my manuscript. A mix of anger and fear balls in my throat.

She snaps her head around. "Hey."

"That's private." I reach over and pull the papers from under her touch, snap my laptop shut and tuck it under my arm.

I can barely see, I'm so full of rage and disappointment.

Writing has become so precious to me that I need to protect it. Protect it from...

At the moment writing is mine and only mine. Yes, Nathan knows I'm writing, but he hasn't read anything I've written. Mrs. Fletcher has, but she's a professional and we're both trying to achieve the same thing. She's in my corner. She gets it.

Ellie is part of my world back on Wimpole Street, waiting for me to start a future I don't want. She's not going to understand, and I'm not prepared to defend myself. Not yet. Not until this book is done.

EIGHTEEN

Ellie

"Shit, shit, shit, shit, shit." I'm chanting to myself as I pull on my bra and fasten up my jeans. I wasn't snooping. Okay, I was snooping. But he left it there.

I crash out of the bedroom, expecting to come face to face with Zach so I can apologize, but I find the living room empty. The shower starts to run. *Shit.*

I feel terrible. He looked so furious and sad at the same time. I didn't mean any harm. I never wanted to upset him. I pace back and forth, waiting for him to come out of the bathroom, but he's taking his time.

Maybe it's better for us to cool down. Or for him to cool down at least. I've seen Zach disinterested and impolite, but I've never seen him furious.

I came here to prove that I'm good at my job. Not to be fired.

But it's not just the job. I don't want to upset him. He's a good guy. And I like him. I *really* like him.

A familiar slurry fills my stomach, chugging guilt and shame and dread into my gut. I just want to crawl into a ball. At least with Shane, I knew his moves. I understood what I had to do to put things right again between us.

I glance at the door. I can't leave. It's too dark out and the snow has already started.

I exhale and try to think but my mind is too fuzzy. Too many memories are crashing together, too much regret and sadness.

I stagger to the kitchen. I need to distract myself. I need to cook. I can show him how sorry I am through my food.

I start to peel vegetables. There's always something so satisfying about removing the skin of carrots and potatoes—tiny bursts of dopamine hit my brain each time I set down a fully peeled one.

I freeze as I hear the door to the bathroom open, but I don't move. There's no point in talking to him before he's dressed. No one wants to get angry in a towel.

Or in a crash helmet, as Shane used to say.

I take a deep breath but it's jagged and sharp. How could I have done this? I betrayed his trust. I should have just minded my own business. I know better than to snoop around, which come to think of it, is why Shane got away with cheating on me for as long as he did. He was always so adamant about me respecting his privacy. He used to say it worked both ways, but I never had anything to hide.

I start to slice the carrots as the door to the bedroom opens and closes, and then a door I can't quite place—it seems too far away to be the bedroom or the study. Maybe it's the bathroom, but no—

The sensation of the knife slicing through my index finger hits me before the pain.

It's not a bad cut. Just a bloody one. I press my thumb down onto the cut to stop the blood flowing and knock the tap on with my elbow.

Of course, it's that exact moment when Zach appears at the door to the kitchen.

Leaving my hand under the running water, I turn my head to look over my shoulder. "Zach, I'm so sorry."

"What happened? Did you burn yourself? Cut yourself?" His expression is gruff and irritated.

"It's nothing." I keep my finger under the tap only because I'm worried the bleeding hasn't stopped and it will look worse than it really is. I don't want to have to focus on my finger right now. I want to fix this with Zach. "I know I was snooping, and there's no excuse. I know you wanted to keep whatever you're working on confidential and I looked anyway. I don't know how to say how sorry I am. I betrayed you and—"

He stalks over to me and takes my hand in his and examines the cut, but it really is nothing.

He frowns but inspects my finger. "I don't think we'll have to amputate."

"I'm so sorry. I don't know how you'll ever forgive me, but I promise I'm trustworthy and I didn't really see anything." I try to remember what it was I actually did see. It wasn't anything medical. I expected to see data charts and spreadsheets but...I frown and realize how near he is, how easy it would be to run my palm down his back.

He shuts off the tap and takes some kitchen roll, patting my finger dry. The blood has stopped.

"I'm so, so sorry. How can—"

He sighs, exasperated. "Get off the cross, Ellie. With this weather drawing in, we really do need the wood." He leans in and pulls out a first aid kit from the kitchen drawer.

"What cross?" I say, just as realization dawns. Was he making a joke or accusing me of being dramatic?

"I shouldn't have left it out if I didn't want you to look."

He presses a plaster over my cut and pulls it tight over my skin. "I'm just protective."

"I shouldn't have looked. I'm not a child. I should have respected your privacy."

He nods. "I guess we're both at fault, then." His tone isn't nasty or venomous. He doesn't sound like he thinks I'm too stupid to live or like he can't believe he actually has to deal with someone as ridiculous as me. He's just...resigned to what's happened, or at least he's accepted his part in it.

"I am sorry."

"I know," he replies. "And I'm sorry I got so angry." He turns to leave. "I need to get on. I've got a deadline."

I hold up my finger like some kind of crazed woman doing her best ET impression. "Thanks."

He lets out a half laugh and leaves the room while I'm still trying to process what just happened.

Was that it? Surely he's going to torture me further? Maybe he'll shout at me later. Give me the silent treatment for the rest of my time here? Although, it doesn't seem like it from the interaction we just had.

Or maybe I've been conditioned to think every misstep and mistake of mine is a huge deal, when in reality it's just... not. I shouldered the blame for anything and everything that went wrong in Shane's world. I used to tell myself it was my job as his manager to protect him from things not going his way. But our professional dynamic bled into our personal one, and I spent a lot of time apologizing and trying to make up for my apparent sins big and small— except nothing I did wrong was small. Cynthia always said she didn't like the way Shane spoke to me, the way be blamed me for everything. I used to brush off her comments, because it didn't matter to me if I had to apologize for something that wasn't really my fault or if I accepted Shane's fury at something that wasn't a big deal. But maybe it should have. Maybe I shouldn't have let Shane convince me —let myself be convinced—it was my job to assume responsibility for everything that didn't go right in the world.

Maybe in this new version of my life, people make mistakes and are easily forgiven.

What an idea.

NINETEEN

Zach

I glance up at the clock and realize I'm working in the dark. The computer says it's seven thirty-five, but that can't be right. I've not had lunch. I lean back in my chair and the gurgle in my stomach tells me that dinner is overdue.

I press save, then do it again, just in case. Before I shut down my laptop, I check the word count. I've added nearly four thousand words since three this afternoon. That's more than twice what I would normally write in a day. Four thousand words of love story between Benjamin and Madeline. I've been so consumed by my characters that I haven't come up for air. I click close and stand.

My legs creak as they straighten, like they've been in the same position the entire day. I roll my shoulders back and then head out to find Ellie. I'm sure her finger's fine, but I'd like to check it out, and I'm looking forward to seeing her. I was furious when I saw her looking through Mrs. Fletcher's comments, but I tried to figure out why it mattered and couldn't find a reason. No, she shouldn't have snooped, but I shouldn't have left it out. She must be a little weirded out by the fact I'm not chasing new clients. I can understand why she'd go looking for clues to my mysterious research project.

The entire cottage smells delicious. As I come into the sitting room, I notice the fire's been topped up with wood and it's lovely and warm. Ellie's so good at making people feel good. I bet she was great at managing her boyfriend's career. I want to hear more about that. Being snowed in might not be so bad after all.

I poke my head into the kitchen. "Hey."

She spins and there's a look of shock on her face, like she wasn't expecting to see me. "You're here."

"Were you expecting someone else?"

"I just want to say how sorry I am, and I know you probably think—"

"Ellie, stop apologizing. We've had this conversation already." I take a step toward her and realize she's shaking. "Are you okay?"

She takes a step back and sucks in a breath. "You've been in there all day and now it's gone seven—I know you must be angry—"

"I'm not angry. I just lost track of time. That's all." I circle my arms around her, wanting to soothe her somehow. "Did you think I was deliberately hiding in there? To punish you or something?" Why has she blown this out of proportion? It's like she's invented an alternate reality in her head.

She shrugs, staring at my shoulder. "I guess. I understand I was wrong."

"It's forgotten," I say, wanting her to forget too. I don't understand why she's beating herself up like this. "You're really hard on yourself. There was fault on both sides, remember?"

She pulls her eyebrows together and finally meets my gaze. "You're not angry anymore?"

"I was never angry at you. At myself for a little bit, but even that didn't last. I was mildly irritated. You didn't set the place on fire—you looked at something you shouldn't have."

She exhales, and I feel the tightness in her seep away. We're silent for a couple of beats before she says, "I made dinner. I wasn't sure if you'd come out, but it's moussaka."

That's what I could smell.

"How could you think I would miss out on any meal cooked by you? I'm not sure how I worked through until now. The hours just flew by."

"Really? You just lost track of time?" She still doesn't believe that I don't want to hang, draw, and quarter her. What in the hell happened to her that she expects that of me?

I press a kiss to her forehead. "Really. Can I help with anything?" I release her and she gives me a small smile and shakes her head.

"No, maybe just open some wine, if you don't mind." Why would she think I'd mind?

We busy ourselves getting dishes down from cupboards, pulling cutlery from drawers and uncorking the wine.

While Ellie dishes up the moussaka, I take the now-empty cup she put the heather in yesterday. I head out to see if I can find more.

The snow is already two or three inches thick and it's falling fast in thick clumps, like the flakes can't get down fast enough. The ground is completely covered, but I know there was heather planted just in front of the cottage. I tunnel a hole through the snow, using my hand. Pretty soon, I've uncovered a small bush of heather. I take three or four stalks and head inside. It's at least minus five out there, and I imagine it's the last time I'll be outside for a couple of days.

I kick the snow off my boots before heading inside and dumping my coat and shoes. I don't want that moussaka getting cold.

"Heather for the table," I announce, holding up my find.

Ellie snaps her head up and freezes, shaking her head. "Who are you?"

I'm confused by her response, but I don't say anything. I thin out the heather I've brought in, dump it in the cup and place it on the table before washing my hands.

"Are we ready?" I ask.

She flashes me the biggest smile and it makes me ache inside. I get the feeling she doesn't use it as much as she should. "So ready," she replies.

We take our seats and she raises her glass. "To surviving being snowed in."

"Oh I think we'll do more than survive," I reply. If I'd been here on my own, it would have been fine. I would have made a lot of cheese and ham sandwiches and soup, I'd have had to relight the fire at least once a day, and I wouldn't have such good company over dinner. Everything about Ellie being here means that it will be better than if I'd been here on my own.

"How is it out there? It looks thick but it's difficult to tell with the lights of the kitchen on."

"It's a few inches thick. But it's coming down fast and the wind is wild."

She laughs. "Why on earth did you choose the Scottish islands in November?"

I smile, not at my ridiculous choice, but at her. She's gorgeous. Now I've reassured her I'm not angry, she's lighter than before. Happy looks good on her.

"I have to say, this is the best moussaka I've ever eaten." I point my fork down at my plate. It's comforting home cooking and doesn't pretend to be anything else, but it's the perfect combination of cheesy and spicy and sweet. "It's incredible. You have such a talent."

She blushes and waves her hand away, like she doesn't believe I'm telling the truth. "Thank you. But care to fill me in on why I'm cooking in the actual middle of nowhere?"

"It's my cousin's place. I needed somewhere at short notice and...he's never even been here. He won the place in a bet."

"What?" she shrieks, her eyes wide like someone just told her *she* won a house. "Who wins a house in a bet?"

"He's American. He's in this regular poker game and...I don't know, I guess someone ran out of cash."

"It's pretty and everything, but if he's never going to come here, why on earth doesn't he sell it?"

"I think he likes to tell people he's got a place in Scotland and have them assume it's a castle." I don't know if that's true. I've just said it to make her laugh. It's the best sound.

"Well, it's definitely not. But in summer I bet it's beautiful. Or spring. Autumn even."

Now it's my turn to laugh. "Yeah, just not the dead of winter. But it's serving its purpose. I'm getting my work done."

She takes a forkful of aubergine and nods.

My work. The work I've lied to her about because it's writing, and there's nothing remotely medical about it.

"I'm not doing medical research," I say.

She meets my gaze but doesn't say anything.

I exhale, put down my fork, and lean back in my chair. What have I got to lose by coming clean with her? Yes, she's going to know there's possibly not going to be a permanent job with me, but she's chasing a different dream anyway, and if necessary, I'm sure we can put our heads together and find another role for her somewhere else. Even if she only glanced at my papers, she'll know it's not medical research. I'm not really telling her anything she doesn't know.

"I'm editing a book," I say. "Specifically, my book." I tell her about Mrs. Fletcher and how she's about to retire, how she wants my book to be the last thing she sells. "Maybe nothing will come of it, but when an opportunity like that comes along, I just felt like I had to grab it with both hands."

"So you're a writer," she says. "Not a doctor."

My heart thunders in my chest. *Not a doctor.* The words hit me like I've walked into a plate glass window.

I've only ever known myself as a doctor.

Medicine has been currency in my family for as long as I can remember, and far before any of us went to medical school. As we grew up, the shelves in my parents' study were filled up with awards and trophies and certificates. Everything and everyone of significance in my childhood was about medicine. I'd hear my father taking animatedly about a breakthrough in his research, during the periods where he wasn't practicing clinical medicine. My mother would come home elated or defeated, depending on how her surgeries had gone that day. Promotions were celebrated over dinner, the pros and cons of various treatments discussed over breakfast. Medicine was the air we all breathed, the language we spoke, the world we knew and understood.

If I'm not a doctor, where is my place in the world?

Of course Nathan figured it out, but not without bumps along the way. It helps that he's borderline famous, fantastically rich, and one of the most powerful men in finance.

Nathan built himself a fortress inside the family, emerging as and when he wants on his own terms.

I am fortress-free.

"I'm not sure what I am," I say. "I know I don't love medicine. Not like you're supposed to."

"Supposed to?" she asks. "Is that a job requirement?"

"I told you all my family are doctors or surgeons. They love it. They're passionate about it. The only thing I've ever been passionate about is writing."

"And this is your chance to make writing into..."

"I've not thought that far ahead. I mean, the plan is still to have a private practice twice a week, try and ignite some kind of spark for medicine that's never been there."

"And you think a private practice is going to help that? How?"

In truth, I don't think it will help. I'm just going through the motions, but it's the story I'm telling myself for the time being. Until I have a better one, there's no point poking holes in it. "I'm going to get this book to Mrs. Fletcher and see what happens. She seems enthusiastic, but that doesn't mean anything."

"You should close down the office and sack me." She takes a bite of her moussaka and looks me in the eye while she chews.

"You're telling me you want to get fired?" I raise my eyebrows.

"No, but it's a waste of money. If I was just your friend sitting opposite you, and not your employee, I'd tell you to get rid of me and close down the office. Honestly, I have no idea why I'm there anyway."

"I guess I'm just...going through the motions," I say, voicing the very truth I've so far only admitted to myself. "Doing what I should be doing."

"*Should* according to who?" she asks, and I don't have an answer. "Even if the book you're working on doesn't work out, you shouldn't get yourself deeper into medicine. Find something else. Or write another book. A better one that will become a bestseller." She shrugs like it's the most logical and obvious solution, and I'm an idiot for not thinking of it before. Of course, I've thought about it. It's just hard to follow through. To pull the plug and actually tell the world, *I'm done with medicine.*

"It's like when I first made cheese souffle," she says. "I thought they were done—they looked fantastic through the door of the oven. But when I brought them out, they completely collapsed. I took them out too early. Doesn't mean I don't love cooking. Doesn't mean I never made cheese souffle again. Of course I did. And I did better the next time. It's the same for you. You've never had anything published and you still love to write. If this agent can't sell this book, write one another agent can sell. If you've found your passion in life, you can't just give up on it."

"And thank God you didn't give up cooking."

She laughs. "I have my uses."

"So why didn't you follow your passion earlier? Surely there's a career in cooking, even if you haven't gone to Le Cordon Bleu."

She takes a sip of her wine, and I can almost see the answers scrolling in her mind. "It took me some time to realize I loved to cook. I started my last job when I was nineteen. I assumed I'd do it forever. I was never going to leave some employee to manage Shane. No one would have cared like I did. So I wasn't looking for anything else. I suppose I didn't realize I wasn't doing what I was passionate about."

Shane. It's the first time I've heard his name, and even though I don't know what he did to fuck things up between them, I already hate him. "Because you were passionate about him?"

She tilts her head, like she's really thinking about her answer. "Because I wanted him to be happy. I wanted to please him."

She sounds like she was his servant, not his girlfriend.

"Yeah, looking back, it wasn't that I enjoyed the job— more that I felt that it was my duty," she says. "It didn't occur to me that there was an alternative." She straightens in her seat. "I've never thought about it like that before, but it's true—I felt I could make him happy by doing the job, and his happiness was more important than mine. And isn't that what love is—putting their needs before your own?"

Other than a semi-serious girlfriend back when I was eighteen, I've never been in love before, so I'm not the expert. Still, I'm pretty sure that's not what love means at all. "I don't think it means sacrificing everything you want. Otherwise, don't you just become their slave?"

She sets down her fork and sits back in her chair.

I nudge her leg with mine. "I didn't mean to upset you. It wasn't a criticism."

She looks up and forces a smile. "I know. I'm just thinking."

"Thinking?"

"You're right. I sacrificed a lot. And it's difficult to recall much he did for me." She's not talking to me. She's talking to herself. I take another mouthful of food while she thinks. This moussaka is so delicious, it would be a crime not to.

"Tell me about your book," she says, changing tack. "Can I read it?"

"Absolutely not," I say immediately. The idea of someone I know reading what I've written is bizarre. "It's a cozy mystery set in a hospital. The main character is a retired football player turned security guard."

"And is he brilliant but entirely underrated?"

I laugh and nod my head. "Am I just writing a giant cliché?"

"Is there any blood and guts in it?" She wrinkles her nose and I want to pull her onto my lap.

"Not really. There are corpses. But you never see how the person became the corpse."

She shivers exaggeratedly. "You say corpse like it's no big deal."

I shrug. "You can take the doctor out of the hospital..." If only she knew the way corpses were treated by med students.

"And what's cozy about all these dead bodies?" she asks. She stands and reaches for my plate.

"Sit down and let me clear the table." I stand.

"I don't mind." I can tell she genuinely doesn't. But it sounds like she's programmed to do everything for everyone else and isn't used to anyone doing anything for her.

"Please." I put my hands on her shoulder and guide her back to her chair. For good measure, I pour another glug of merlot into her glass of wine. I set about taking our plates and stacking everything by the sink. "And cozy just means you don't read the violence on the page."

"And who is your hero's Watson?"

"Oh, the inevitable sidekick. That's who most of my edits are about. Madeline. She's brilliant, but has a day job so can't take a starring role. But he relies on her. Respects her and...is attracted to her."

She stands and heads to the sink. "I like it. A little romance in the mystery."

"And they're both a bit awkward and don't know where

it's going to lead. It takes a while to build up to any physical intimacy, but their chemistry is undeniable."

I don't realize until I finish speaking that I could be describing Ellie and me.

She slips the rubber gloves on in silence before turning to the sink.

"Let me wash up," she says. "I can't have you do everything."

"I've done nothing. You've cooked this incredible meal. I've made no contribution at all."

"That's not true." She lifts her chin toward the cup with the heather in it. She's not joking.

"I'm not sure that counts."

"It does to me." Her voice is quiet, but I can't contradict her. Whoever Speedway Shane is, he is clearly a complete dick.

We wash up and I tell her more about the book. She asks me questions and I enjoy talking about the writing and the writing process, how I plan out what I'm writing for the day. I enjoy talking with her about anything.

"It was Mrs. Fletcher's idea to develop the romance between Benjamin and Madeline. And it works. I like the additional element of working together to solve this mystery but at the same time having this underlying sexual tension."

"Is she married?" she asks.

"Only to her job. And he's a widow who's never really gotten over the death of his wife."

"And is that based on personal experience?"

The question is unexpected. "My girlfriend never died, if that's what you mean. And I've never been married."

"Sorry," she says.

"You don't have to keep apologizing, Ellie. You can ask me anything you want." If any member of my family were here, they'd have cartoon eyes out on sticks right about now. I'm renowned for being more private than my brothers, quieter. Probably because I've been wearing a persona that didn't fit all these years. But Ellie doesn't care if I'm a doctor or not.

"I suppose I was fumbling for some relationship history. You know mine in its entirety."

"There's not much to tell. Last serious girlfriend was at university. And then...medicine is pretty all-consuming. When I had any free time, I was thinking about how I didn't want to be a doctor. There've been a few things that each lasted a few months, but nothing serious really."

"You're more of a one-night kind of guy?" She groans. "I sound like I'm asking for a ring—I'm not. I just don't know how to navigate anything outside of...you know. We were together for such a long time."

She's not asking me for a ring—I know that. She just wants to feel safe, because she never has before.

I reach over her into the sink, pull off her gloves and then take a couple of steps backwards and sit down on my chair, pulling her onto my lap. "I've had one-night stands. I've attempted to turn one-night stands into something more. And sometimes that works—for a while—but mostly it doesn't. All I've learned is that if there are hard and fast rules, no one's told me. I only want to see what's right in front of me at the moment. I don't want to look too far ahead, but I know I like you. I know I like talking to you and looking at you and that you have an arse that I can't pull my eyes from. And I know I want to kiss you again. But that's only one side of the story. This isn't just about me. It's about you, too."

She rearranges herself on my lap so her legs are astride me and my heartbeat levels up. "I like your bottom, too."

I laugh but she silences me as she strokes her hand down my cheek. Her eyes dip to my lips and then back up to meet my gaze, as if she's asking for permission, but I don't respond. I want her to take what she wants.

Cupping my face, she licks across my bottom lip and it's about the sexiest thing that's ever happened to me. I feel myself thicken beneath her and I wish I had more self-control—I don't want to put her off. Then she dips her tongue inside, just for a second, before pulling back and pressing her lips to mine. It's like she's hit the reset button.

I open my mouth a little and she captures my upper lip, nibbling and sucking before letting her tongue taste and explore.

I've never enjoyed a kiss so much. Never given up control of a kiss like this. But something tells me it's what she needs.

TWENTY

Zach

She stills and her mouth leaves mine. Is she expecting me to take over? I mirror her, wanting her to set the pace. She clearly bears scars from her last relationship, and I don't want to do anything that would add to them or make them worse.

"You're unbelievably sexy," I whisper.

She pulls back to look at me, her expression incredulous. "I am?"

She shifts in my lap and I smooth my hands over her arse, then groan at the feel of her. Even fully clothed, there's a softness to her.

"Absolutely you are." How could she doubt it? "And that's the best kiss I've ever had."

She blushes and my chest expands with pride. I want to see more of that blush. More of that glow she gets when I give her a compliment.

I cup her face, sweeping my thumb over her cheekbone, and wonder what's going to happen next. Whether this kiss was a precursor to more, or whether I'll have to try and get content with the best kiss of my life.

"We should wash up," she says. "Or I can do it. You've been busy all—"

"You're not washing up right now, and neither am I. It can wait."

She glances over at the sink as if she's expecting the dishes to argue with me.

"You want to grab our wine and sit in front of the fire?" I ask, fighting the urge to lift her up, carry her into the bedroom, and start work on her body—pulling out all the sounds I know she's capable of making.

"Is that what you want to do?" she asks.

I laugh. She doesn't want to hear what I want to do to her. "What do *you* want to do?"

She sighs and squirms, like she might be able to read my mind. Fuck, I've got to get a grip. I have so much pent-up need for this woman, I feel like I'm about to burst.

"I want you to kiss me," she whispers.

I meet her gaze and she pokes her tongue out and wets her lips as if preparing herself. I slide my hand into her hair and guide her head to mine. Our mouths meet and I take the opportunity to taste her, explore her, *devour* her.

Animal instinct takes over and I stand, holding her, and turn to sit her on the counter. I'm semi-aware of things hitting the floor, but nothing seems to break. I work down her neck, sucking and licking. When I get to her collarbone, I realize I have to stop.

I pull my mouth away and brace myself against the counter, my hands either side of her. "Fuck. I need to cool off."

"I can't remember kissing ever being like this," she says.

Kissing *isn't* usually like this, I don't say. I don't want to say anything I don't mean, and I don't want to come across as a guy who'll say anything to get a gorgeous woman naked. I don't want it to sound like a line, because it's not. It's a truth that feels like it's branded onto my skin. She feels too good. Better. Different than anything I've ever felt before.

Maybe it's because it's just kissing, and for the first time in a long time, I don't know if there's anything else after the kissing.

She threads her fingers through my hair. "Let's go and check the fire."

An intermission, a break—good. As long as it's not the end.

I hold her hand as she slips from the counter and I can't take my eyes off her. It's like every movement is the sexiest thing I've ever seen. Every glance, every touch is like magic.

What's the matter with me?

I take our wine from the table and she leads the way into the living room. The fire's still going, but I throw on a couple more logs. Not that we need any more heat in this room.

"So you'd never been to this place before you came up to edit your book?" she asks.

"No. It's a running joke that Vincent won this place, but none of us have ever been. I knew I had to get away from everything if I was going to make Mrs. Fletcher's deadline. I didn't want to be distracted by my normal routine or my brothers dropping in. I didn't want to think about anything but writing and editing."

She winces. "Sorry I interrupted things."

"Don't be."

You're just what I need.

I don't say it out loud because I'm not quite sure what it

means, but the words float in my head as if they want to be spoken.

Side by side on the sofa, the sexual tension between us has settled to a simmer but I slide my hand into hers because I can't not touch her.

"Tell me more about what you want to do when you finish at the cookery school."

She brings her legs up onto the sofa and leans against me. I nearly groan with pleasure at the feel of her body against mine.

"I've been thinking maybe I'd like to be a private chef. There are plenty of jobs in London, and they pay pretty well. Who knows. It's a long way away. All I know is that I love to cook. That's when I'm at my happiest. It's where I find solace and peace."

"You're an exceptional cook."

"We should do the apple pie tomorrow. Unless you don't have time. I know you're busy."

More cinnamon. I couldn't think of anything better.

"I should be able to carve out some time."

"You should get your rest." She shifts, lets go of my hand, and stands. A wave of disappointment moves through my body. I'm not ready for her to leave.

"You must be tired," I say. I'm so wired, I'm not sure I'll be able to sleep at all tonight.

"You need to be fresh for tomorrow. You have a deadline to hit," she replies.

We both stand and I cup her face and press a kiss to her lips. "Sweet dreams."

I watch her walk to the bedroom. She lets out a small smile as she closes the door. If we weren't snowed in, I'd go for a walk, then let out my pent-up desire in the shower. I glance out of the window. The snow is at least knee-high now, although it's difficult to tell. Regardless, it's not running weather. It would be foolish to even go for a walk. It's pitch black and windy as fuck. You'd have to have a death wish.

There's nothing to do except go to bed. I can't even do the dishes because I know the sound will bring her right back out here to help, defeating the purpose of the distraction.

I sigh and pull my shirt over my head, when I hear the creak of a door. I snap my head around and she's in the doorway of the bedroom, standing in her underwear and a t-shirt that skims her waist.

My entire body begins to buzz with need as her gaze flickers over my chest. I turn full on to her so she can take it all in.

I want her, and I can't hold back much longer from telling her all the filthy things I want to do to her.

"Ellie." My voice is throaty and hoarse—I can barely form words through the desire.

She transfers her weight from one leg to the other and I can't help but stare between her thighs and wonder how she tastes.

I exhale, unable or unwilling to hold back any longer. "Come here."

I can't be sure, but something like relief passes over her expression. As she walks toward me, I can tell by the sway of her breasts that she's not wearing a bra. I clench my fists, trying to keep myself on a lead.

"Ellie," I repeat. It's a question—is this what she wants? Is she ready? Is she sure?

She steps toward me and stands as close to me as she can without touching me.

"Zach." She fumbles for the bottom of her t-shirt and pulls it over her head.

I groan. I'm dizzy, my senses fighting for supremacy, each one trying to elbow the other out of the way. There's too much to take in.

"You're beautiful," I manage to say.

She looks up from under her lashes. "So are you."

I skim my palms down her sides, settle them on her waist, and hook my thumbs over her hip bones. "Couldn't sleep?" I ask.

"Didn't want to," she says.

I let out an *I-know-that-feeling* chuckle and maneuver us so she's sitting on the sofa. She reaches up for my jeans fastening, but I open her thighs and kneel between them.

"I want to taste you, Cinnamon."

I hook my thumbs under the sides of her underwear and remove the white lace in one swift movement. Immediately she goes to close her legs.

I just shake my head and lean over her, kissing her once on the mouth, once on the neck, and once between her oh-so-perfect breasts. I could spend hours lost on her breasts, but I'll come back to that later. I take one of her nipples in my mouth and release it, giving it a scrape of my teeth, causing her to let out a shocked yelp.

She covers her face and I chuckle. I pull her bottom towards the edge of the sofa, but I'm not going to be able to do what I want to from this angle. I stand, scoop her up and lay her flat between the sofa and the fire.

Now I get to have all of her.

She pulls her legs up and I press her knees wide, bending down to lick her from one end to the other before she has a chance to get embarrassed.

Her hand slaps the rug beneath us as she lets out a cry

and I dive into her so deep, I don't ever want to surface. I lick and suck and press, learning what makes her whimper, what makes her moan and what makes her scream.

I want to hear it all, over and over.

Her clitoris is throbbing under my tongue, and I can feel her inching closer and closer. I slide my thumb inside her and she screams.

"Zach, stop."

I snap my head up to see the expression of shock on her face.

"I think I'm going to—"

I grin, press my fingers flat over her G-spot and circle her clit with my tongue as she dissolves into pieces in my hands. Her legs shake and her shoulders shudder as her orgasm convulses through her body.

I crawl over her, watching as she comes back down to earth.

"What was that?" she asks.

I smile—she looks like she's never experienced anything like the orgasm she just had. I feel honored I was the one to give it to her. "*That's* just the start."

I hover over her and she licks her come from my lips, and I think I might climax right here and now. How can anyone so sweet and kind be so fucking sexy? I cover her mouth with mine and we kiss as she pulls and paws at my jeans until we're both naked and I'm lying over her, her legs either side of my hips, my dick hard as stone, nestled on her clit.

"You feel good," she says, sweeping her hands up my arms, braced either side of her head. "Hard. Safe. Good."

"Definitely hard," I say and let out a laugh.

She shifts underneath me so my dick grazes up and down her clit. "Yup. Definitely hard."

I grin and dip my head, trailing my tongue along her throat, over her breasts, circling her nipples. Using my teeth, I tease her until her nipples are hard against my tongue.

"How do you know the exact right amount of pressure?" she asks on a sigh. "It's like you've unlocked a code and know everything about my body."

"Your body tells me," I say. I take her nipple between my teeth and press and release, press and release, biting a little further each time.

"Holy shit," she cries out. I see a look of panic cross her face, but it's chased away by an expression of bliss, so I resume my play. With my hand I tease the free nipple, squeezing and flicking, pulling and pressing. "Zach."

I shift on top of her, my dick sliding against her clit, my fingers, my mouth, my teeth all working to bring her pleasure.

She throws her hands over her head, grabbing for something, reaching for something, until she lets out a scream and arches her back, shuddering under me as her climax rattles through her and vibrates against me.

I've never enjoyed making someone come so much.

But I'm about to burst.

I roll over onto my back and push the heels of my hands into my eyes, trying to distract myself from her taste, her sweet sounds, her body so responsive and needy and perfect, I'm not sure I'll ever get over it.

I feel her move over me and I open my eyes to see her about to straddle me. One look at her on top of me will push me over the edge, so I grab her wrists and flip her to her back.

"You ready?" I ask.

She sinks her teeth into her bottom lip and nods.

"Tell me."

"I'm ready. For you. Inside me."

I close my eyes and take a couple of steadying breaths so I don't come all over her stomach before I've even managed to get the condom on.

After a couple of seconds, I sit back on my knees and reach for my wallet on the coffee table.

"Please, Zach. Hurry."

Fuck. I swallow, my hands shaking as I pull out the foil square.

Anticipation dances in my veins and adrenaline makes me fumble as I cover my dick. I turn back to her and she's watching my erection, her mouth parted, an undisguisable look of lust on her face.

Insatiable.

We'll see who falls first.

I lick my lips and crawl over her. Her hands guide my hips between her legs as she slides them wide to welcome me. As soon as my crown reaches her entrance, my vision tunnels and I squeeze my eyes shut. I push in, slowly, oh-so-slowly. I want this to last as long as humanly possible.

"I can't move I'm so full," she says.

"Who would have thought you'd have such a dirty mouth." I grin at her as I slide out and then push in, quicker this time.

"If what I say shocks you, you should hear what I'm thinking."

"Oh yeah?" I choke out.

A little chat is just what I need to distract me from her tight, wet pussy and the way we seem to fit so perfectly together. At least it allows me some semblance of pretense that the woman under me doesn't completely own me right now.

"Yeah," she huffs out. "You'd hate hearing about how

hard you are and how thick you feel, how I'm being stretched out—"

I cover her mouth with my hand because one more syllable would send me over the edge. She groans into my palm and her hot breath against my skin just ratchets up the need in me. Every nerve ending in my body has hit maximum capacity and is calling out in surrender.

I don't have long. This slow, seductive dance we've been doing these last weeks has hit hyperdrive and there's no going back.

I slowly begin to piston my hips, pressing and dragging —following the animal instinct to nail her to the floor as hard as I can.

She pulls me closer, her cheek against mine, her lips covering me, stealing sloppy, desperate kisses, flesh slapping against flesh, breaths intermingled and desperate.

She clutches at me, arches her back, and groans, and just as I realize she's coming again, my vision blurs and I hear a distant roar—the stampede of my orgasm tearing free and exploding from my center, across my body, through each and every cell.

A kaleidoscope of sounds and sensations roll across my awareness and I collapse over her, wanting to share it, to hold her closer.

Holy. Fuck.

She squeezes me tighter, wrapping her legs around me, and it feels like she'll never let me go.

TWENTY-ONE

Ellie

I've never felt so completely and utterly seen by someone.

Yes, it's great sex. The one, two, three, four orgasms so far testify to that. But tonight is way more than just an orgasm tally.

"You okay?" Zach asks, peeling himself away from me where we're lying in front of the fire.

"I'm perfect."

"That's for sure." He sighs. "I couldn't hold back when I felt you start to come."

"The second time," I say to clarify. "You must have missed it the first time."

He chuckles. "You came twice? Just then?"

How are we talking so matter-of-factly about orgasms? And how in the hell have I had four? So far. That's never happened to me. Ever.

But then, I've never met a man like Zach before.

He kneels back and deals with the condom and I can't

stop staring at him. He's so physically perfect, it feels idiotic that social convention forces him to wear clothes.

"You have a really nice body," I say.

He glances over at me from under his floppy hair. "You have a body specifically designed to drive me wild."

I force back a grin. "Oh yeah?"

I sit and reach over and circle my hand over his dick. Immediately, it twitches under my touch.

He gives me a glance as if to say, *you see?*

He reaches for my breasts, stopping them swaying as I move my hand up and down his lengthening cock, but I'm not quite close enough. I need more of me to be touching more of him. I shift and he takes my chin, gives me a dirty, *I'm-going-to-fuck-you-so-good* kiss and then lets me move him so he's lying on his back.

"I couldn't let you do this earlier," he says, as I lift my leg to straddle him. "It would have been over in seconds. Watching you above me like that. It would have been game over."

I glance away, not wanting him to see how much I enjoy his compliments. It must be so obvious to him that I'm not used to this kind of sex. I'm not used to two people getting pleasure out of pleasing each other.

I take a condom and put it within reach. I want to have a little fun first, but I want to be ready.

"Watching me like this?" I reach behind me, pull my hair up behind me and then let it fall, then press my hands to his chest, completely aware what the movement does to my breasts.

He grabs my hips and pulls my forward. "You're a fucking siren."

"You think I'm luring you to the rocks of destruction?" I lift up and slide myself along his erection.

"If you are, it will be the greatest way to go."

I laugh. He's so sexy lying beneath me. I think he's right. "I think you made me this way. I've never felt..."

I don't finish my sentence. I don't want tonight to be about anything but him and me and what our bodies can do and feel, but there's a far-off chanting that could be the wind, but I swear it's my own voice saying *It was never like this with Shane.*

I shake my head, wanting to rid my head of anything but the man in front of me.

I grab the condom beside me. "Do you mind?" I offer it to him.

"Do I mind?" One side of his mouth lifts in a small teasing smile.

He takes the foil square, rips it open, and I watch, mesmerized, as he stretches it over his erection. I'm pretty sure penises aren't meant to be as pretty as Zach's, but I guess he's pretty all over.

Tentatively, I take him in my hands.

"It doesn't break." His teasing tone is still there as he lies with his hands behind his head.

I wonder if he realizes how I've rarely done this—been given the control to do what I want in bed. Sex with Shane was never really about me.

But tonight is, it's about Zach *and me.*

I kneel forward and Zach sweeps his thumb over my bottom lip and hooks his hand around my waist.

He lets out a sharp "Fuuuck" as I slide back and take him inside me, pressing my lips together, trying not to let him see how much I enjoy making him feel good. Seeing him undone by my body heightens my pleasure and all too quickly, and already I can feel another orgasm building.

How is that possible? I'm tempted to pause things and

get into it. How can he make me come so much? Is it just me, or does he do this to every woman? Maybe I just physically fit him somehow. We're two sides of a perfect orgasm, and when we come—pun intended—together, we just can't help but make each other climax.

Both hands are on my hips now and he's rocking me back and forth. Maybe he knows I need him to guide me, senses that I don't have the strength to do it myself.

We stare at each other as I move on top of him, and I can feel sensation twisting around us both, building and building, taking us higher and higher.

I tip my head back and he shifts, sitting and licking a line between my breasts that makes me shudder. We're chest to chest now, not an inch between us, and somehow this feels more intimate than having him between my thighs or having him over me. Now, looking at him, eye to eye, equal to equal, it makes me feel safer and more cared for than I ever thought possible.

I wrap my arms around his neck as our movements get more desperate, more jagged and needy. We half-kiss, our mouths on each other's, swallowing each other's sounds. Each moan is created and shared; each movement is both of ours. Sweat combines and I pull back just before I climax to see him come at exactly the same time. It's like one orgasm passes through both of us and we cling to each other, neither wanting it to end.

TWENTY-TWO

Ellie

I'm aware of every bone in my body. Each one aches slightly differently, but aches all the same. I've been on my feet all day, cooking, fixing the cacophony of cushions and discarded clothes from last night, and keeping the fire topped up with logs.

At some point we made it to bed, but when I woke, I jumped in the shower. When I got back and found Zach awake, I didn't even let him touch me. "You need to work," I said. I can't get his look of disappointment out of my head. I've tossed it around in my brain all day. But I'm not going to be the reason he misses his deadline.

I delivered a sandwich just before one, and other than fleeting glimpses of him on his way to the loo, I haven't seen him all day.

When the kitchen door creaks open just after seven, a bubble of excitement rises in my chest.

He pushes his fingers into his hair. "Hey."

As much as I try and act like his appearance is no big deal, my entire body buzzes like a zillion cells have suddenly woken up from their nap. I can't help but beam up at him. "Hungry?"

He strides toward me and circles my waist. "Always." Goose bumps sheet my skin at his touch and I know it would be so easy to skip dinner and get to the good stuff.

But not yet. He needs to eat. And I want to hear about his day. I want to stretch this evening out to be as long as possible because this time in Rum can't last forever. I'll have to leave soon and I want to experience as much of Zach Cove as I can.

"You feel good," he says, pulling me closer and pressing a kiss to the top of my head.

"How's Benjamin Butler?" I wiggle out of his arms and set plates on the counter.

"I think he's falling in love and doesn't even know it," he replies.

I turn my head to look at him and he's surveying the countertops, looking at the food I'm about to dish onto our plates.

"This looks incredible and smells better," he says.

"Ossobuco," I explain.

"Can I do anything?"

A simple question shouldn't fill me with such a deep thrill. But I know I could ask him to do anything and he'd be happy to help. Even though I don't need any help, it's just nice to be with someone, sharing a meal with a man, who offers it willingly and means what he says.

"I have it handled."

"Of course you do," he replies. The thrill that's gathered in my chest grows and spreads along my limbs. More contrast to Shane: he thinks I'm capable.

"Did you make the progress you wanted to today?"

He pulls in a slow breath and lifts his arms, stretching

out his body from being cramped behind his computer all day. I have to turn around because the sight of him is almost overwhelming. "It's difficult to say. I think so. I'm just making tiny changes, a look here, a note of his appreciation of her there. He's been closed off for a long time and he's gradually reawakening."

"So you don't want to be too heavy-handed." I place our full plates on the table and he grabs the bottle of Barolo and the corkscrew and comes to the table.

"Exactly," he says, removing the foil from the wine bottle. "It's about being realistic. These people are professionals. They're not batting their eyelashes at each other over a corpse."

He pours the wine, I get the red cabbage, and we both sit.

"Bon app," he says, stealing my phrase and lifting his glass before resuming his thoughts on his characters. "It's about balance. More than anything, I've added more of Madeline on the page. I figure, if he likes her—even if he doesn't realize it—he's going to be drawn to her. He's going to make up reasons to be near her."

"I can see that." I can't really comment. The only thing I can take away from my time in a ten-year relationship with Shane is that I'm not sure I know what a man in love looks like. "And Mrs. Fletcher's comments are still useful?"

He nods. "This is so good," he says on a groan after his first mouthful of stew.

I pause to watch him enjoy my food.

"Did you learn how to make this at home?" he asks.

"Ossobuco?" I ask, a little confused. When he nods I try not to spit out my wine. "No, my parents aren't big cooks. Dad likes to barbecue twice a year and Mum's a spag bol kind of gal."

"You see them much?"

Regret dives in my stomach. "A little more now." Shane never wanted to visit.

"*Now* meaning since..."

"Since I broke up with Shane." I take a slug of wine, quickly followed by a mouthful of dinner so I don't have to say anything else.

"They didn't like him?"

"The feeling was mutual. I abandoned university to manage him and they didn't like that decision. He resented their resentment. He said they never thought he was good enough."

"Was he?" His eyes are on me, dark and serious, and I have to remind myself to breathe.

I shrug. "No one is ever good enough for their daughter, right? It was *my* decision to leave university, not his. He just suggested it and it made sense. Plus, it meant we got to spend more time together. I could make sure things were done correctly; opportunities weren't missed."

"And you never wanted anything for yourself?"

"It was for me, too. In the beginning anyway. Practical experience in talent management sounded exciting. It could have been a stepping stone to me being some kind of agent or at least an HR professional or something. I enjoyed it at first. I was happy for a time and then...I spent a lot of time trying to make it how it *was*, trying to convince myself that things would be okay *if only*...you know."

"Was there a turning point when you realized you weren't happy?"

His question hits me like an exorcism. I haven't realized it until right this second, but yes. "A few years in, we were arguing a lot. He seemed to be less and less happy with the things I was doing and the opportunities he was getting. I would try and explain that the appetite for anything Speed-way-related was waning, but he didn't want to hear it. It was easier to blame me. I definitely considered going back to university then but...it seemed too difficult." I twist my fork around and around my plate, moving my food from point to point. "By then, my relationship with my parents was strained, so I couldn't ask them for financial support. The thought of getting into debt at that stage of my life was over-whelming. I didn't get paid a salary—we just shared Shane's income. There was no way I could have asked him to pay for it." I exhale as I remember—that's when I'd started putting money away in a savings account. Small amounts every month. "Challenging the status quo seemed like an insurmountable obstacle."

"So you stayed."

"So I stayed."

"And you convinced yourself you were the problem."

Our gazes lock and it's as if he's spoken a truth I've been keeping a secret until now.

"Maybe," I say. "I don't think I really understood how bad things were until we were over. It sounds ridiculous, but I lost perspective. My relationship with my parents was an annual visit and a phone call on birthdays. My friends had moved on with their lives. Even my best friend, Cynthia, and I barely kept in touch. I got used to the temper tantrums and the dressing-downs. The silent treatment and the name-calling. His behavior got more and more difficult to explain and excuse to people on the outside, so I avoided everyone. That, together with the fact that I didn't have any qualifications or experience outside working for him...how could I defend myself against his criticisms?"

"He bullied you." It's not a question, just a flat summa-tion of the situation from his perspective.

"He'd get frustrated about the lack of progress I was making."

"Did it ever turn physical?" he asks.

I shake my head. "Absolutely not." I blink and blink again as I think back. "He never hit me," I clarify. There were a couple of times where I'd moved out of the way when I thought things might turn physical. And he pushed me once. At least, I think he did. He told me I stumbled, and things were so heated and hazy, it's difficult to be sure. "He used to throw things."

"But eventually, you left?" he asks.

I look down and shake my head. "He left me for someone else—one of the PR girls that used to travel with the riders when they competed abroad." Nausea rises in my stomach and I take a swig of wine to try and wash it away. How could I have been so stupid? Why didn't I get out sooner? "You must think I'm an idiot for staying with him all those years."

He reaches across the table and links my fingers with his. "You were the frog in slowly boiled water."

I narrow my eyes in challenge. "I was the what now?"

"They say if you put a frog in a pan of boiling water, it will jump out. But if you put a frog in cold water and slowly heat it up, the frog will be cooked alive. Shane wore you down over years, chipped away at your confidence and isolated you from your friends and family."

I sit back in my chair, startled by his sharp description.

"I'm sorry," Zach says and I look up from my plate.

It feels like I can breathe again after years of not taking in enough oxygen. My body shifts gears from *high-alert* to *everything's-going-to-be-okay* for the first time in a long time.

I look up from my plate. I want to thank him for helping

me see something I'd been blind to for too long, but I don't want to come across as dramatic. "There's nothing for you to be sorry about. It's a helpful way to think about it." It hadn't occurred to me that it was natural to be oblivious to small changes. It makes perfect sense. I would never walk into a relationship like the one Shane and I had by the end, but the change from good to bad had been too gradual to notice.

"It's all in the past now. I need to focus on my future."

"Does that future involve the chocolate brownies I saw?"

I laugh because I'm exhausted from our discussion about Shane, but somehow feel lighter for it. "The future should always involve chocolate brownies."

We work together clearing the table, and just as I reach for the plate of dessert, he pulls me in for a hug and we stay pressed together, our arms wrapped around each other in comfortable silence. There's no need for words because I know what his touch is saying.

I'm sorry you had to go through that.

You're worth more.

He was an idiot.

I'll never do that to you.

TWENTY-THREE

Ellie

If I had an internet connection, I'd Google how long habits take to form. I'm sure I read somewhere that it takes a month, but I've only been on Rum three days and already I'm in a routine of sorts. I spend the day buried in thoughts about food, thinking about what a weekly menu would look like for different types of households. If I were a private chef, how would I feed a family of four? A busy single executive with an unreliable schedule? What options would I offer on holidays? Later, I figure out a menu for the evening. And I think about Zach.

A lot.

More than I should, considering how little time we've really spent together. I keep telling myself it's just our forced proximity or the sex or something in the Scottish air. Things would be different if we were in London. I'm not sure if I've convinced myself though.

His appearance at the kitchen door takes my breath away. It's like every time he leaves a room, my brain has some internal dialog where it tells itself he can't possibly smell like fresh pine needles or make my insides turn to molten lava when he looks at me. I must be imagining the way he listens to me like I'm the most fascinating person he's ever met.

And then Zach reappears in an epic facepalm to my brain because he's just the man I thought he was.

He scoops me into his arms and presses a kiss on my head.

"I've made truffle chicken, and apple pie for dessert," I say, trying to ignore the buzz racing through my veins at his touch.

He releases me and scans the kitchen. "You did?" He inhales and groans, the vibration hitting straight between my thighs. "Shall I open some wine?"

"Absolutely. It's my last night here. We should raise a glass to unexpected houseguests."

"Your last night?" He pulls together his eyebrows in confusion.

"The snow's cleared. You probably didn't notice, but it's been raining all day. There's no snow left."

"But it will all turn to ice." He pulls out his phone and waves it around to see if he can get a signal.

I shake my head. "Nope, it's going to be way above freezing tomorrow." I managed to get enough connection to find the weather forecast at exactly eleven forty-four.

"Wow," he says and I hand him two wineglasses to remind him that he's on alcohol duty. "So you're really going home?"

I dish up the truffle chicken and green beans and set them on the laid table. "I even picked us some new heather." I don't mention that I've kept a sprig of the heather he picked the night I discovered his manuscript. I've already hidden it away in the zip pocket of my suitcase.

A little memento from the Isle of Rum. A keepsake from a thoughtful man. A memory of a wonderful trip.

He pours the wine in silence, places the glasses on the table next to our plates and takes a seat.

"Bon app." I raise my glass and he clinks our glasses together, not taking his eyes from mine.

"Do you want to go home?" he asks.

"Well, I think my vagina could do with a break." I grin and he ignores it.

"Because you could stay. If you wanted."

Of course I've been thinking up reasons to stay. Excuses that would prevent me leaving. He won't eat properly if I'm not here. He'll get lonely. If he got sick, who would look after him?

"You want me to?" I ask.

"Sure," he replies casually as he cuts into his chicken. Then he meets my eye. "I'd like you to stay."

My insides turn liquid and I bite back a grin.

"If you want to," he adds.

His words clang in my ears like he's dropped a roasting dish onto the wooden floor.

If I want to.

I'm not used to putting what I want to do first. I spent so many years as Shane's manager—creating opportunities for him, organizing him, facilitating his easy life—that it became second nature to shroud what I wanted in what Shane wanted. I became adept at burying my needs and dreams, and watering and pruning his.

"If I stay...what...what would I do?" I say it out loud but I'm asking the question of myself. If I stay, I'll spend my days cooking and cleaning for Zach while he works. Maybe I'll go for a walk—but not with him. Perhaps I'll pop into the village to buy more food, but what I'll be doing is sitting around, watching. Waiting, while Zach pursues his goal of finishing his book.

I've done that before.

"There's not much to do," he says. "Except share food, a bed. Be. It's not like there's much back at Wimpole Street for you to do, either."

He's right—there's not much to do back in London. Maybe I'm no worse off if I stay. I enjoy being with Zach, and maybe I won't just be watering his dreams but our newly sprouted relationship. That wouldn't be a bad thing. "I suppose I could stay."

He grins. "Great." His tone is light as if it's no big deal if I stay or go. I suppose it doesn't really matter to him.

A knot rises in my stomach. Something doesn't feel right. Saying I'll stay seems to be more than just spending more time in Scotland. Would I spend two more weeks here?

"If I was to leave..." I say the words carefully and take in his expression. I don't want to upset him, but I'm not sure staying is the right thing to do. "Would it bother you?"

"Bother me?" he asks. There's a beat of silence before he continues. "You should do what you want to do." His words aren't sharp, cut through with an undercurrent of accusation about me being selfish. "If you need to get back, then go." He shrugs. "I enjoy your company." He gestures at his plate. "Your food." He holds my gaze. "Your body."

My insides swirl with indecision. The desire to please him is almost overwhelming, but I can't help doubting if staying is the right thing to do.

"But I'm only gone two weeks. After that I can enjoy all those things about you back in London. Whatever you want to do is the right choice."

My heart inches higher in my chest at his casual reference to the future. He's not trying to get his own way. He's just suggesting possibilities.

This is new territory for me—and it feels good.

I need to go back to London. If I stay, we'll start off this relationship in the wrong place—with it being all about me pleasing him. Maybe whatever is between us won't last, but if it does, this isn't how it should start.

"I want to go back to London." I have to take a breath because I can't quite believe I've said the words. "It's not about not wanting to be with you." I want to make that very clear. "It's not about not wanting...whatever this is between us. But you need to work and I...I need to be pursuing my dreams too. I need to find another job. A good one that pays well."

"You have a job," he says.

I tilt my head. "I resign."

"You don't like the idea of an office romance?"

I smile and shake my head at him and his lopsided grin. He knows I can feel his lips on every part of my body right now.

"You need to close the office. You know that more than anyone. And I can't—I won't enable you to stifle your dreams anymore. When you leave here, you'll have a completed manuscript. You won't need a pretend consulting room in a very expensive and real office on Wimpole Street."

He groans and pushes his fork into his plate. "So on Thursdays and Fridays, what am I going to do?"

"What you've been doing every Thursday and Friday since I met you. You're going to write."

"It seems like you're making a lot of decisions for me right about now." He doesn't sound angry, more disappointed.

"I'm making a decision for me, not to stay here to prop up your dreams but to go after my own. In relation to Wimpole Street, I'm just telling you what you already know."

He nods his head. "I know. But don't worry about your job. I'll keep you on the payroll until you can find something else."

I'm grateful to him, but I don't want his charity. I want to do things for myself—I want to get on with the rest of my life.

"I'll be fine, Zach. I'll take a look at your lease if you send it to me. I can work out how you give notice."

"Sure. That would be great. I suppose I just want to suspend reality a little longer. I want to do nothing but write all day, hang out with you in the evenings. It's selfish, but I want you to stay."

His words warm me from the inside out, but I have to hold firm.

"If it makes you feel better, when you get your book deal, we can come back and get snowed in again."

He looks up at me from under his floppy hair and his expression tugs at my insides. My instinct is to cave and tell him I'll stay, that I want to make the next two weeks as easy as possible for him. But I've been that girl, I've done that. And it didn't work out. It's time to put what I need first for once. "Is that a promise?"

"Absolutely," I say. "I can't wait to be snowed in with you again."

TWENTY-FOUR

Ellie

It seems entirely ridiculous that I'm sitting in front of a laptop in Zach's waiting room when I know we don't have any patients and we won't have any patients.

Zach insisted on paying me a month's notice, so I'm going to cancel the website and work out how to service notice on his lease. Until the month is out, this is where I'm going to stay—even though he told me to work from home. It doesn't feel right while he's paying me. Anyway, I have so little to do, I can trawl through the jobs on LinkedIn and ring the agencies from my desk.

I'm halfway through an application for an executive assistant role at a dental practice when Jen sticks her head around the door. "Hey, stranger. How was the trip? I've not seen you for ages." She comes in and plonks herself on one of the visitor chairs by my desk.

I don't want to get into how I messed up with the ferries and ended up snowed in with only my hot boss for company —Jen would assume we got naked, even if we hadn't.

"Got him his reports and then he said I could take some annual leave while he was up there working."

Not the truth, but easier to explain.

"Nice. Did you do anything with your time off or just veg?"

I hope the warmth crawling up my neck isn't visible. "Not much. Cooked, cleaned. That kind of thing."

"Oh yes, you like to cook, you told me. I had a boyfriend once who was a chef. I put on two stone while we were together. I would have ended it months before, but his crème brûlée was out of this world. Can you do that stuff? Crème brûlée? Desserts and things?"

I nod. "Yeah. I've made it before. Just followed a recipe I found online."

"Maybe bring some in for Dr. Newman. That's what I came to tell you—Dr. Sanders's assistant, Marigold, is leaving. Moving to France. Her boyfriend bought a place that makes wine—you know, with all the grapes."

"A vineyard."

She points at me and then slaps her thigh. "Vineyard. I always forget. It really should be called grapeyard. Anyway, Marigold is leaving. I'm going to apply for her job—she earns more than me. The job is busier and Dr. Sanders is a fucking nightmare by all accounts, but I'll let it slide off my back, nothing much gets to me. But I was thinking, maybe you can apply for my job. The practice is busier—it's a permanent role. More money. What do you think?"

I should be delighted.

But my heart actually sinks at her idea. I just want to cook.

"Wow," I say. "That seems..."

"Perfect, right? You know the setup here, the maintenance guys and stuff. I don't have to worry about working with a complete cow. It's a win-win."

This is fate handing me an opportunity and I can't bring myself to feel enthusiastic about it. But I have to be practical. "How do I apply?"

"Send me your CV. I'll have a word with Dr. Newman. As long as I get the Dr. Sanders job—which I will, because Marigold will only show him my CV and then a bunch of shit ones she gets off LinkedIn. Then I'll get you the job with Dr. Newman and we'll all be good. Dr. Perfect here will have to find someone new." She bounces up from her chair. "Brilliant. That's sorted, then. Obviously don't tell the agency or Dr. Cove until it's all lined up."

"I won't." I wonder if it's perfectly obvious that I'm faking my smile.

She twirls out of my office and I abandon the application to the dental surgery. Jen has got me covered for jobs I don't want.

Scotland shifted things for me. Being with Zach brought into stark contrast how flawed my relationship with Shane was, and how much of me had withered while I was with him. Even though I knew what my parents and Cynthia had been telling me all those years was true, I'd not seen it—not clearly. Or maybe I hadn't wanted to really see it, because what would it say about me?

Zach helped me realize it wasn't my fault.

The understanding ignited something in me. I've always known I want to go to Le Cordon Bleu, but now I'm determined and impatient in a way I've never been before.

I want to claw back the life I should have had. I deserve that. I'm not going to go from one pan of boiling water and sit idly by in another one.

What I need is a plan to get to Le Cordon Bleu more quickly.

I stand, head over to the door to the waiting room, and lock it. I don't want Jen coming in here again when I'm not expecting her. I need to focus.

I open Zach's office door and root about in his desk. It doesn't take long to find the whiteboard pens I ordered for him. Those and the whiteboard behind his desk are exactly what I need.

It's time to brainstorm a miracle to get me to Le Cordon Bleu.

I make the list.

Take out a loan, I write first. My head starts to swirl with all the reasons why that won't work. I don't have any kind of decent credit rating because for the last decade, every bank account, credit card, and rental agreement was in Shane's name. I cut myself off. If I focus on all the reasons things won't work, I'm going to spiral. I just need to keep throwing out ideas.

Win the lottery.

Steal the money.

Convince a billionaire to set up a scholarship I successfully apply for. Le Cordon Bleu in London used to have a Julia Child scholarship but it's been closed. If Shane had left me for his PR woman a couple years earlier, I might have been in with a shot at that one.

Have someone pay for me.

I take a step back and examine the short list. I can't get the word "scholarship" out of my head. I've checked the website over and over—I even called the London office. There are definitely no scholarships available. In London.

But there's a Cordon Bleu in Paris, right? And maybe other places?

I bolt back to my desk and bring up the website. Yes, there are schools all around the world, from Peru to Canada.

I start going through the different schools and find scholarship pages in Shanghai. And India.

My heart inflates in my chest and my heartbeat bangs in my veins. This could be it. I really think I could have found something.

My instinct has me reaching for the phone. I want to tell Zach. He'd think this was a brilliant idea. But he's working and I shouldn't disturb him, even if by some miracle he had a signal. I'll email him tonight.

I pull out my notebook and start to make notes on the closing dates of each available scholarship. Some I don't fulfil the criteria for because I'm not Spanish or I don't have a certain number of years in the industry. When I've finished going through all the various websites, I am eligible for three scholarships: Wellington, New Zealand; Melbourne, Australia; and Paris, France.

Excitement chases up my spine and I set to work.

All the scholarships have deadlines for applications at the end of the year, so I don't have long. But if I'm successful in any of them, it means starting in January—less than two months away. All three are full scholarships, covering all fees. My current savings would cover accommodation costs, so I'd be able to press fast-forward on my future.

It's not until five hours later, after writing twelve thousand words about why I want to study at Le Cordon Bleu, that I realize I need to pee, have a coffee, and take a break.

I also need to check emails. I know Zach is closing the office down, but I could at least pretend I have a job to do.

When I click into my inbox, my pulse trips in my neck. There's one from Zach.

I open it. He tells me he misses me, and how he's taken a trip to the post office to make sure I get the email.

It's so romantic.

I imagine him, bundled up in his coat and scarf and gloves, a thousand layers unable to hide how beautiful he is. How sweet he is, to interrupt his writing time to think about me and reach out.

He says he sent a text this morning but doesn't know if it's come through. I check my phone but see nothing from him.

It's good to hear that he's made good progress on the book and I laugh when he gets to the bit where he burnt some toast this morning.

He asks me to write to him and tell him about my day, even if it's just a few lines about how little I had to do.

I go to the loo, make a coffee, and sit down to reply when it hits me: If I end up with a scholarship and have to go to Australia, that will be it for Zach and me. Hell, even Paris is likely to spell the end for us.

I'm deliberately vague when I reply. I tell him I'm looking into scholarships and sponsorships to try and speed things up. Then I tell him I miss cooking for him, that I miss the noises of appreciation he makes when he eats my food. I tell him I miss him naked, over me, watching me as I come.

I press send and then go back to the beginning of my application to read through everything, including the recipes I've devised in accordance with the brief. The website says they're looking for someone who can put flavors together and has "flair"—whatever that means. All I know is that I like to cook.

Just before I leave the office, my phone rings. My rib

cage squeezes when I see it's Zach. How did he manage to get reception?

I slide the phone open.

"Hey, where are you? Hanging out of the bathroom window?"

There's no answer.

"Zach?"

"Ellie? Hey, I wanted to hear your voice."

My stomach swoops and I squeeze my eyes shut, wanting to drink in the sound of his voice. "I miss you," I say.

There's just silence in response. I think of something I can say to backtrack. "I miss cooking for you," I say, as if correcting myself.

Still there's silence.

Then finally, "Ellie, can you hear me?"

I laugh and pull the door shut, the lock clicking behind me. "Yes, can you hear me?" Of course he can't hear me. He's in the middle of nowhere, right where he's meant to be.

And for now, here is where I'm meant to be. I just hope that in January, I'm meant to be in Paris.

TWENTY-FIVE

Zach

Mrs. Fletcher's grin tells me that I did a good job, but I want to hear what she has to say, just to make sure.

"This is excellent," she says, nodding. "Really good. I couldn't put it down last night. You've really captured the way Benjamin falls for Madeline without really realizing it at first. I like the way his thaw is so gentle that he doesn't even notice he's not so cold anymore. Excellent work. I couldn't have asked for more."

Mrs. Fletcher reminds me of my dad—tough to impress. It makes her praise, when won, all the more valuable.

"I'm pleased. I'm really happy with how it turned out."

"It's remarkably...nuanced. I love what a slow burn it is. Although we know these two are destined for each other, I'm glad it's left open ended. There's no happily ever after for them. At least not yet. Not until a few books into the series, I hope." She widens her eyes, taps her pencil twice on the printed manuscript she has in front of her, and sits back.

"I've had some off-the-record chats with publishers. I'm

certain we're going to auction. This is just what the market needs at the moment and your background as a doctor, working in a hospital, just like our protagonist—it's all going to add to your salability. Very good."

"Great. So, what's next?"

"If you're happy for me to send this out, I've got my assistant working on the package. Have you given any thought to what the next book will be?" she asks.

"The next book?" Have I missed something?

"Obviously this is going to be a series of mysteries. We're not going to stop at one, right? It would be good to have a summary of the next one worked out. I'd like a three-book deal, if we can get it. But it's got to be two-book, at a minimum."

I'd not really thought beyond this one. "You think they'll want me to write something else?"

"I know they will."

"I've had some ideas, but nothing concrete." The ideas for another book flowed thick and fast while I'd been up in Scotland. The first two days back at the hospital had been frantic—the levels of understaffing were borderline danger-ous. I'd had four endoscopies cancelled this week, but been called down to A&E much more—nine times alone on my Tuesday shift. I'd left work every night exhausted and miserable, unable to think about anything other than how much I hated my job and how grateful I was that I only had to do it three days a week. Last night, I didn't get home until ten. I've not even managed to see Ellie since I've been back in London. She's coming to mine this afternoon for the first time. We're going to spend the afternoon and evening together, and just the thought of pressing my lips to her neck relaxes me.

"When do you think you can have something for me?"

she asks.

"I can work on something tomorrow and this weekend. How long do you need it to be?"

"Not long. I'm going to put you in touch with a free-lance editor who will help you craft it into something I can use. She'll identify any issues before we put it in front of publishers. Call her. She's a cantankerous witch, so beware. She's also the best at what she does, so tread carefully."

"Don't worry, I'm used to cantankerous." Images of my dad flash through my mind. Whatever will he say when he finds out his son is a writer?

"Good. So we'll be formally submitting at the start of next week. I'm warming editors up before then. By the time they get their hands on the manuscript, they'll know they have to act quickly."

Mrs. Fletcher seems so sure of how this is going to play out. She's so certain that everyone's going to want to sign me up. But medicine has taught me that there are no guarantees.

"But there's a chance no one's going to want it, right? It's not like I'm a bankable name. No one's heard of me. And it's not as though I have any background."

"But I do," she says without missing a beat. "I don't make promises I can't keep, and I like to under-promise and over-deliver. I'm telling you, this book"—she lifts the manuscript in the air—"will go to auction and make you a lot of money. And, unless someone seriously fucks up, it will be a bestseller. So strap in and let's enjoy the ride."

Except there's one major hurdle I have to get over before I strap in anywhere. I have to come clean to my family and tell them everything. That I've written a book, that I have an agent, that I don't want to make a success of my new private practice. That what I want to do is write. That, and hang out with Ellie.

TWENTY-SIX

Ellie

I buzz up to flat C and wait. I don't expect him to come to the door, but as I watch him approach the Victorian glass inlaid at its center, the ache I've felt since I left him in Scotland disappears. All the nerves I've had about being here today, outside of the bubble of an isolated cottage on a Scottish island, just dissolve.

He opens the door and I fling my arms around him. He reaches around my bum and hitches me up so he's carrying me.

"Hey. I missed you," I say.

He chuckles. "I missed you too."

"The office has been quiet without you." He backs into the hallway and I wriggle down. "I brought ingredients." I head back outside and grab the bag I brought.

"Of course you did."

I've got so much to tell him—the scholarship applications, the fact that Paris is by far my favorite option. I also need to give him details of how he needs to surrender the lease. And I want to hear about Mrs. Fletcher. But I know if my hands are free, I'm not going to be able to keep them to myself. So I'm going to cook.

He bends to kiss me and I know it's meant to be a small peck on the lips, but I can't help pulling him closer and sliding my tongue to meet his. Something unleashes in him and he backs me up, pressing me up against the wall.

"Fuck, I've missed you," he breaths against my neck between delicious kisses.

I can feel my body disintegrating under his touch, and when he slides his hand up my skirt and between my thighs, letting out a groan of relief and lust, I remember that we're in a public hallway.

"Hey," I say, pushing a little at his shoulder. "Should we go up to your flat?" I say as he undoes the buttons of my shirt. "Someone could walk by."

"Who?"

I pull the sides of my shirt back together and try to ignore his hand pressing against my clit through my underwear.

"People from flats A and B, and who knows, D and—"

"Oh, no," he says, straightening and taking my hand. We turn to the left and straight through the door. "I combined the flats and haven't gotten round to swapping out the buzzer. The C buzzer is the only one that still works."

We enter into a gorgeous kitchen/living room, which is all exposed brickwork, stainless steel countertops, industrial exposed electrics, and brown aged leather. It's like something out of a magazine.

"You combined the flats?" I don't know much about the London property market, or about doctors' salaries, but I know this flat wasn't paid for by his hospital wages. "Did you sell a kidney or something?"

"Just fucked around with Bitcoin back in the day."

"You fucked around with Bitcoin. That's not code for anything, is it? I don't keep up with the kids. Is Bitcoin an older woman who liked to treat her boys to houses when she's done with them?"

He laughs and heads to the fridge. I plonk my bag on the counter and unpack what I've brought with me.

"My brother Dax and I got really into trading Bitcoin a few years back. And we got out at the right time. I bought this house. It's between him and God what he's done with his money."

"Your brother's name is Dax? There's too much I'm learning about you today."

He sets a glass of wine on the counter next to me. "Dax is one of the four. They each have their own names."

"You're hilarious." I press a palm against his abdomen and he shrugs as if to say, *obviously I'm hilarious, it's effortless.*

He takes my hand and kisses my wrist. "There's a lot of getting to know you we still have to do. But it's just filling in the gaps. I know your heart."

No one has ever said anything as kind... romantic...sweet.

"You do?" I ask. I'm not fishing for compliments; I'm just wondering if he's as perceptive as he thinks he is. My heart is open to him, but it's still tender from years of misuse.

He nods. "I know you're hardworking and kind and loyal and..." He narrows his eyes. "An excellent kisser."

He steps up to me, as close as he can get, and cups my face, smoothing his thumbs over my cheeks before sliding his lips over mine. "It's good to have you here."

My body sags against his, relaxing at his touch, his

words, the way he seems to like me and isn't afraid to say it. I'm not sure if it's because Shane and I got together so young, but I'm not used to feeling like the man touching me can't *not* touch me. I know everything with Zach is fresh and new and exciting, but it's difficult to remember examples of how Shane showed me his love. Looking back, it's not clear to me if Shane even liked me, let alone loved me.

There's no doubt about Zach's affection, despite the tiny bombs of doubt about the future that intermittently detonate in my brain. Each time the dust clears, he's still there, looking at me like I'm the best thing he's ever seen, touching me like I'm to be cherished.

Kissing me like he wants to ruin me.

I end our kiss. "I need to cook, or we're going to go hungry."

"We could get sweaty instead," he growls.

Shivers flutter up my spine, but I don't want this just to be about sex. I mean, there's no way I'm going home *without* getting naked, but I want to talk too—I want to hear more about his book and I want to tell him about the scholarships. I grab the potatoes I brought and start to prepare them. "Tell me more about your meeting with Mrs. Fletcher."

He exhales and leans against the counter, like he's in some kind of dilemma, rather than being told he's written a blockbuster, breakout novel. "I told you everything."

We spoke on the phone after his meeting, ostensibly to arrange tonight, but we'd ended up talking for over an hour.

"I knew she'd love it."

He laughs. "You haven't even read it."

"But you worked so hard on it. And she loved it before you even made the edits, or she wouldn't have asked you for them in the first place."

He presses a kiss to the top of my head.

"Tell me why you're not excited?" I ask. There's something bothering him. Something about the situation isn't sitting right, but I can't tell what.

"I am excited." His voice is flat and unconvincing. I can't help but laugh. "I am," he says again. "It's just the way she's talking, things aren't going to take long. She's sending out the manuscript on Monday. She says we might have offers before the end of the week."

I turn my attention from the potatoes to look at him. "That's amazing, but you think it's too fast?"

He frowns like he can't quite understand why he's not more excited either, and he's trying to figure it out.

"You want more time to work on the book?" I suggest. I'm not quite sure why he's not playing air guitar and punching the air.

He takes a large swig of his wine and sets his glass on the counter. "I need to tell my family."

I put down my knife and toss the potato I'm holding into the pan. "You don't want to?"

"They're all medics. My dad—I'm not sure how he's going to react."

"But this is *your* life, Zach, I—"

He cuts me off. "I know. But...it will be a shock to them and...I'm not sure they'll..."

I wipe my hands down my jeans and step towards him, circling my arms around his waist. "What you've done is amazing. If they don't see that..."

"I want them to be okay about it." The expression on his face tells me he wants them to be more than okay about it.

"It's Dax's birthday this weekend. I'm going up to Norfolk. I'll tell them then."

"Good. It will be okay."

"Do you want to come with me?" he asks.

I'm aware of every part of me touching him. I don't want to move and give away my shock at his question. "You want me to?"

"It would be great to have someone there who gets it."

My instinct is to accept instantly, but my instincts haven't served me well in the last few years. Does that mean I automatically say no? For the first time since Zach and I kissed, I feel a little awkward. "Will Nathan be there? You said he was supportive when you told him."

He glances down at me. "Yeah."

"But of course I'll come," I blurt. "I'd love to meet your family."

I don't want to meet Zach's family. It's too soon. We're barely dating. I can still count the number of times we've had sex. Every instinct is telling me no.

But I like him. I hate seeing him uncomfortable, and my knee-jerk reaction is to make him happy.

"I can't wait for you to meet them too."

He dips his head and presses a kiss to my neck, and his touch is like an override button. I relax back into the moment and enjoy the press of his lips, the scrape of his teeth, the tumble of compliments. It all washes away my nerves about my bad instincts and meeting his family.

I fumble at his waist, searching for the edge of his t-shirt. I want to be closer to him, touching more of him. I push my hand under the cotton, but he takes over and pulls his top over his head.

Bare-chested Zach is like something out of a fragrance advert. He's solid muscle—round, broad shoulders, hard flat pecs, and chiseled abs. Every time I see him in all his naked glory, I'm surprised. Not that he looks out of shape under his clothes—more that he just looks so perfect without them.

"It makes it worth it," he says as I run my hands over his chest.

I tilt my head, silently asking for clarification.

"The work I put in to having a body like this," he clarifies. "It's worth it because you like it. *You're* worth it."

It's like he's set my vagina on fire—the idea that he's in the gym thinking about me. About me touching him and enjoying his body.

"You're gorgeous," I say.

He pulls my t-shirt over my head and unclasps my bra. "It's like you're made for me, you're so perfect."

We fumble at each other's clothes like it's Christmas morning and we're eight-year-olds trying to unwrap everything at warp speed. In seconds we're naked in the middle of his kitchen.

He's found a condom from somewhere, rips it open, and spins me around so I have my back to him. "Put your hands on the counter." It's an order and I'm happy to comply.

Just as I curl my fingers over the side, he pulls my hips toward him and I lose my balance. He steadies me.

"You're going to need to hold on," he says.

I grip the countertop and he presses my back so it's flat, level with the counter. His hands smooth over my bottom and down my thighs and then his tongue is on me, at the base of my spine. He licks up, up, up, and my body shivers and writhes against him. It feels like he's claiming me, tattooing me with his tongue, making me his.

He leans over me, his front against my back, and with one hand braced on the counter next to mine, his breath against my cheek, his free hand roams, finding my breasts, my stomach, my clit.

"I want to be as good for you as you are for me," he whispers.

I replay his words, trying to remember exactly what he said. He wants to make *it* good for me? What's he saying? Is this about sex, or more than that?

I'm pulled back into the moment by him sliding into me. It winds me, and I'm not sure if I'm going to be able to catch my breath. It's like someone's stamping on my lungs and I might pass out if I can't find oxygen from somewhere. I let out a cry as he reaches the end of me and my knees start to buckle. To steady me, he hooks his hand around my waist.

But he doesn't let up.

He pulls back and then slams into me, and it's only his hand keeping me in place that stops me falling. I try and pull in a breath and keep my position, because although it's almost too much, I'd do anything for more.

He stills deep inside me and I grip the edge of the countertop, preparing myself for what's to come. I'm so full of him, I can't move now.

"Breathe," he growls against my ear.

I do what he says and I manage to fill my lungs until his hand underneath me finds my clit.

It's game over. Any semblance of control I thought I had dissolves under his touch and I have no say anymore in my body's reaction. I can't will myself to breathe, stand with my legs straight, or keep my hands clamped to the counter.

I don't have room in my brain to think about anything.

All I can do is *feel* everything.

He starts to work in and out of me as his fingers slide and press, and it's been just a few minutes but my orgasm bursts out of me, rolling through my body like a stampede of horses. But Zach doesn't stop, he doesn't even slow down, and I'm barely conscious from my first orgasm when I feel the stirrings of the next one.

"You feel so good," he says, smoothing his hands over

my shoulders, cupping my breasts, pulling at my nipples in a way that's bordering on painful but just the right side of *how-did-I-not-know-anything-could-feel-like-this?*

"I'm going to make you come again." His voice is rough, and it doesn't sound like him. He sounds sexy but a little desperate—like he wants me as much as I want him. The thought that I might be capable of making him feel even a small part of how he makes me feel shifts things. It gives me the strength to straighten my arms and I push against him, just slightly.

He groans and I feel my power grow. We move like we're two parts of a machine made to fit each other, working together perfectly.

"Can you feel that?" he asks. "Can you feel how good this is?"

I can't answer. My voice has gone, my thoughts are jumbled. All I can focus on is the threatening orgasm drumming against my spine. My skin tightens across my body and he speeds up behind me. Whatever lid has kept me from boiling over slides off and I call out his name.

My orgasm pours over me like hot chocolate sauce and Zach latches his hands over my shoulders to hold me in place as he pushes his hips up, up, up.

He groans and collapses over me, spent and exhausted.

My knees finally give way and he catches me just before I fall. He pulls me onto the floor where we recover in a naked heap, hot and sticky, limbs intertwined.

TWENTY-SEVEN

Zach

As we pull up in front of my parents' house, the front door opens just a fraction and Dog shoots out like water from a pistol.

I open the car door and hear my father shouting. "Dog, get in here!"

The black Lab crashes into my calves and I bend and pet his head. "Hey, crazy boy."

"Bring him in here, will you?" Dad calls from the door and then disappears back inside. Some welcome.

Ellie slides out of the car and shuts the door. "Sorry about him," I say, nodding at the door. "His 'people skills' gene was removed at birth."

Ellie laughs and I pause to watch. She's so fucking beautiful. A blush has crawled across her cheeks, like we've just finished a walk along the coast. Her t-shirt and jeans cling to her, revealing nothing and everything. Her hair is down and reaches that part of her lower back I like to run my fingers down when I'm behind her. My dick twitches, and she shoots me a look like she knows exactly what I'm thinking.

I pull her hand into mine. "Thank you for coming." Even the journey up here was better because she was next to me, talking about her scholarship applications, her hand on my thigh as we sat side by side.

"Thank you for inviting me. Oh, let me get the thing I made."

"The thing you made?" I ask.

She opens the back door of the car and pulls out a cake tin.

"You didn't say you made anything. I could have done with a snack on the way up here."

She grins. "Hence why I didn't tell you. It's French apple cake. Your mum won't be offended, will she?"

I laugh and we head inside. "Pretty impossible to offend my mother. She's had five sons. That's five boys trying to offend her to make her and each other laugh on a daily basis. A cake is better than your sons learning to fart in unison."

"You farted in unison? How is that possible?"

"A lot of baked beans. That's all I'm saying."

"Zach!" My mum throws up her hands, a tea towel in one of them, and beckons us into the kitchen. "And, Ellie. It's so lovely to meet you. How are you, my love?" She pulls Ellie in for a kiss and takes the tin from her. "I do hope this is something you've made. Zach has told me you're a phenomenal chef."

"Just a self-taught home cook."

My mum peels off the lid of the tin Ellie has brought. "Oh, that looks delicious."

"It's French apple cake."

"French apple cake?" Dad asks as he enters the kitchen. "Have you made one, Carole? I've not had that since we went to that place down in Dorset. What's it called?"

"Dad, this is Ellie."

He turns around sharply, as if he's encountered an intruder. "You're with Zach, are you?"

Ellie glances up at me.

"She's my girlfriend, Dad, be nice to her."

Dad takes her hand in both of his. "My deepest condolences. Any woman that has to put up with any of my sons deserves a place in British history."

I roll my eyes. "You'll get used to him."

"It's tough," Ellie says. "Getting him to even speak to me in the beginning was like getting blood from a stone, but I wore him down. Turns out he's one of the kindest, most thoughtful, loyal men I've ever met."

Dad pats her on the shoulder and my heart lifts. Dad spends at least ninety-eight percent of his time moaning about the five of us, but I know he loves us all. I know not because he's always telling me, but because I've overheard him talking to my mum about how he worries about various issues we're having, and because he always asks us when we're next coming up to *bother him*, and because his hand on Ellie's shoulder is him agreeing with her.

"You better keep a tight hold of Ellie, Zach." He starts to laugh. "I'm going to say the same thing to Nathan when he arrives."

"What, that he needs to keep tight hold of Ellie?" I grin, proud of my deliberate misinterpretation of what he's saying. My mother laughs. She's always my very best audience. I hope I don't see that light in her eyes dim when I tell her my news.

"You'll be laughing on the other side of your face when your cousin arrives..." He checks his watch. "In about an hour."

"What cousin?" I ask.

My dad holds his stomach and starts to chuckle.

"John, stop it. I've told you, Vincent isn't going to be stealing his cousins' wives and girlfriends."

"Vincent is coming?" I shoot a look at Ellie. "Since when?"

"He won't need to steal them," Dad says. "They'll go willingly."

I roll my eyes, but on instinct I sling my arm around Ellie's shoulders.

She looks up at me. "Is this the cousin who lent you the Rum house?"

"Oh yes, you were there too," Mum says. "How was it? Zach said you were snowed in."

"It was beautiful. I did a lot of cooking while we were snowed in and Zach was working."

I move from Ellie to go and make some tea, leaving her to chat to Mum.

"How's the new practice going, son?" Dad asks as I stick the kettle under the tap and he starts munching on the vegetables that have been left mid-chop on the chopping board.

This would be the perfect time to just get it over with and tell him about the book, but with everyone arriving, I'll probably get interrupted. "It's early days," I say. It's a cop-out and I know it.

He pats me on the back. "You've always been successful. This will be no different."

The problem is, I don't want more of the same.

"Thanks, Dad."

"Can I make any calls?" he asks. My dad isn't a showy man. He doesn't talk about his connections and contacts, but I'm certain there's not an influential person in medicine he doesn't know.

"Thanks, but no, thanks."

"Of course. You always wanted to do everything by yourself." He shakes his head while he chuckles. "You're a good boy."

It's been a long time since I was a boy, but having my dad's appreciation always takes me back to the eleven-year-old, sixteen-year-old, eighteen-year-old, taking exams, wanting to make my parents proud.

The dog starts barking from outside and I glance out the window. It's Nathan and Madison. The other black sheep in the family has arrived.

"Go and help your brother and Madison in with their stuff," Mum says to me.

"Why? Nathan's perfectly capable of lifting an overnight bag himself."

She shoots me with a look that says, *don't mess with me*, so I head out and Dad follows.

As Nathan gets out of the car, he glances between me and Dad and then back again. He's trying to figure out if I've said anything yet.

I give a little shake of my head.

"You need to rip the plaster off," he says as I pull him in for a hug.

I ignore him. "Did you know Vincent is coming?"

"To Norfolk?" Nathan asks.

"Apparently."

"Is he arriving by yacht or something?" he asks. It's ironic that Nathan is joking about Vincent's wealth, given how rich Nathan is. It says a lot about Vincent.

Madison comes over. "I thought you were bringing Ellie?"

"I did." I'm confused. "She's inside." Her eyes light up with mischief and she heads toward the front door.

I groan and start after her. Unsurprisingly, I'm not carrying anything.

I arrive back in the kitchen to see Madison practically strangling Ellie in a hug. "It's so good to meet you. Zach needs an amazing woman in his life, and from what he says, you're it."

"She baked French apple cake." Dad leans in to kiss Madison on the cheek. I'm not sure how, but Madison has managed to charm my father. I swear he would do anything she asked.

"Well, if you didn't have my vote already, you would do now. I heard you're a cook. Are we trying it?"

A hand settles on my shoulder, and I turn around and see Jacob. "Hey, I didn't realize you were here." I pull him in for a hug.

"Came up yesterday. Sutton and I wanted to get a couple of long walks in." He grins. "So you brought a woman to Norfolk. You know what that means, don't you?"

"It doesn't mean anything," I say. I know that's not true. None of us are the type to introduce women we're casually dating to our families.

"Yes it does," Jacob says. "But we can talk about that later. Shall we do a fire pit tonight?"

"Absolutely not," Mum says. "It's going to be freezing tonight. No one is going out in that weather, because by then we'll be several drinks down and making bad decisions. Or talking Dax into making bad decisions. He told me the other day he's still limping because he jumped down from the top of the barn the last time he was here."

Nathan, Jacob, and I exchange looks and try not to laugh.

"Stop laughing. It's not funny. You know that boy will accept a bet from anyone."

"It's not us you need to worry about," Nathan says. "Vincent's the gambler."

Mum groans. "You'll have to have a word, John. I'm not making any middle-of-the-night A and E trips."

"He's never listened to me his entire life," Dad says. "He's not going to start now."

"I'll sort it," I say and put my arm around Mum. "Dax is going to be fine."

"I'll sort it," says Nathan.

Jacob starts to laugh and I know we're all imagining all the ways we can stop Dax being destroyed by Vincent's bet suggestions. We could tie him to a chair so he can't move. We could gag him so he can't accept any bets. We could put something in his food so he's so ill, he spends his entire evening in the loo.

"We might need some duct tape," I say and Nathan and Jacob both laugh.

My mother turns and points her finger at me like she did when she found I'd eaten an entire apple pie one Easter. "No torture."

"Are you sure? Isn't that better than him accepting a bet from Vincent?"

She lets out a breath like she wants to kill someone. "Just don't cause any serious damage at least."

"Jesus, Carole," Dad says.

Mum starts to giggle. "I'm not advocating torture. I just don't want Dax getting into trouble that he can't get himself out of."

"Again," the entire kitchen choruses.

I glance over at Ellie who's looking between us, smiling. She meets my eye and her smile amplifies; it's like someone is trying to yank my heart from my chest.

I weave through my family members and slide in behind her. I bend to whisper into her ear. "You okay?"

She turns to face me. "Yeah. This is..."

"Crazy?"

"Nice. And I don't think you have anything to worry about."

The way she's looking at me is like a ball of warmth radiating in my chest. It just makes me feel good. *Being with her* makes me feel good. I'm not sure when I've felt this good about life ever. It's partly to do with the book, but it's not just the book. It's her. It feels like we're in each other's corner. We're a team. We have each other's back. That feels more intimate to me than any sex I've ever had.

"Hey." Sutton comes over, grinning at us both, and gives us a joint hug. "Lovely to meet you, Ellie. I can't wait to hear all about how not-perfect Zach is. I'm convinced he has a flaw, I just haven't seen it. And if anyone's going to see it, it's his girlfriend."

I might be imagining it, but I swear Ellie tenses at the word *girlfriend*. I make a mental note to make sure she's not getting freaked out by Sutton and Madison assuming she's basically a member of the Cove clan now. We can be an overwhelming bunch even when we're on our best behavior. And we're never on our best behavior.

"Zach!" Nathan waves from the other side of the kitchen and gestures out to the hall. I know he's going to tell me to tell Mum and Dad about the book sooner rather than later, and I don't want to hear it. But maybe I need to hear it.

I nod back to him and press a kiss to Ellie's head. "I'm just popping out to speak to Nathan. Sutton, don't scare her off."

She smiles up at me and I head out.

"Have you done it yet?" Nathan asks as soon as we're out of the kitchen.

"Shhh," I say.

"What's going on out here?" Jacob comes out and I shoot Nathan a *fuck you* look. He just shrugs as if to say, *he's going to find out anyway*.

Which is true, but...

"There's never going to be a perfect time. If you tell Jacob now, at least you've got us both onside when it comes to Mum and Dad."

Jacob's eyes widen. "You're proposing? How long have you known Ellie?"

"I'm not proposing." I turn down the hall. We need to go somewhere more private.

"The study," Jacob suggests. Just the place to tell Jacob I hate medicine—the place that documents every career high of two of the most successful medics in the UK.

"The snug," I growl.

Nathan comes in last and shuts the door behind him.

"She's pregnant?" Jacob guesses.

Nathan sighs. "Zach hates medicine, wants to write detective novels and is about to sign a huge book deal."

Fucking Nathan.

Jacob starts laughing. "What?" He looks at me. "What?"

I shrug. "I would have said it slightly differently, but those are the highlights."

"Okay. And Ellie's pregnant?"

I lift my hands in exasperation. "This has nothing to do with Ellie."

"Then why is she here?" Jacob asks.

"I like her. I like hanging out with her. I wanted her to come."

Jacob stills. "Right. So what, you're going to be a tortured writer now instead of a tortured doctor?"

"Something like that," I say.

"I've never seen him so happy since he's been writing regularly," Nathan says. "It's unnerving."

"Cheers, mate," I reply.

"Just saying."

"So why are we in here hiding to talk about this like you're waiting to tell Mum and Dad Ellie's pregnant? I don't get it."

"Of course you don't," Nathan says. "So speaks the natural heir to the Cove name."

"What?" Jacob says.

"You're medicine's golden boy," Nathan says. "Zachy here's worried that Mum and Dad are going to be pissed off that he's leaving medicine—"

"I'm not leaving medicine."

"Yes you are," Nathan says.

"No, I'm not." I don't have the energy to tell him all about how my agent says it will be good marketing to stay as a working medic. And anyway, it might temper Mum and Dad's disappointment. An image of their disappointed faces flickers in my head and my stomach flops and churns. "Maybe I do need to get it over with."

"Why do you think they're going to be pissed off?" Jacob says. "Dad won't give a shit as long as you've not dug up his leeks or upset the dog. Mum...she'll just worry about you, but that will be true whatever job you have. Why are you making this into a big deal?"

"You don't get it," Nathan says.

"It's fine." I put an arm on Nathan's shoulder. "Let's just—"

We all freeze as the door to the snug creaks open and Dad appears.

"What are you lot up to in here? If you do something to Dax that upsets your mother, I swear I'll—"

"We're not going to torture Dax," I reassure him.

"We are going to try and make sure he doesn't get drunk enough to agree to do something stupid though," Jacob says.

"Good," Dad says. "Maybe swipe his drink all the time. Or fill it up with watered-down something. You know how Vincent gets. He holds no prisoners. He's a bloody nutcase —he'll have Dax doing God-knows-what. And make sure no one involves Dog in anything."

"Promise. It will be fine, Dad. When's Beau getting here?" I ask, trying to distract him.

"God knows. He's on shift, so probably sometime just before midnight." The brutal schedule is one of the worst things about being a doctor. More proof that you really have to love your job.

"Jacob, can I show you something?" Nathan says. "Zach, you stay here with Dad."

I roll my eyes, but I don't need to say anything because Dad just follows them right out of the room.

"You okay?" Ellie asks as I get back to the kitchen. "Yeah, just my brothers being...them."

"So you haven't..."

"No. I want to pick a time when everything's a bit...calmer." That was wishful thinking in our house. It was never calm anywhere the Cove family gathered in numbers.

MUM WAS ALWAYS the first one up, so I'd set the alarm for six.

I'd been consigned to Mum's sewing room in the outbuilding on the pull-out sofa, but at least it means I haven't woken Ellie. I open my phone and drop a message to Ellie telling her I missed having her sleep next to me, then plod into the bathroom.

I'm pretty sure no one will be up for hours, but given Vincent's flight is delayed and we don't know what time he's getting in, I want to make sure I get some time with Mum.

After a quick shower, I pull on some clothes and head over to the main house. I must have had too much to drink last night because I didn't wear a coat over here and it's cold, even with my jumper on. It's misty, the house surrounded by fog so thick it feels strange that I can move through it without being able to feel anything.

I toe off my boots when I get into the boot room and then head to the kitchen where Mum's at the Aga.

"You're an early bird," she says. She must see something in my expression. "What is it?"

"Thought we could have a coffee and a chat together before everyone else gets up and things descend into chaos."

She smiles. "I love the chaos. I miss you boys being home all the time."

I flick the switch on the kettle, put the tea in the teapot, and take some mugs from the cupboard.

"Ellie's lovely," she says. She's opening the conversation she thinks we're about to have, but she's barking up the wrong tree. "It's been a while since I met one of your girl-friends."

I don't know if what I told Ellie was true, that I was really too busy at work to connect with someone. Maybe I just never met anyone I was serious about. But I can't help but think I wasn't open to anything when I was in a job I didn't like, looking at a future I didn't want.

"Yes, she really is. We haven't been together long but..."
I pour the boiled water into the teapot. "She's great."

Mum is trying hard to be relaxed, but I can tell she's
bracing herself.

"She's really good for me. And I hope I'm good for her."
I take the teapot to the table and Mum brings over the mugs.

"I'm certain you are." Her mouth is pulled into a forced
smile—a sure sign she's worrying.

"But it's not Ellie I want to talk about."

She snaps her head up.

"Maybe next trip."

Her face breaks into a warm, genuine smile and I can't
help but chuckle.

"No marriage proposals. No grandchildren on the way."

"So it's work?" she asks and I nod.

I pour the tea and realize Mum has gotten the milk out
of the fridge without me even realizing. She's always been
there, picking up the pieces and filling in the gaps when we
don't even realize the pieces are missing or the gaps have
appeared.

"I don't know if you remember when I was a kid, I used
to like to write." I've deliberately not rehearsed what I was
going to say today. I'm not sure if any of it is going to make
sense.

"I remember. You even thought about doing English at
university."

I wonder what my life would have been like if I'd never
studied medicine. I can't have any regrets. "Yeah, but I went
into the family business," I say, smiling, but she's not smiling
back. I take a breath. "I've sort of kept up with the writing—
on and off, through the years. Just bits here and there when
I can fit it in. A short story, developing characters. I've done
a lot of reading about craft and technique."

She sits patiently, holding her mug in both hands. There's never going to be an easy way to tell her that I'm rejecting everything about her professional achievements. I've just got to grow a pair and get on with it.

"As you know, the private practice hasn't taken off yet and I've been using the free time I've had to do more writing. I've actually written a book."

She lifts up her hands. "You always were a polymath. That's wonderful, darling." I'm not sure she'll still think it's so wonderful when I tell her the rest. "Oh, is that why you went up to Scotland?"

"Yes. One of my patients turned out to be a literary agent, and she read what I'd written and gave me some notes. I spent the time in Scotland incorporating them into my draft."

"Right," my mother says. "So you've finished it now?"

"I have." I glance out of the window. I'm not sure I've ever done anything I'm as proud of as finish the first in the Butler Mysteries. "And she really likes it. She thinks it will get a lot of interest from publishers."

"That's wonderful, Zach. I'm so very proud of you."

It's not that I expected her to react badly. My mother has never been the type to throw things or even raise her voice. And at this point, I'm an adult. It's not like she can ground me or take away my bike for a week. I just don't want her to be offended. Or worse, disappointed in me.

"Thanks," I reply. "It means I'm going to close down the private practice."

"Ahhh," my mother says, like things are clicking in for her. "So you can write more?"

"Partly, and also because I'm going to have publicity demands from a publisher—that's if they even buy it."

"But you're still going to keep your job at the hospital?" she asks.

I'm quick to reassure her. "Absolutely. I'm not giving up medicine completely."

She takes another sip of her tea. "Is that because you need the money? I thought you still had some left over from that coin thing you and Dax got into. I know you bought the house—"

"I still have some, you don't need to worry. I'm not working for the money. I guess I thought you'd be pleased that I'm not giving up being a doctor."

"And I'd be pleased because...?"

I'm a little confused by her question. "You know—it is the family business after all."

She presses her lips together, the same way she did when Dax put a ball through the glass of our front door when we were kids. That's about as bad as it gets from my mum. "I'd be very displeased if you were in a job just because it's the family business. I know you've always been a natural student. You've always been top of your class; you've always excelled at medicine. You're great with patients, other members of staff—Zach, you really are incredible."

I can feel the weight in my stomach grow heavier as she details all the reasons I should be happy to be a doctor. My entire body seems to slump and I check my shoes to see if I'm actually sinking into the floor.

"But none of that means anything if you don't enjoy what you do."

I glance up to meet her eye. Did I just mishear her?

"I've always had my suspicions that medicine wasn't your first choice. That's why when we were visiting universities and went to look at Oxford, I insisted we stop by the

Bodleian to see if you connected with the...feel of it." She sighs and shakes her head. "But out of all my boys, you've always been the most difficult to read."

"I felt conflicted," I say. "There was such a clear path in front of me with medicine. And then there was Jacob on his way as well. Medicine felt like the path that was chosen for me. To do something else—I didn't quite know what—was a risk."

She sets her mug down on the table. "I should have pushed you more. Been clear that medicine wasn't the only option."

I can't lie to her and say it worked out fine—I enjoy my work. "This isn't your fault. It's just...medicine is what this family is. It puts food on the table, it's the language at the dinner table, the reason Dad misses your birthday. It's so familiar that not to have done medicine would have felt like rejecting my entire upbringing."

My mum shuts her eyes for a second, then two. "I'm so sorry."

I shift my chair round so I'm next to her and I put my arms around her. I expected to have to shoulder her disappointment, not her guilt. "Don't be. You don't have anything to feel bad about. It's not like you actively pushed any of us into being doctors. And becoming a gastroenterologist isn't the worst thing I ever did."

"Stamping on Dax's Transformer and lying about it doesn't count." We laugh and she leans her head on my shoulder. "All I've ever wanted for you boys is for you to be happy and to be good people."

The kitchen door crashes open and Dad stumbles in. "Morning. Where's Dog?"

"Still sleeping," Mum says. "Speaking of, what are you doing up so early?"

"Couldn't bloody sleep. Expecting to be woken up by your bloody nephew at any moment." He lifts his chin in the direction of the table. "Is that tea hot?"

I stand. "Yeah, I'll get you a mug."

"So what's with this Emily girl. Is she pregnant?" Dad sits down and pushes his bushy white hair back from his face.

"What? No." I plonk the cup in front of Dad. "And her name is Ellie."

"Zach's happy," Mum replies. "I'm not sure if Ellie instigated the happiness or has appeared because Zach's happy. But she's lovely, so it doesn't matter."

"That cake certainly was lovely. So what's this big heart-to-heart about?" He nods at Mum and me sitting side by side. "Have you told her you're giving up medicine?"

My stomach somersaults and my lungs are punched free of air. "I'm going to kill Nathan."

"John, how did you know?" Mum asks.

My dad rolls his eyes and takes a sip of tea while we both stare at him, waiting for an answer. "Nathan's not said anything. I've been waiting for you to decide not to be a doctor since you graduated medical school."

"Dad!" I'm used to his dramatic statements, but this feels more dramatic than usual because it's true.

He just shrugs and I scan his face, looking for a trace of disappointment or sadness, but he's just sleepy and grouchy, so there's nothing new there.

"Have you really, John?" my mother asks.

"We both knew his heart wasn't in it. We used to talk about it. You were all for banning him from going to Oxford if you remember. But then you came back from visiting and you said that if being there didn't make him a writer, nothing would."

"Did I?" she asks.

"Did you?" I echo. How is it my parents have known for longer than me that I should never have become a doctor?

My dad shakes his head. "You only remember the bad things you've done. If it casts you in a positive light, your memory is terrible."

"It's a mother's curse," she says on a sigh.

"I said to you, he needs to discover what he wants on his own, without any intervention from us. We would have supported you, whatever you wanted. What we know outside of medicine isn't worth knowing, but it was your life. It was up to you." He takes a sip and I wait for him to finish. "You chose medicine. I never thought it quite fit you, but that was up to you to find out."

He seems calm—like he's unconcerned whether his sons follow in his footsteps. But other than Nathan, we all did. It's easy to be relaxed when you don't have to face the reality.

I'm going to rip the plaster off.

"Dad, I'm giving up the private practice. I wrote a book and it's going to be published."

"What kind of book?" he asks, without missing a beat.

"A mystery. A cozy mystery. Set in a hospital."

"Sounds good. So you're giving up your practice entirely? Or just the private stuff?"

He still sounds so calm.

"Staying three days a week at the hospital." I'm exasperated. "Aren't you angry?"

He grimaces. "Why would I be angry? It's your life. But if you're not enjoying it anymore, I'm not sure why you wouldn't give it all up."

"I thought you liked having your sons follow in your footsteps," I say.

"It certainly makes things easier because we talk the same language, but it's your life." He glances at Mum. "Honestly, Carole—anyone would think we shunned Nathan because he dropped out of medical school. We never made any demands of you boys in terms of what you wanted to do with your lives."

"I've just said the same thing," Mum says. "But Zach obviously feels pressure, even if we didn't purposely apply it. They all probably do to some extent."

"You're Carole and John Cove," I say. "You're inspirational to so many people, including your sons. It's no wonder we wanted to emulate that."

Dad pats my knee. "We're there cheering you on, from the sidelines, whichever path you choose. You never need to worry about that. So what's this book all about. Can I read it?"

"Not before me," Mum says.

Dad groans. "You're such a slow reader, Carole. I'll be waiting for next Christmas if I have to wait until after you've finished."

"Maybe you can both wait until it's published. I might even sign a copy."

Paws against the terracotta tile pull our attention and a sleepy Labrador joins us.

"Absolute scoundrel," Dad says. "It's like having a sixth child."

Mum shoots me a look that acknowledges Dad loves to complain more than he likes apple pie, then she smiles at me. It's a smile that tells me she's proud of me and there was never anything I could do to change that. It's a smile I've seen a thousand times before, but I've only just understood its meaning.

TWENTY-EIGHT

Ellie

Today's the day. I'm a jumble of nerves and excitement as I pace in front of the sofa in my flat: Cordon Bleu Paris scholarship results are due out before three this afternoon. What is more unexpected than the nerves is the low hum of dread I just can't shake.

What if I don't get it?

And what if I do?

There's a part of me that wants to get a yes from Paris more than I want to breathe. It's a *big* part of me. Finally I'd have the fresh start I'm ready for. It will mean I've done something for *me* for the first time since I met Shane. Getting this scholarship feels like the final piece of healing that I need to be able to move on with my life.

But it would be the end of Zach and me. He's going to be in London, working long hours, trying to juggle two jobs. I'll be across the sea, working my tail off, finally investing in my future. Cracks are going to show and I don't trust myself not to want to fill in those gaps by sacrificing things that are important to me—namely, my spot at Le Cordon Bleu. I need to relearn how to prioritize my needs. Until then, I can't be with Zach if I'm in school.

But if I don't get the scholarship and my dream takes a little longer, because I have to save the money, maybe that wouldn't be a bad thing. Which probably explains why I haven't told Zach that the results are out today. There's no point in creating a problem between us before there needs to be one.

I can hear Cynthia's voice in my ear without having to call her and she's screaming at me. There's no way I can give up on even *wanting* the scholarship. I certainly couldn't turn it down. It would be madness. I'm not going to repeat the same mistakes I made at nineteen with Shane. I've learned not to give up on my future to invest in someone else's.

But Zach isn't Shane. He's the kindest, most generous human I've ever met. Not to mention handsome—could I ever forget the handsome? Am I supposed to give up on him —on us? Relationships should mean compromise, but I don't understand how it's meant to work and I don't have time to learn on the job. Le Cordon Bleu is too important.

Either outcome today comes with a downside, and I don't know which way is up.

I jump as my mobile rings. For a second I think that's the school calling, but of course it's not. They've stated very clearly that we'll get the results by email.

It's Zach.

"Hey," I say as I answer the phone. It's Monday and Zach's at the hospital. If I hadn't known his schedule, I'd be able to tell by the muted yelling and wheeling of trollies in the background.

"You okay?"

"Yes, of course," I say, deliberately shifting my tone and

trying to sound light and bright. "What's going on with you?"

"Well, I just got a call from Mrs. Fletcher telling me she has two offers on my manuscript."

Joy blooms in my chest. "That's fantastic. Good offers?"

"Even more than she expected. She's now saying she'll switch gears and go for a round-robin auction."

I'm not sure what that means, but I make a mental note to Google it when I get off the phone. "That's exciting."

"Being here makes it feel like cheating."

I laugh and then stop abruptly. Cheating isn't funny. I wonder if Shane started his affair when he was traveling. He'd often point out why it wasn't practical for me to come along to his expos and appearances abroad, even when he was away for weeks at a time. I had appearances to arrange, finances to manage. How could I do all that and "tag along" as he put it?

But she—the woman he left me for—would have been there.

Maybe he cheated because it was convenient. Maybe to punish me. Maybe it was because he just couldn't keep it in his trousers.

Whatever the reason, it happened. And it taught me a valuable lesson: long-distance relationships don't work.

"I'm super excited for you. Shall I cook tonight?" I ask.

"I'll leave that to you. Are you at mine now?" We came back from Norfolk last night and I stayed at Zach's place. In fact, since I first went to his flat after Scotland, we haven't spent a night apart. It hasn't felt like too much or that we're moving too fast—it's just felt right.

"No, I'm back at my place."

"You should use the key under the plant pot on the step to let yourself in. Use a slightly bigger kitchen."

I laugh at his use of the word *slightly*. His kitchen is about ten times as large as mine. But it's not as well equipped.

"When do you hear about the auction?" I ask.

"Apparently it can take a week or so."

"So before Christmas," I say. By then we'll both know what we're doing. "I'm so happy for you, Zach."

Someone shouts his name. "Look, I'm going to have to go. Shall I pick you up?"

I hear the email notification on my phone. It could be details of the Selfridges sale. And it could be the decision on how the rest of my life is going to turn out. "I'll meet you at your place at eight thirty," I say.

"Use the key if you're there before me." He hangs up and I sit where I'm standing, landing on the sofa right in front of my open laptop.

It's not Selfridges that have emailed. It's Le Cordon Bleu.

This is it.

I double-click on the email and the less than a second that it takes for my laptop to realize it's required to wake up from its snooze feels like five months. In that short space of time, I relive the last five months in my head. Shane announcing we were over, me moving out, me crying a lot, looking for a job, finding a job, not understanding why in the hell I had nothing to do in my job. And then the Isle of Rum and Zach.

In the last five months, I've gone from hopeless and heartbroken to emboldened and excited. I'd like to stay here awhile—enjoy the view and breathe in the fresh air from this peak, but when I open the email, there'll be no standing still. Whatever the answer is will bring joy *and* sadness.

I draw in a breath and click.

I can't read the whole sentence. My gaze fixates on certain words:

Delighted.

Welcome.

Paris.

My hands are shaking and it's difficult to focus, but I start to read the email from the beginning, because I have to be sure.

I haven't imagined it. They're offering me a place to begin the Grand Diplôme in Paris. On a full scholarship. Term commences 6th January.

They want me?

January.

I read the email again, from the beginning, with laser focus. There's no mistake. They're delighted to award me a full scholarship. Term begins in four weeks.

Zach and I can't survive this, but for *me* to survive, I need to take this incredible opportunity.

Don't I?

TWENTY-NINE

Zach

I kick off my shoes at the door and a thrill shoots up my spine at the idea of seeing Ellie *right now*. Not just that—I also get to share the good news about my book with her. It's like my body has been holding back and I can only appreciate the great things that are happening to me if I'm with her. It's like she's become a part of me and I can't imagine what life used to be like before her.

I step into the kitchen and she's setting a bottle of champagne on the counter.

"You think it's too early to celebrate?" I ask her.

"Never." There's something in her smile that seems a little forced. A sense of uneasiness wedges into my buoyant mood.

The smell from the oven is incredible—garlic and something delicious. When I get to her, I slide my hands around her and press a kiss to her neck. She softens against me and lifts her gaze, and I drop a kiss on her lips.

"I have news," she says and inexplicably my stomach

dives. Maybe it's the tone of her voice or the way she's avoiding my eye.

Nothing can be that bad if she's by my side. "Good news, I hope." I pull her closer.

"I found out about some scholarships for Le Cordon Bleu. You know the ones I told you about?"

I hold her at arm's length, my hands on her shoulders so I can see her expression. Is she happy? Sad? Did she get it? "Ellie, stop stalling—did you get a scholarship?"

A shy grin unfurls on her face and she nods. "I just found out today. I still can't believe it."

I lift my hands and cup her face, placing a rushed kiss on her lips. "This is amazing." I must have misread her. This is incredible news.

"But it's not in London," she says, her smile dissolving in an instant and that wedge of discomfort in my mood thickens.

"Right." I shrug. It doesn't change how incredibly happy I am for her. London would have been easier, but nothing's impossible. "But where? Wellington? Sydney?"

"Paris," she replies.

My heart inches higher in my chest. "That's great. It's a train ride away. I'm being selfish here, but you're only going to be a couple of hours away." She sighs and steps away from me. My hands stay suspended in the air for a moment before I drop them to my sides. "You don't seem excited."

"I am excited. Of course, I'm thrilled. I mean—Le Cordon Bleu in Paris? That's more than I dreamed of. And a full scholarship? It means I can get started on my future straightaway."

"Right!" I say, trying to drum up a little more enthusiasm in her. "This is great news." I strum my knuckles over her cheeks.

"It is. And we should celebrate. Do you want to open the bottle?" She nods at the champagne. "I'll get the glasses."

I don't move to open the wine. Not yet. I want to figure out what's bothering her. "Ellie?"

It's nice having her here and having her know where things are. I've never lived with a woman. I haven't even been able to imagine it. Not until now. I wait as she takes two glasses from my kitchen cupboard and sets them on the counter.

She glances up at me when I don't reach for the bottle.

"What's going on?" I ask. "You don't look like a woman who just won a scholarship to her dream school in Paris."

"I do," she says, smiling blankly.

I fix her with a look that says *stop*.

"It's just that...it's a big decision."

"Is it?" I ask. "This is what you want, isn't it?"

She sighs. "I think so. I'm just gun-shy, I guess. I haven't made a big change like this—made a big decision like this—since I left university. That didn't turn out so well."

"But you were giving up your future to manage your boyfriend. This is different. This is for you."

"That's what my parents said."

"You called them? That's great." That wouldn't have been easy for her. I'm pleased she's building back her relationship with them. "What did they say?"

"They were happy for me. Delighted."

"And you know they just want what's best for you."

"I guess," she says, clearly still uncertain. "And if I turn it down, it's not like I've got anything here?" She glances up at me as if asking for confirmation.

"Why would you turn it down?"

"Right," she says.

"You love to cook, Ellie," I remind her.

"I really do," she says on an exhale. "You're right. It's ridiculous that I'm even thinking about turning them down. It's just that I know we haven't been...we've not been sleeping together long, but...I like you."

"I like *you*." I step towards her but she steps back, like she's not done and doesn't want to be interrupted.

"I *really* like you. But I don't think I can give up on such an amazing opportunity."

She's acting like we can't be together if she takes the scholarship, and frankly, I'm confused. "I would never ask you to." Just like Shane should never have asked her to give up university.

"Right," she says. "But if I'm going to be in Paris, and you're going to be in London...in my experience, long-distance relationships don't work. Being apart a lot can lead to people getting...distracted by other people." She looks down.

Things start slotting into place. Her hurt, her disappointment, her lack of belief in herself always leads back to one person: Shane.

This time when I move to touch her and she steps back again, I follow her, lift her up onto the counter, and step between her legs. "We're not talking the other side of the world. You're going to be in Paris. And how long's the course? A year?"

She closes her eyes like she's trying to blink away what I'm saying.

"It can't work," she says and it feels like a clap of thunder in my chest.

"Of course it can."

"No. I'm going to be working crazy hours. When I'm not at the school, I'm going to be wanting to practice and test recipes and do my homework. You're going to be working your NHS job, plus you're going to be doing publicity. Your second book won't write itself. There's no room for long distance in either of our futures."

The way she rattles off the reasons we won't work tells me she's thought about this. She's been rehearsing this conversation in her head. I don't get it. Why hasn't she talked to me about this before now? Why has she been keeping these thoughts and feelings to herself? If she had, we could have taken each potential issue one by one and thought of solutions, and work-arounds. This way it's like she's hitting me with an arsenal of objections and my shields are down. I'm not prepared.

I step back from the counter. "So what, that's it? We're not even going to try? We shake hands and say, nice to have known you?"

She presses her fingers to her forehead. "I start in *January*," she says, like this explains everything. "In four weeks. I have to find a flat. I have to prepare."

"So I'll go with you."

"You're going to Norfolk for Christmas."

"So we'll go to Norfolk and then we'll go to Paris. Or we'll go to Paris on Thursday this week to start looking. That way you can get something sorted before the holiday."

She groans and tips her head back. I step in close again and slide my hands up her thighs. "You're going to be busy."

"So I can't have a relationship?" I ask. There's no way I'm going to ask her to stay in London, but at the same time, I don't understand why she's calling time on our relationship just because she's going to Paris for a year. We're meant to be on the same side, working together to achieve the same thing—being together. But now it feels like we're on opposing teams.

"You're going to be meeting a lot of new people."

"I'm a doctor. I meet a lot of new people all the time. I'm not interested in anyone else. It's you I want." I'm trying to rebut her arguments, but it feels like I'm trying to break down a brick wall by launching cotton swabs at it.

She sighs. "It's not the same. You're going to be meeting glamorous people. People in PR. And you're going to be on book tours and staying overnight in hotels and I'm going to be in a different country."

"You say different country—but it's a couple of hours on a train."

She sighs. "No, it's not. It's half a day once you add in travel at either side. And it's two lives moving in opposite directions."

"No, it's two lives living, Ellie. That's what we're talking about." It's early in our relationship, but it feels like we've known each other a lifetime. She feels it. I feel it. We both *know*. If we didn't, we wouldn't be having this conversation. We'd be happy for each other's success, and if things ended a couple of months after she moved, maybe we'd be sad about it, but maybe we'd be expecting it too. One of us needed to mention the *we-like-each-other-a-lot* elephant in the room. "Yes, we're not going to be in the same city for a year. But I like you. I like you a lot. And I'm willing to do what it takes to make sure things work between us. Are you saying you're not?"

She grabs the bottle of champagne and pulls off the foil that covers the cork. I take it from her. She's going to drop it or at least spill some of this shit and I could do with a drink. As I finish uncorking the wine, she begins a new sentence three or four times.

"I like you a lot too, Zach."

I try and ignore the twitch at the corners of my mouth

when she speaks. It feels like a big concession, despite the fact that she's not telling me anything I don't already know.

"But that's not enough," she continues. "I thought I was going to marry Shane. We were together a decade and shared a life—our home, our friends, our bank account. It didn't stop him from cheating."

I take a beat before I reply. I can't imagine how much a decade-long relationship that ends in betrayal can dissolve and destroy someone's confidence. Shane has left scars worse than I've ever witnessed on someone's skin. "If someone wants to cheat, they're going to cheat. I don't want to cheat on you. I won't cheat on you."

"But being apart makes it easier," she says. "That's all I can think about." She presses the heels of her hands over her eyes. "If I were a couple of years down the line from the lies and deceit, then maybe every time you came over to Paris, I wouldn't be thinking about what you'd been doing the week I hadn't been with you. But right now, that's all I'll be able to think about. I don't want us to end with me being paranoid and you being weary from my questions. This has been *so good. We've* been so good. I don't want to ruin it."

I swallow and take a breath, trying to assimilate what she's saying. There really is no response. She wants to end while things are good—before we have a chance to know if they would have gone bad. I have no defense, because there's nothing to defend myself from.

"So that's it?" I ask.

"We can still be friends," she says. She looks like she's in pain as she speaks—but it's all completely unnecessary. I don't know if I'm more frustrated at her for not believing in me or for not having more faith in us.

"I'm not him," I say.

"I know," she says, pulling her eyebrows together. "You're ten times the man he was."

"Then trust me."

She stares at the floor for a beat, then meets my gaze.

"I'm sorry."

"In twelve months, you're back in London. Then what? I can swipe right if I find you on an app or ask you out if I happen to bump into you crossing Waterloo Bridge? Or you're fucking some French twat with bad dress sense and an accent."

She tilts her head as if to say, *you sound like a spoiled teenager*, and I know I do. But it seems so fucking pointless. Such a total waste of something that was on track for fucking amazing.

"I should go," she says and slides off the counter. "Honey garlic chicken's in the oven. I'm sorry."

She starts to leave, but I'm not ready to give up. Not yet. I just need time. Time to think. Time with her. Time so she sees who I am and who we can be together. I grab her hand. "I shouldn't have said all that. I'm just...disappointed. But you said we could be friends, right?"

She turns and narrows her eyes. "Yes."

"Then stay." I pull back my shoulders and stand tall. "Let's eat. Let's celebrate. You bought champagne, after all."

If I have to pretend to be just her friend to remain in her life, that's what I'll do. And slowly, surely, I'll make her see that I'm not going to cheat on her. I'm not going to meet anyone else. I'm not going anywhere.

"Is that a good idea?"

"Yes," I say. "You've cooked already. We might as well eat. Even though I'd prefer to end the evening with us both naked, if that's not on the menu tonight, I'll settle for honey garlic chicken and a conversation."

THIRTY

Zach

Being at work feels tortuous since finishing the book. Even if I didn't have offers on it already, or it wasn't going to auction, I'd still be struggling to get through my shifts because I know there's something I love to do. And it sure isn't being here.

I nod at one of my colleagues as they pass me in the corridor. I'm meeting Dad for lunch. We can't possibly use the hospital cafeteria. There'd be too many people staring and interrupting us. Everyone still wants a piece of the man, the myth, the legend. Dad never liked being the center of attention before he retired. He certainly doesn't now.

It's not often that Mum and Dad come to London anymore, even less often that Dad comes on his own. But he called me this morning to tell me he's *got a meeting*. That level of vagueness usually means he's going to 10 Downing Street. Even in his retirement, his opinion is sometimes the only one that matters. The sliding exit doors of the hospital buzz open and I spot Dad in the car park speaking to the head of general surgery.

He sees me and gives me a wave before saying his good-byes to Giles.

"You look tired," he says.

I kiss him on the cheek and nod in the direction of Pret. "Let's grab a sandwich. How come Mum's not with you?"

He guffaws. "When has your mother ever followed me around like a dog?"

"I know, but you're both retired now. I thought you might want to come down on the train together."

"Dear boy, we've spent the last forty years grabbing moments together here and there. Trying to bring up five boys and work shifts—we've been grateful for every spare second. Since retirement, we see each other all the time. I'm not saying it's not wonderful—it is. I was very often tempted to give it all up just to spend more time with your mother. But we see plenty of each other. And anyway, she's been waiting until I'm out of the house for the day so she can lock the dog out and pin together that quilt she's making for Nathan and Madison."

"What quilt?" I can't imagine Nathan compromising his uber design-conscious interior for a homemade quilt.

He shrugs. "No idea. I thought you might know. It seems to be some big project. Anyway, I'm in London. She's still in Norfolk. I'll be home for nine. When you boys were little, I swear we'd go weeks without really seeing each other. We were relay childcarers and doctors. I think there was a good five to seven years where I spent far more time with the postman than I did with my wife."

I laugh. I'm never sure if Dad knows how funny he is.

"How did you know you would survive? Did you ever think that you two wouldn't make it?"

"We loved each other," he says. "We knew we wanted

to be together. And we knew we wanted to have successful careers. So we did what we had to do."

He makes it sound so easy. "At the beginning was it easier? You were young when you met. There must have been less pressure."

"I don't remember it being like that. Even at university I remember having to sit down with our diaries and create blocks of time to spend together. Of course it got worse once we were on the wards."

"So you knew from the beginning that you wanted to be with Mum forever."

He glances at me and I can tell he's wondering why I'm asking.

"I knew I'd never do better than her. She was smarter than me. Quicker. And...sociable. People liked her. I've always been a grumpy so-and-so, but with her...I was less gruff. She made me better."

"I'm not sure I would have finished the book without Ellie," I blurt. It's never occurred to me before now, but I think being with her in Scotland—it made me see what a life as a writer could be like. And I liked it. I like my life with her in it.

"She seems like a good girl," he says. "Woman," he corrects himself, and I can't help but love him for it.

"She dumped me."

"Oh," he says. "What did you do?"

"She's going to Le Cordon Bleu in Paris in January. I have to be in London because I'm still working Monday to Wednesday. Then I've got the book stuff on top of that."

"Nothing there seems unsurmountable. I presume you're going to be giving up medicine entirely at some point."

"My agent wants me to stay working at the moment.

Says my publisher will want the credibility of me as a doctor to market the book. This is my debut novel. I want it to be successful, and if staying working as a doctor for a little longer is what it will take, so be it."

"Sounds like the sensible plan. And you've always been the most sensible of my sons."

I groan. If being sensible means losing Ellie, I'm not sure sensible is the best option. "Ellie doesn't want to do long distance," I tell him. I never talk to my parents about my relationships. Not that there's been much to talk about recently. But I can't *not* talk about Ellie. She's all I think about. I can't force her to have a relationship with me, but I want to show her how possible it is. I'm hoping our trip to try and find a flat for her at the end of the week will help her see how the distance isn't so much.

"Hmmm," Dad says as I open the door to Pret. He strides inside and we scan the open fridges, deciding what to eat for lunch. "She's got to want it, too," he says out of nowhere.

Of course he's right. But I'm sure her ending things wasn't about us and all about the way her relationship ended with her ex.

"She's frightened of getting hurt. She's been burned by the long-distance thing before."

He takes the egg sandwich I'm holding and heads to the counter. I trail after him like a kid, having his sandwich paid for by his dad.

"I can pay, Dad," I say, reaching for both sandwiches, but he slaps my hand away and hands them to the guy behind the till, who has an Italian flag on his name badge but no actual name.

Dad pays and we find a seat by the window.

"There must have been a time with Mum that you

thought, she's special, she's the one I want to make the effort with." Ellie's right—we're only a few weeks into our relationship—but nothing about it makes me want to give it up. All I want to do is be with her.

He opens up his sandwich. "There wasn't a buzzer that went off and that's how I knew she was the one I wanted to marry. There was just never a time when I didn't want to make the effort with her."

That's how it's been with Ellie. Not in the beginning—not before Scotland. When she was sitting outside my door at Wimpole Street, I thought she was attractive, but since Rum, I've craved her presence in my life. "And you knew it was a two-way thing? With Mum?"

"I don't remember us having a conversation. But she made the effort to see me as much as I did with her."

"And when did you realize you wanted to marry her?"

He lifts his gaze to meet mine. "You're going to marry Ellie?" He fixes me with a stare.

"I haven't really thought about it. I'm not saying I'm *not* going to marry her. Would that be so bad?"

He shakes his head and puts down his sandwich. "Your bloody mother. She's always bloody right about these bloody things."

"Mum thinks I'm going to marry Ellie."

He shrugs. "Yep. And I told her you hadn't known each other long enough."

"I haven't planned a proposal or anything. Yet." We've not been together that long, but how long is long enough? "But I'm not ruling it out either." Ellie is the first woman in a long time...maybe ever, that I want to find time with, that I resent being away from, that I look forward to seeing at each and every opportunity. But we've only been together just over a month. "How long did it take for you to know you wanted to marry Mum?"

This time he's the one to take a beat before answering. "There isn't a set time. It's not like you're waiting for a year to pass and then you know. You'll know when it's right. You'll feel it in your gut."

I feel in my gut that we'll withstand a twelve-month long-distance relationship.

I feel in my gut that I've never been with anyone like her.

I feel in my gut that Ellie is *it* for me.

But I can't force it if she doesn't feel the same.

"It's always felt very even with your mother. There have been periods of time when she's been working longer hours or I've been deep in research—but over time, we balance each other out. One person isn't being taken care of by the other—or maybe, we're both being taken care of equally. Neither of us saw our careers as more important than the other. We were and we are a team. That's important."

"I don't see my writing as more important than Ellie's cooking."

"Maybe she's concerned that *she'd* start to see your writing as more important than her cookery."

That was it.

All the pieces slotted together. At every turn, the answer was the same: it wasn't me Ellie didn't trust. It was herself.

It made more sense than Ellie being worried about me cheating—although I'm sure that's true as well. But the over-riding concern she has is about losing herself in another relationship. She doesn't want to give up herself for someone else. Again.

I understand now, but does it change anything? How can I get her to trust herself?

The answer is obvious: I can't. The only choices I have are to pull back and be her friend until she learns to trust herself on her own, or I can walk away completely and hope she comes back to me eventually.

I don't like either option.

THIRTY-ONE

Ellie

The cab pulls up in front of the modern six-story building in the fifteenth arrondissement that's a twenty-minute walk to Le Cordon Bleu school. I insist on paying for the cab, and Zach and I get out and pause to take in the structure. From the size of the windows and the shape of the building, it's clear that it's trying to be sympathetic to the surrounding architecture. But it's failing.

"It looks like a hostel," Zach says.

I know I should have been firm and told Zach he couldn't come to Paris to flat hunt with me, but he was so enthusiastic. Even though I know it's a bad idea, I value his opinion and I love his company. And I'd really prefer not to do this on my own.

"It's more modern than the others I'm looking at," I say. "It's good to have a contrast. And it's close to the school."

"But further from Gare du Nord," Zach says.

I don't remind him I won't be commuting from London to my flat, but from my flat to the school.

"I don't suppose that matters," he says. "It's not like St

Pancreas to Paris takes long." Zach's being as subtle as a brick. He's been very careful not to cross the line between friends and lovers in terms of physical contact, but it's clear he hasn't given up on us. Although I don't want to give him false hope, it's sort of nice to pretend it would be possible for a little while longer, even though I know it's not. "It's only twenty-three minutes longer than London to Manchester," he says as if he's talking to no one in particular.

Honestly, I'm surprised. I assumed that when I told him I was going to Paris for the year, he'd agree we have to go our separate ways. We're so early on in our relationship, it would be much easier to quit while we're ahead rather than try to force something. He's agreed to be just friends, but it doesn't take a genius to figure out he wants more.

"It's a lot of traveling to come here and back in a day."

"But not for a weekend," he says.

A man in a shirt, jeans, and no tie approaches us. His hair is even floppier than Zach's and he's showing at least a week of stubble. "Ellie?" he calls out.

"Jean-Luc?"

"Oui, oui."

We shake hands. I introduce him to Zach and Zach shakes his hand as he towers above him by almost a foot. "Let's see, shall we?" he asks.

The flat is on the ground floor and it's a little dark. The bedroom is so tiny that the small double bed is pushed against the wall and the kitchen is just two cabinets and a separate cooker. The curtains are a shade of blue you see in hospitals and there's a two-seater red sofa. It's not glamorous and it's not big. It certainly doesn't feel *Parisian*, whatever that means. But it's clean, modern, and fully furnished. "It's available from the first of January?"

"You can rent it from now, but yes, the landlord is happy with first of January."

There's not much to see, so we end the tour quickly. Jean-Luc doesn't spend time trying to sell the unit to me. He probably knows it will get snapped up. "Call me, Ellie," he says as he spins his keys around his index finger.

"Thank you," I call after him.

"And you were worried about me cheating? You're going to be in Paris, with all these...Parisian men."

"Which you don't have to worry about," I remind him. "Because we're not together."

"Oh yeah," he says flatly. "What's next?"

"I have another appointment in just under half an hour. It's only about a ten-minute walk east."

"Lead the way," he says.

I bring up Google maps and we cross the road toward the next flat. "What did you think of that one?" I ask.

"You don't want to know," he says.

"Aren't you here to help me decide?" I ask.

"No, I'm here as your friend, to keep you company. That's it. I don't want to be accused of...I just want to be here."

"Accused of what?"

He shoves his hands into his pockets. "I don't want you to think I'm concerned about how comfortable it will be for...us. Whatever place you choose has to feel right to you, not me. I accept your decision to end things."

I stop and look up at him. "Have you?"

"You said that's what you want, so I have to. That means I'm not going to offer my opinion on these flats because I don't like any of them."

Familiar guilt rises in my stomach and I bow my head and sigh. "I know. You don't want me to live here at all."

He cups my face and lifts my chin so I meet his gaze.

"Of course I want you to live here. A year at Le Cordon Bleu on a scholarship is all your dreams rolled into one. And I don't know if you realize this, but *your* dream for you is *my* dream for you." He swallows and I dip my gaze to catch the bob of his Adam's apple. He can't mean that, can he? If he's faking it, he's doing a mighty good job. "I'm only sorry I won't be here with you every weekend."

It's like his words tug at a cord in my stomach. I can't regret that I've won this scholarship, but I can regret I'm going to have to walk away from Zach.

He releases me and we continue our walk.

"You're right though," he continues. "I wouldn't be able to come out *every* weekend. Sometimes I'd have to cover shifts. Sometimes I'll be writing or doing publicity. If I wasn't working, it would be a different matter," Zach says. "I'd move to Paris with you."

I can't help but laugh. "You would?"

"Why not?"

"I don't know, maybe because we've known each other for five minutes?"

"That's not true. We worked together for what, a month before Scotland? Then we lived together for almost a week. And since then it's been...what? Three weeks?"

"Exactly. It's been a month."

"Is there a set amount of time you have to put in before you feel serious about a person?" he asks. His tone isn't joking, more interested and inquisitive.

"Of course not..." I don't have much to compare my relationship with Zach to. "But a month is too short a time to put your life on hold for someone."

"I agree, but we're not talking about putting our lives on hold."

I know what he's saying sounds logical. I really do. He wants to keep going and see where we end up. If long distance doesn't work out, it doesn't work out.

But it's not that simple.

I *know* it won't work out, and I'll be bracing myself for the end for the entire relationship.

I can't live like that.

THIRTY-TWO

Zach

Nothing much raises an eyebrow in London. There's a place for everything and everybody. Still, I get more attention than I expect as I head towards Mrs. Fletcher's office on Lower Regent Street carrying the bottle of champagne she instructed me to bring along to our meeting.

There's a group of girls gathered around Eros's fountain, all wearing plastic tiaras, and I can see them pointing at me and whispering. "Need someone to share that with?" one of them calls out.

"Give my mate a kiss, will you? She's getting married next week."

It's not like I'm about to kiss a stranger, but suddenly the idea of kissing anyone ever again other than Ellie seems utterly ridiculous.

"Have a good night, girls," I say as I pass them by with a smile and a two-fingered salute.

I turn left into the lobby of Mrs. Fletcher's office. She told me to be there at three forty-five on the dot with a bottle of chilled champagne. I check the time on my phone. So far, so good. I've got five minutes to spare.

I sign in with reception and head toward the stairs to the third floor. I go to tuck the champagne under my arm and change my mind. This trip should be made by lift or I'm going to end up wearing most of this champagne.

By the time Mrs. Fletcher meets me at the entrance to Fletcher and Associates, it's three forty-five on the dot.

"Just in time," she says. Holding out her arm, she guides me through the door with a sweeping gesture. "Your auction ends at four sharp. We'll see where we're at."

"I never did ask what a round-robin auction is."

"Well, round robin is how it started off. Now we're down to best and final because it was all taking too long." Her office overlooks Piccadilly Circus and it's almost silent, compared to the chaos down below. "Take a seat. Let's leave the champagne until the top of the hour. I might have sneaked something into the fridge myself too."

"When you say things were taking too long, do you mean people were slow with their offers?" I ask, taking a seat in the camel-colored chair that's exactly the same color as Mrs. Fletcher's rollneck jumper and skirt. I glance down. Even the carpet is camel-colored.

"WHI Books have this long and laborious process for making offers and it was tiresome. I think it takes two board meetings to get anything approved. This way, they can really think about what the manuscript is worth to them and put their best foot forward. It was the best way in the end."

"So WHI is one bidder. What about the others?"

"The thriller and mystery imprint at Collins and Simons. And RedPrint."

"And whoever bids the most will win," I say flatly.

"That's up to you," Mrs. Fletcher says. "You'll have the

top bids from three of the four biggest publishers in the world. You can accept any one of them, or you can accept none of them. Next stage, I would suggest, is to meet with their teams. See if the editor is someone who shares your vision for the book. You can talk to their marketing people. Then you either pick the offer you feel most comfortable with, or you say no to everyone."

"And then what?"

She laughs. "You burn it and have a story to tell at dinner parties for the rest of time. Or you self-publish it." She shrugs. "It's completely up to you. I don't want you to feel any pressure from me to accept any particular offer. You'll know in your gut what feels right."

People keep telling me to listen to my gut, but I've always been driven by science and data. I look at evidence and facts. That's what scientists are trained to do. "I'm not sure what my gut will say."

"You'll hear it, mark my words."

Before I can disagree, the glass door of Mrs. Fletcher's office opens and a woman enters, pushing a trolley topped by two glasses and a bottle of champagne in an ice bucket.

"Thank you, Bridget," Mrs. Fletcher says and glances at the clock on the camel-colored wall. "We have offers from RedPrint and Collins and Simon, but we're still waiting on WHI." She glances at her computer screen and rolls her eyes. "Nope. They're leaving it until the last minute."

Bridget is standing behind me against the wall, her hands behind her back, like a soldier awaiting orders.

Mrs. Fletcher's mobile rings on her desk and she rolls her eyes again. "How they get anything done, I have no idea."

"Fletcher," she answers. "Yes. No, I don't have it. Yes, I've refreshed." She clicks her mouse a couple of times.

"Hard copy would have been fine too. Yes." She keeps clicking on her mouse, her face a picture of utter disdain for whoever is on the other end of the line. "Here it is," she says. "Yes, I can open it. Very good. I'll be in touch."

She doesn't wait for a goodbye before pulling the phone from her ear and ending the call. "WHI were just under the wire. Of course if they were late, we still would have let them participate, but it doesn't hurt to make them sweat."

This woman is a complete and utter baller.

She leans back in her chair and grins as excitement rises in my veins. "So, Dr. Cove. You have three mid-six-figure offers for the first two Butler Mystery novels. Any one of them is going to make you the next big thing in genre publishing."

THIRTY-THREE

Zach

Apparently, friends don't spend Christmas with each other's families. That's according to Ellie. I suggested we spend the holiday in London together, but apparently friends don't do that either. She's pulling away from me, and there's nothing I can do. And I miss her already.

Instead, I'm in Norfolk with two of my four brothers, contemplating whether it's acceptable to put brandy in my coffee this early in the morning on Christmas Eve, while Vincent, who's inexplicably visiting *again,* is typing away at his laptop.

"Dr. Perfect," Beau says as he comes into the kitchen. "How goes it? I hear you're not content with being the best doctor the UK has ever seen—don't tell Jacob I said that— but now you have to lay bare your polymath skills and become a famous author."

"Is he related to us?" Vincent asks me in a growl.

I'm not quite sure why Vincent is here for Christmas. He comes to the UK a few times a year, but if I see him, it's always in London. Yet the twice he's been over here, he's come to Norfolk. When I asked him about it before, he muttered something about a tax issue. But here he is, laptop open on the kitchen table as people mill in and out of the kitchen.

"I can only pray he's not. They must have switched him in the hospital."

"You can't rain on my parade, Vincent," Beau says.

"I'm surrounded by Americans all day," Vincent says. "And not one of them is as upbeat as you are."

"I'm different when I'm at work. Given you don't do anything *but* work, you're not used to seeing people in a social setting." Beau's annoying, but he's not wrong. Vincent's work ethic since he got here makes the rest of us look like slackers.

"What's so important that you have to work on Christmas Eve?" I ask. Jacob is stuck at the hospital, since other people's health is, of course, the only exception. Growing up, we rarely had a Christmas with both parents at the Christmas lunch. But we got it—they were saving people's lives.

Vincent rolls his eyes. "Typical doctor, who doesn't think any job is more important than his own."

"Is it?" I ask. "I mean, I don't enjoy what I do, but I accept it has value."

"Is it more valuable than the people who collect the trash from the sidewalk once a week?"

Beau groans. "It's *rubbish* from the *pavement*. Don't pretend you don't know. You went to uni here, mate. Or you could just ask, are doctors more important than bin men."

"Sexist," I tell him.

"Bin *people*," he corrects himself.

"It's not about being more or less important," I reply. "But one person is trained to save a life. One person isn't."

"Doesn't mean they're not important for the functioning of society. We need scientists to develop the drugs you administer. We need the pharma companies to manufacture the drugs. We need the truck drivers to deliver the drugs to hospitals."

"But those people have to have holidays, and their jobs don't tend to be time critical in the way a doctor saving a life is time critical. And anyway, you're not any of those people."

"No, but I'm the guy who invests in the start-up that creates the technology that enables the scientist to create the drug, or the software that the logistics company uses to make sure everything gets delivered on time and on budget. And come to think about it, I'm also the shareholder in the lab that's developing some of the drugs and—"

"We get it," Beau says. "Society would fall over if it wasn't for you."

"Not fall over exactly." The corner of his mouth turns up. "Maybe bend and sway a little."

Beau catches my gaze and nods over to Vincent as if to say, *isn't he arrogant?*

The answer's yes, he is. But he's a self-made billionaire who got kicked out of medical school for failing his exams because he was too busy making his first billion. That kind of thing leads to arrogance even when not combined with the Cove family genetics. Arrogance runs through our veins —it has to, or none of us could practice medicine.

"If this book thing fails, can I have a job?" I ask him. "I don't want to go back to medicine," I say as I take a bite of my cheese and cucumber sandwich. If Ellie had made this sandwich, she would have added herbs or some kind of seasoning which would have elevated it to restaurant-worthy. My stomach misses her too.

"Really?" Beau asks. "Not even if the writing thing doesn't work out?"

"Is that news?" I ask. Our family aren't the best secret keepers. There's no way they don't all know I've never enjoyed what I do.

"So you'd rather go and do something in an office than be a doctor?" he asks.

"No, I'd rather be a writer than be a doctor," I reply.

"I thought you're having a book published?" Vincent asks.

I groan. "It won't come out for years. Or eighteen months anyway." It's not like I expected it to happen right away, but when they talked about releasing autumn next year, I couldn't think of what they could possibly be doing between then and now that could take that long.

"So you're just sitting around for eighteen months?" Beau asks as he swoops in and grabs half of my sandwich, takes a bite, and then puts the rest back on my plate.

I push him away. "Not exactly. They want me to write another one." I try and push away the pride that rises in my stomach. It still doesn't feel exactly okay that I'm making a career change. It's like I've bought a new mattress and I know it's going to be comfortable, but it's just going to take a bit of getting used to.

"Hope they're paying you."

"Yeah," I say. "It's a two-book deal." Before Ellie arrived in my office, her skirt up around her ears, I'd only scribbled a few chapters here and there. She'd been with me through the entire process of crafting my book and kick-starting my new career, even if she didn't know it at the beginning. It feels weird to be working on something else without her by my side. There's nothing I want more than a couple of weeks with Ellie, snowed in on Rum.

"Then what are you asking me for a job for? Sounds like you've made it."

"There are no guarantees. You never know when things are going to go pear-shaped." There were no warning signs that Ellie was going to call things off. Everything between us was better than anything I've ever had before. And still she walked away.

"Way to look on the bright side," Beau says.

"The more you risk, the bigger the reward," Vincent says. "It's true in investing, it's true in life. This writing thing is a risk, I'll give you that. But the reward is getting to spend your days doing something you love. Plus, you're going to be rich and famous."

"I'll skip the fame part, if that's okay."

"Are authors really famous?" Beau asks.

"Nah," I reply. "Never heard of Stephen King or J.K. Rowling."

"Yeah, but not many get famous, do they? I think you'll be consigned to obscurity. You don't need to worry."

"Thanks, Beau."

"It's not scalable," Vincent says, as if I understand what he's talking about. "That's the problem with writing. Even J.K. Rowling—she's got a ceiling on what she can earn."

I tear my gaze from my sandwich to Vincent, who's still focused on his screen. I want to check that he's really saying what I think he's saying. "She's done okay," I offer.

"Absolutely. And the merchandising has been smart—of course kids' books lend themselves better to that. Then you've got the film and the theme park rides and all the other spin-offs." He stops typing and looks up. "You're right. I think she's done well. But not the same genre as you."

I chuckle. "I have no desire to be the next J.K. Rowling." Mrs. Fletcher has told me I've signed a really good deal for a debut author. But my family don't know that. Neither does Vincent.

"Where's Ellie spending Christmas?" Beau asks. "Or have you dumped her already like all the others."

"What?" I ask. "What others have I dumped?" Beau is talking shit, as usual.

"There was that girl, Susie, I saw you with once. And the one with the really long blonde hair."

Susie? I've never dated a Susie, have I? All the women before Ellie seem to blend together. "I haven't dumped Ellie. She's dumped me, if you must know."

"Is that why you're even more miserable than usual?" Beau asks, and out of the corner of my eye, I see Vincent crack a smile.

"Probably," I reply. It's more than misery that has cloaked my mood. It's an emptiness that I've never experienced before. It's an unshakeable feeling that something's missing. Someone's missing. I have a thousand thoughts a day I want to share with her, plans I want to talk about with her, experiences I want to have with her. Instead I'm here, surrounded by people, but lonely without *her*. "Just wait until you fall in love with a girl who doesn't want to be with you."

"Fallen in love?" Beau shrieks, half laughing and half choking. "Hey, Vincent, did you hear that?"

"Fuck you," I reply and take another bite of sandwich. "And you." I lift my chin at Vincent.

"I didn't say anything. I'm far too busy making money. And if you did the same, you wouldn't be nursing a broken heart right now. Get your priorities straight."

I stand and dump what's left of my sandwich in the bin before heading to the living room to get some peace. The fire is on in the inglenook fireplace and Madison is lying on one of the two sofas with her feet on Nathan's lap.

"What's that ruckus about?" Madison asks.

"Nothing," I say, collapsing on the sofa opposite them. I lie lengthways, tucking a cushion under my head and putting my socked feet up on the arm of the sofa, where they'll be warmed by the fire. "Beau's being a twat. Vincent doesn't help."

"There certainly is a lot of testosterone here at the moment," Madison says. "Would be nice to have another woman about."

She's not subtle.

"I don't disagree with you. If it were up to me, Ellie would be here." I know Nathan thinks I've given up. I haven't, but I can't force her to spend time with me. I can't force her to love me back.

"Have you actually checked with your publisher that you being a practicing doctor is something they want?" Nathan asks.

"I don't need to. It was practically the first thing any of them said to me." I'd had conversations with all three editors, just as Mrs. Fletcher told me I would. All of them liked the fact that I was still working in a hospital.

"Could you drop down the number of days you do?"

I shake my head. "Already checked. Hospital says they're already paying too much to locums." As soon as the words are out of my mouth, realization dawns. I sit up and swing my legs around so my feet hit the floor.

Nathan and I speak at the same time. "I should locum."

"Yeah," he says. "Can you do a couple of days a month or something?"

"I can do what I want because I won't be contracted," I say. "I've got a mate from med school. Locuming is all she's ever done because she's A and E and hates night work, so she just takes day shifts that need filling. I don't know why I didn't think about it."

"Saves you from doing a job you hate that keeps you away from the woman you're in love with." Madison's absentmindedly playing with the hem of her jumper—no one would ever know she's completely hit the nail on the head.

What am I doing? I'm forcing myself to do a job that makes me miserable and it's the cause of the breakdown of my relationship.

"Fuck it," I say. "Even if I can't locum, I'm handing in my notice. I'll tell the publisher my girlfriend's moving to France and I'm going with her. If they don't like it...I had three fucking offers for that book. If they don't like it, I'll find someone who does."

I stand, ready to take action, but I'm not quite sure what my next move is. I don't want to ambush Ellie and call her to tell her. But at the same time, I don't want her to think me resigning is some kind of leverage to get her to take me back. No, I'm resigning and moving to Paris. It's a done deal.

THIRTY-FOUR

Ellie

I deliberately didn't bring much, but it seems a bit pathetic that I'm confident I can live with what's in the two suitcases I brought with me.

At least I have a view. Of Paris.

I glance out the floor-to-ceiling windows to an unmistakably Parisian street. The wrought iron Juliet balconies, blue oblong street signs, the boulangerie on every corner. Yes, I'm definitely in Paris.

It's wonderful.

And it's lonely.

I miss Zach.

I'm furious at myself. He was the first man I'd cared for since Shane, and I had to go and fall for him in such a short space of time.

I unzip my suitcase and start to pull out what I've brought with me. It's mainly clothes, but of course I have paperwork, toiletries, and the keyring I bought in the general store on the Isle of Rum.

I hold it up to the light. It's just a grey, polished stone

with slivers of white quartz running through it. Simple but beautiful. I pull out the keys to my new flat and transfer them onto the keyring. The ring itself is sprung so tight that I break my thumbnail, but eventually I manage to slide my new keys on.

My phone buzzes in my pocket and I pull it out. My face flashes with heat and my stomach burns when I see the name.

But without thinking, I answer it.

Because I've never said no to Shane.

"Ellie, Ellie, Ellie." His voice is a wave of cold water, cooling me instantly, turning me to stone.

"Why are you calling me?"

"A favor really. I've gotten myself into a mess. Fifi is... you've probably heard, she's pregnant."

I hadn't heard but I feel nothing. I'm numb. Has he really called to tell me this?

"So?" I ask.

"So she can't handle all the admin anymore. Pregnancy brain, she says." He pauses. "To be honest, she was never as good as you with that stuff. And now she's pregnant. She's going to be busy with the kid. I'm not going to be able to handle everything." He pauses. What is he waiting for? Congratulations?

"I need you to come back."

My stomach heaves and I stagger to the sofa and perch on the arm. He can't be serious. He can't be asking me this. Not now. Not after everything.

"Obviously we'd need to sort out salary and that kind of thing. I'd pay you fairly—although, you know there's less money in this game than there used to be. You know the job. You're good at it. It's the perfect solution for both of us."

Us? When was there ever an *us*?

"Ellie, Ellie, Ellie," he says again. I used to think it was cute when he'd address me like that. I'd never deny him anything when he spoke to me like he is now: demands disguised as requests. Petulance disguised as dependence. Not that I denied him much no matter how he spoke to me.

"What, Shane?" I ask. I want to put the phone down, or throw it down the loo or out the window. I want to stamp on it and make sure he can never contact me again, but I don't. I keep the phone pressed to my ear and I listen.

"Come on, babe, what do you think? It's perfect, isn't it?"

What do I think? I think a lot of things.

"I can see how it's the perfect solution for *you*," I say.

"Exactly. I know the kind of girl you are—you're not one to hold a grudge. You're not one of those psycho girls. We were over long before Fifi came on the scene. You know what's good for you."

I replay what he's just said in my head. He's manipulating me—trying to position me as having a mental issue if I don't want to go back and work for my cheating ex-boyfriend and his knocked-up new flame. Has he always done this? It's so transparent.

Why would he think after everything he's done to me that I would come back and manage him? Because I've always done everything he's ever wanted. I've been his unwitting servant ever since we first got together.

"You're right," I reply. "I'm not holding a grudge." It's true. I don't wish him harm. I realize, I don't even hate him anymore.

But I'm done being hurt by him. I'm done being manipulated by him. I'm done being his servant.

"Good girl," he says. "You can start as soon as you like.

You know we always work well together, you and me. It's going to be great. Just like the old days."

Oh. My. God. He actually thinks I'm going to say yes.

"Shane, I'm not coming back to work for you," I say.

"What?" he says. "But you said yourself you're not holding a grudge. I hope you're not lying to me." His tone hardens a little, and I recognize the change in approach.

Familiar nausea sloshes in my stomach, but I push it away. He often used to accuse me of something I hadn't done, and now I realize it was to get me to do what he wanted. I'm not lying to him—there's no need, but guilt still grips me around the chest. I haven't done anything wrong. I'm not sure I ever did. I take a breath, and when I exhale, the feeling eases.

If he doesn't get his way by pretending to be nice, he'll try gentle manipulation. If that doesn't work, he'll try and make me feel bad. If that doesn't work, plain old shouting and calling me names used to do it.

"I hope you find someone, Shane. There's no reason to call me again."

A calmness settles in me and I zone out from what he's saying. I can tell by his tone that he's agitated, but I don't tune into the words. Whatever tethered us together has been broken. His power over me has dissolved. And I'm no longer afraid.

The emotional bruises have faded and I'm healed. I'm not the woman I was when I was with him.

I'm about to be a student at Le Cordon Bleu.

I live in Paris.

And I'm in love with Zach Cove.

With that last thought, I hang up.

THIRTY-FIVE

Ellie

How do you tell someone you wish you'd never called things off? It's the kind of thing that really should be done in person, but I don't know the next time I'll be back in London. Who knows what could happen in the meantime?

I've been such an idiot. All the while I was trying to protect myself, when the wounds from my relationship had already healed.

I'm not the same person who put up with the shit Shane dealt out. I know better now. And Zach is partly why. He showed me how low my bar was, and gave me a new benchmark for what to expect from a man.

Not that any other man could ever hope to reach it.

My cases are half unpacked and I just want to repack them and run back to Gare du Nord. Just for a few days, so I can see Zach again.

But I can't. Classes start tomorrow, and anyway, Zach is unlikely to forgive me. He tried to tell me again and again we could make it work, but I shut him down time after time. Why should he give me another chance?

But a wise voice inside reminds me that Zach isn't Shane. He's not interested in punishing me. He wants me to be happy.

I pull out my phone and I bring up his number. I can't wait—I've got to talk to him and tell him how I feel. My heart is thundering as I press call because everything has changed. I always wanted to be with him, but now I'm prepared to take the risk of doing everything I can to make sure we're together—whether we're in the same city or not.

"Hey, I was just thinking about you," he answers.

His smooth, velvety voice slips down my spine and my face heats at the thought of the things I want to do to the man.

"Same," I reply. He's all I can think of. I need to find a way to tell him I want him. And I trust him. I trust *us*.

"That's nice to hear," he says. "I was going to call you. Wish you good luck for tomorrow and tell you some news."

A knock at the door interrupts my thoughts and I head over to unlock it. "Hang on," I say. "There's someone at my door. Let me just see what they want."

I fiddle with the unfamiliar brass knobs and locks, trying the door several times before I manage to yank it open.

A mixture of joy and relief spills over me as Zach stands before me.

"You're here," I say, not really believing what's right in front of me. My life is too good to be true right now.

"Wanted to wish you luck."

I want to throw myself at him and jump into his arms. But we need to talk. I open the door wide and he passes me, that now-familiar frisson of electricity sparking between us.

It's so good to have him here. The flat instantly feels more like home.

"That's nice. And you came all this way."

He's grinning when he turns to face me. "Of course I did. Nice place," he says.

"It's small." *But big enough for two*, I don't say.

"Great view." He's looking right at me when he says this.

"I wanted to...tell you something." I don't know how to say, *I think I made a monumental fuckup by ending things between us and I've changed my mind.*

"Talk to me," he says. He takes a seat on the bright red sofa and pats the cushion next to him.

"I've realized a few things," I say.

"Like how much you miss me?"

I move to the sofa but I hover, unready to sit down just yet. "Yes, as a matter of fact."

He nods, a small smile on his lips, as if he was expecting me to say this.

"Have you changed your mind? About being together?"

Is he actually in my head? Or maybe my body language is giving me away. Or maybe he was expecting me to be lonely in Paris and reach for something familiar. But that's not it. It's not company I want: it's him.

"Yes," I say in a half whisper.

He reaches for my hand and pulls me down on the sofa next to him, but he doesn't let go of my hand. He threads his fingers between mine and sweeps his thumb over my palm.

"And not because I don't know anyone in Paris and I'm lonely."

"So why now?" he asks.

"Because of the man you are. And the woman you make me."

He pulls me onto his lap and cups my face in his hands. The electricity sparks and crackles until it just becomes white noise—it's just who we are together. "I think this is long overdue, don't you?"

As if being held back on a lead, my pulse throbs under my skin in anticipation. I nod and he sweeps his lips over mine, so gently that I can barely feel him.

I groan. I need more. I need all of him.

I sink into him, giving myself up to his lips, his tongue, the press of his fingers. I should have known from that first kiss that there was no going back. I hadn't figured it out then; I have now. What I have with Zach is rare. And it's not to be given up because I'm afraid. Or because I don't feel worthy. It's to be cherished and nurtured and brought out of the fog and into the sun and worshipped.

He trails soft kisses down my neck and I whisper, "I love you."

He stops and pulls back. "I love you, Ellie."

"I want to do the long-distance thing," I say, just to make sure he knows I'm all in. "London to Paris isn't such a big deal, and it's only a year."

He smooths my hair around my ear. "We don't need to."

My heart starts to bang against my chest. He can't have meant this to be a goodbye. Not after that kiss? He's come to Paris, after all. "I want to," I say. "Really, it will be fine. We can alternate weekends in London and Paris."

"I don't think so," he says. My stomach twists into knot after knot after knot.

I clamp my hands to his shoulders. "Zach, I'm—"

He must see the panic in my eyes. "Ellie, it's fine," he says. "I'm moving to Paris."

"What?" I say. My heart seems to stop beating and I forget how to breathe. What did he just say? "But your job. The book."

"We're only here for a year. My book won't even be

published by then, and I refuse to give up being with you just to work in a job I don't enjoy."

"So you're going to resign?"

"I already have. I've told my publisher, too. And anyway, I'm going to locum. I'll do a few days here and there, and they can still say I'm a practicing doctor."

Blood starts to flow around my body again but I don't know what to say. I don't know why I ever doubted Zach. He's never given me any reason to doubt him and now, when I've pushed him away, half drowning in my past, he's pulled me out and done whatever it took to make everything okay. "I love you," I say. It's all I can manage to convey how much I appreciate him.

He smiles, and it's the best thing about being in Paris.

"So, did you bring a case?"

He shrugs. "Just my backpack. I don't need much and I have to go back to London tomorrow. I have work."

"So you just came to say good luck?"

"That, and to tell you I love you, and that I'll be moving to Paris."

"So this time it's me with an unexpected houseguest." I can't think of anyone I'd rather have turn up on my doorstep unannounced.

"No chance of being snowed in unfortunately," he says, a devilish twinkle in his eye.

"We can always pretend."

"My thoughts exactly."

THIRTY-SIX

Zach

I'm trying to keep my breathing steady, but it's not easy being this close to Ellie, my hands on her, her hands on me. I gave up my job to move to Paris in order to save a relationship that's too precious to lose, only to find Ellie is prepared to overcome her biggest fears to do the same. To know she wants this as much as I do, cements things between us. Not that we were ever casual, but this—now—it's permanent.

"Thank you for not giving up on me," she says between rushed kisses as we unbutton and unpeel, strip and pull our clothes from ourselves and each other.

"Thank you for not giving up on us," I say. "I know how difficult it must have been for you to consider long distance, to trust that you wouldn't lose yourself."

We both still. Naked, facing each other, she strokes her palm down my cheek. "I wouldn't let me." The corners of her mouth curl up in a half smile. "And *you* wouldn't let me."

She knows me. She trusts me.

"We're both on the same team." I cup her face and press

my lips to hers, breathing in the familiar scent of sunshine and lilacs.

She nods, rounding her hand over my arse. I lift her up, grab my wallet, and walk us over to the bedroom. This isn't going to be a quick fuck. I want to take my time with her, like we're snowed in and have nowhere to be.

I lay her down and brace my arms either side of her head. I take in her deep brown eyes. They've lost the glaze of anxiety they had when I first met her and gained a softness that wasn't there before. Her hands slide up my sides and she bends her knees to rest on either side of my hips.

"We fit," I say.

"Perfectly," she replies.

I bend and press a kiss to her neck, just below her ear, and the scent of lilacs drifts over me afresh.

Her fingers scrape the back of my neck and I work my way down, pressing kisses slowly and deliberately over every dip and curve. I need to reintroduce myself to her body and let it know that this time, I'm not going anywhere.

She wiggles beneath me and I press my palm flat across her stomach, smoothing the other one down, down, down, finding her warmth, nestling my fingers into her folds. She tries to arch her back, pressing into my palm, but I keep her in place as I work my fingers into her, my thumb on her clit circling and pressing.

I close my eyes for a long moment, reveling in her sounds. The gasps and the moans, my whispered name on her breath.

It's been too long.

I shift and she reaches for me. I'm already hard, but the feel of her fingers on my cock pulls the blood from my entire body, as if every drop is fighting to be near her.

"You feel like velvet and stone all in one," she says and I let my head fall back as she works her fist up my shaft.

Pressure builds in my chest, leaving me breathless, and I capture her wrist before she can move any more. I'm dangerously close to spilling all over her and I need this first bit, the bit before forever, to last a little longer.

"Are you trying to spoil my fun?" she asks.

"Just prolonging it for both of us," I reply, dropping her wrist and removing my hand from between her legs so that I'm not touching her. I sit back on my knees and blow out a breath.

I need a second.

She presses up on her elbows and I have to look away at the movement of her breasts. She sees my struggle and kneels up opposite me. "Let this be about both of us," she says, her tone soft but determined. She reaches for the wallet discarded on the bed beside us and takes a condom from where I keep them, tearing the foil open. I reach to help her but just a small shake of her head tells me she's got this.

Tentatively at first, she positions the condom over my crown, lifting her gaze once to reach mine, but I have no notes. She gets back to it, rolling it down my shaft, and I squeeze my eyes shut, trying to block out the sensation. She shifts onto her bottom and hooks her legs either side of where I'm kneeling and lies back.

"About both of us," she says. "That means you too."

"Ellie," I say. She should know how close I am. Being back near her, this close to her, knowing that we've both sacrificed for and committed to each other, is the biggest aphrodisiac I have ever experienced. I feel like I'm trying to stop myself from falling into a cloud of pure joy.

"Me too," she says in reply.

I growl in gratitude and lean over her, guiding my cock to her entrance. I glance back at her.

"I love you," she says.

I push inside, feeling her engulf me body and soul. "I love you too."

I move slowly and surely, drawing out every second, but within minutes we're both breathless, panting and crying out with pleasure and understanding.

We're living our futures. Together.

EPILOGUE

Three months later

Zach

It's just gone seven. The rattling of the doorknob on our bedroom door as Ellie heads to have a shower is my cue to save my work in progress—the second in the Butler Mysteries—and close my laptop. I've written some bloody good words today, as well as all the other stuff I've done to prepare for tonight.

We settled into our Paris routine quickly. As soon as Ellie gets home from the school, she hops in the shower and then we meet in the kitchen, share some wine and food, and talk about her day. I don't ever have much to say. Even though I spend part of each day walking the streets of Paris, my mind is so occupied by plot and characters, I sometimes forget where I've been. Ellie, on the other hand, is full of stories about the people in her class, the lack of patience of some of the French tutors, and particularly, Chef Jean-Paul, their main instructor and personal torturer.

"Hey, baby," Ellie calls into the living area. I open the

study door. I may have insisted on a bigger, upgraded flat, given I was working from home each day and we needed two people to live together and not kill each other. The new place is about four times as big as Ellie's previous accommodations, with a roof terrace overlooking the Seine and the pretty Parisian lead roofs and winding streets.

I lean against the wall, watching her as she busies herself in the kitchen. I think Parisian light must be different to London light. Ellie looks even more beautiful to me in Paris than she did in London or Rum.

"Hey, gorgeous," I say when she looks in my direction.

She grins at the compliment and half skips toward me, jumping into my arms.

"You smell delicious," I say. "Like lilacs."

"You *are* delicious," she replies as she presses a kiss to my lips. Her legs wrapped around me, her fingers in my hair, I can't help but growl. This could turn into something more really fast, but I'll have to pull back. Dinner first.

"I warmed up the duck from yesterday," I say.

Ellie braces her hands on my shoulders and narrows her eyes. "You did?"

"Yeah, and I made those potatoes you showed me a couple of weekends ago."

"The Hasselbacks?" she asks.

"Are they the ones that look like hedgehogs? If so, yes, the Hasselbacks."

"Did I turn you into a cook?" she asks, sliding out of my arms and taking my hand as we walk over to the kitchen.

"Not in any sense. I just thought it would be nice for me to cook for you this once. Although I don't know what it's going to taste like."

She runs a finger over my jaw. "I don't care what it

tastes like. It might be the nicest thing anyone has done for anyone in the entire history of the world."

"Really? Well, wait until you taste it." I set about taking the duck from the oven and putting it on plates, while Ellie dishes up the potatoes and the green beans.

"Why do I always associate you with green beans?" she asks.

"I have no idea. Take it up with your therapist," I say.

She laughs and I pause what I'm doing to take it in. Watching her happy. With me. It never gets old.

"Shall I set the table?" she asks.

"Hmmm, I had a different idea."

"The balcony?" she suggests. "The sun and the blue sky make it feel like June."

"I think Paris is having its summer early. I swear I need to start putting on sun cream before my walks."

"Watching the sunset from the balcony will be perfect," she says.

"Let's go upstairs to the roof terrace," I say. We've never eaten up there. Up until today, there hasn't been anywhere to sit. But I've fixed that. The sunset over the Parisian rooftops is just the right atmosphere I'm looking for.

"Sounds good," she says. "I'll bring the napkins, cutlery, and some water."

I take the plates and follow her up the spiral staircase to the roof garden.

"What?" she says as she gets to the top of the stairs, her voice filled with shock and wonder. I have to bite back a grin. "When did you do this?"

I managed to find the same tartan that was on the sofa in the cottage in Rum—it's taken me a while—but I got some blankets made and they're on the floor, along with some oversized cushions and a low table.

We set our things down on the table and she puts her arms around my neck. "Is this the same as the sofa in Rum?" I nod, pleased she's remembered. "Gosh, the view is so pretty up here."

"It's beautiful," I say, looking right at her. Watching her in the setting sun over Paris, I can't hold it in any longer. "Marry me, Ellie."

Her eyes widen and her mouth slides into a smile. She shrugs one shoulder. "Of course."

"Of course."

"Of course I'll marry you. But you know that." She strokes my face and I sink into her touch, knowing I'll have it forever. "We've both known we're going to be together forever since..." She looks at me to fill in the missing word.

"The first night in Rum," I add.

She nods and we both sink onto the cushions facing Paris below. "Yeah. Definitely that first night in Rum. Married or not—it doesn't change anything. For me."

"I don't want you to do anything you don't want to do," I say. I understand the history with Shane now and I don't want her to agree to marry me if she doesn't want it for herself. But if it were up to me to choose, I'd marry her. I'd tell the world this woman promised to be mine forever.

"I want to be with you forever," she says. "I have no doubt about that. But I don't care to get married. If you want to, I'm happy to."

I start to protest, but she places a finger on my lips to silence me.

"Doing things because they'll make you happy, makes me happy. Not because I don't know anything but to sacrifice myself, but because we're a team. You do things to make me happy. You moved to Paris, for goodness' sake. We're equals. We give and take. That's what a partnership is. That's what a marriage is—ring or no ring."

It's almost exactly how my father described his marriage to my mother, and we could do a lot worse than have a marriage like theirs.

"I love you," I say.

"I love you," she replies. "And I'll stand up in front of our friends and family in a white dress and tell everyone that I plan to love you forever. It's not such a sacrifice." The smile she beams up at me warms me, like she's the sun and I'm just along for the ride, soaking up her rays. "And I'll wear your ring—as long as it's pretty."

I take the ring box from under the table and glance at her as she shoots me a look that says I've surprised her, and she's not sad about it. I open it and she gasps. I hadn't realized that was the reaction I was looking for until now.

"Yeah, I'll wear *that* ring," she says, and now it's my time to chuckle.

I take the oval diamond perched on a platinum band and place it on her finger. It fits perfectly.

"I do," she says. "Until the end of time."

A WEEK *after that*

Ellie

From the passenger seat, I hit loudspeaker and answer the second call from my mum within half an hour. We're going to Norfolk first and then heading south to my parents in a couple of days. It's the first time my parents will meet Zach, but we've done video calls. When I first told them that Zach and I were together, I could tell from the sighs and the punctured silences that they expected Zach to be a lot like Shane. But unbeknownst to me, he called them before he proposed, and things shifted. Since then, it's like Zach's the son they never had.

"I didn't ask whether there's anything Zach doesn't eat," she says.

"I'll eat anything, Mrs. Frost." He glances over at me with a grin and I can't help but reach for his thigh. He's done nothing but encourage the rebuilding of my relationship with my parents. He was the one who invited them to Paris, and they're coming in a couple of months.

My mother laughs. "Oh good. We'll probably have toad in the hole."

"My favorite," Zach says, shooting me a smile that warms me to my core. "I'm so looking forward to meeting you both."

Zach starts to indicate and slows as we approach his parents' house.

"Can I call you later, Mum? We're just arriving."

"No problem," she says. "Have a wonderful time."

I hang up and Zach's hand is on my thigh now. "You okay?" he asks.

I couldn't be better. I can't remember being happier than I am right in that moment, the sun on my face, Zach's ring on my hand, and the future filled with promise. "I love you," I reply.

The side of his mouth curls up. "I love you too."

We pull into the driveway of Zach's parents and the sun is shining so fiercely, it feels like the south of France, not East Anglia. Dog is the first to meet us. This time he comes racing towards me, completely ignoring Zach.

"You're definitely part of the family now," Zach says.

I bend down and scratch Dog behind the ears. He twists his head so my fingers go deeper and I laugh. He knows how to get what he wants from women—typical Cove man, from what I've witnessed.

Before we've even got our bags out of the boot, Madison and Nathan pull up. They've been to see us in Paris and I've grown really close to Madison. It's fun hearing about her cravings.

"Oh my gosh, you're really showing now!" I say as she slips out of the car.

"My cankles are matched only by my huge belly."

I pull her in for a hug and her bump presses against my tummy. "Can I touch?" I ask as I release her.

She nods, rounding her stomach with her palm as if clearing the way for me. "I'm massive for five months," Madison says, pulling her black jacket across her as if it might close—which it won't, as there's at least a ten-centimeter gap between the sides. "If I didn't know better, I'd say it was twins."

"It's not twins," Nathan barks. "Definitely not twins."

I start to laugh. He looks horrified at the thought, even though he knows it's not true.

The sounds of a helicopter come into focus and I grab the tin of brownies I brought with me from Paris, as well as one of our weekend bags. Zach goes to help Nathan with their own things.

The flickering sound of the blades gets louder and we all look up as the black helicopter appears in the sky.

"It looks like it's headed right to us," I say. But no one can hear me, it's too loud.

We all stand and stare at the bright blue sky as the helicopter lands in the fields just across from Zach's parents' house. I glance over at Nathan and Zach, who exchange a speaking glance.

The door to the helicopter opens and a tall, dark-haired man in a suit gets out. He looks familiar.

Zach nods toward the house and we all go inside.

"Did you know he was coming?" Zach asks Nathan.

Nathan shakes his head. "No idea. He was here at Christmas. And now Easter too? It's not because he loves Mum's apple pie."

"Who doesn't love my apple pie?" Carole sticks her head around the kitchen door and sees us all dumping bags and taking our shoes off.

"Did you know Vincent's here again?"

"He called yesterday. Wanted to know if he could spend Easter here."

"Is he running from the mob or something?" Nathan asks. I've learned Nathan is definitely the most suspicious of the Cove brothers. When I asked Zach about it, he said one day he'd fill me in. There's obviously a story there.

"Running from the mob?" Carole says, turning and heading into the kitchen, the four of us following like we're toddlers playing trains. "He likes my apple pie. And he's spending a lot more time in the UK at the moment. Business something-or-other."

"Is he allowed to land in that field?" Nathan asks.

"No," Beau says as he appears in the doorway. "I looked it up after he nearly blew the roof off at Christmas."

"Blew the roof off?" Carole says. "You're exaggerating. The noise doesn't last long and it's a lot quicker than driving up from London."

"Don't encourage him," John says as he follows Beau in.

"He could get fined if he was reported."

John laughs. "Like he cares. He's got more money than —and be careful," he interrupts himself, prodding his finger at Zach and Nathan. "He likes the women, that one. Keep hold of Madison and Ellie. They're good girls and I like having them around."

Warmth grows in my stomach.

"Dad," Nathan and Zach groan.

"They're not our prisoners," Zach says. "Madison and Ellie aren't with us by accident, ready to fall under Vincent's spell if he so much as looks at them."

"Weeeell," Madison says. "He's *very* good looking. And rich as holy hell."

Zach, Beau, and I laugh. Nathan's the richest man I know and also one of the most handsome. Just slightly less so than Zach.

Nathan rolls his eyes, and as he passes Madison, she pulls him toward her and kisses his cheek. "But you're stuck with me at least until this kid hits eighteen. No way I'm doing it on my own."

I set the tin of brownies down on the side by the kettle and Carole grabs my arm. "Thank you, Ellie. It's very sweet of you to bake for us. Zach says your brownies are the best he's ever eaten."

She's so warm—the entire family is *so warm*—it's a wonder Zach ever thought any of them might be unhappy with him for not wanting to be a doctor.

"You okay?" Zach whispers in my ear as he comes up behind me and snakes his arms around my waist.

How could I be anything but okay? Despite my indifference about getting married, it turns out I quite like some of the perks, especially the ring I'm sporting. We're both facing away from the room, so I place my hand over Zach's and we both look at it.

"Have you got something you want to tell us?" Carole asks us. I snap my head up and she's looking at us and then nods toward my finger.

"We're getting married," I say, breaking into a grin and wiggling my hand in her direction.

Madison squeals and I'm pulled into a hug by her and the baby, as Zach hugs Carole.

"I knew it," Beau says. "Totally called it. As soon as you brought her home, I knew it."

John thwacks Beau with a tea towel. "We all saw it, Beau. We're not blind."

Everyone hugs us and takes a peek at the ring.

"Hey, everyone." The commotion silences for a second as we all look up to see American-accented Vincent standing in the doorway, ducking so he doesn't hit his head.

"What's happening? Is Madison in labor?"

"Zach and Ellie are engaged, and I called it," Beau says.

"Mazel," Vincent says. "Take the house in Rum as my engagement present."

I laugh. He can't be serious.

"What are you doing here?" Nathan asks.

"Business," he replies. "And to spend some time with my British family."

"It was your idea to have five kids," John says to Carole. "It will be nice to have a big family, you said. All I get from a big family is a small portion of apple pie and a headache. And now apparently we've adopted another one. Like five isn't enough."

Carole rolls her eyes but ignores her husband.

"Did I tell you I bought a vineyard?" Vincent says, ignoring John's complaints like he didn't hear them. "In Argentina. Turns out a great Malbec." He holds up two bottles.

"Vincent," John says, his tone serious as he steps forward to inspect the wine. "This is my favorite wine. Young man, all is forgiven. You're definitely my favorite son from now on. Get that bloody bottle open and pour me a glass." He spins around and points his finger. "None of you lot touch it. Two bottles won't go very far."

"Good job I have a vineyard," Vincent says. "There's a case in the hallway and a hundred and forty-four bottles will arrive tomorrow by courier. We're not going to run out."

Carole shrieks as John thwacks her on the bottom with a tea towel. "Did you hear that, my love?" he says. "A hundred and forty-four bottles."

Vincent comes up to Zach and me and kisses me on the cheek, congratulating us on our engagement. "You know, I'd really like you to have that place in Rum. As you know, I've never been there. And you began there. It's right that you should have it."

"You can't gift us a house," Zach says. "It's...weird."

"Okay," he replies. "Then you can give me some advice later in exchange. There's a couple of business issues I'm having a little problem with. Wouldn't mind your and Nathan's take. Then you can take the house in return. If you don't, I'll only deliberately lose it in my next poker tournament."

"We'll take it," I say. "You never know—we might retire there."

Zach laughs. "If you say so. And I can chase you around the kitchen with a tea towel, complaining about the dog."

"I can think of worse things," I say. I already know growing old with Zach will be the best future I can possibly hope for. He might hate being a doctor, but he's brought me back to life. I'm better with him, and what's wonderful is that I know he's better with me, too. Neither of us are perfect, but we fit perfectly together.

. . .

READ VINCENT'S story in **Dr. CEO**

Read Nathan & Madison's story in **Private Player**

Read Jacob & Sutton in **Dr. Off Limits**

If you like enemies to lovers office romances, try **The British Knight**

BOOKS BY LOUISE BAY

All books are stand alone

The Doctors Series

Dr. Off Limits

Dr. Perfect

Dr. CEO

Dr. Fake Fiancé

The Mister Series

Mr. Mayfair

Mr. Knightsbridge

Mr. Smithfield

Mr. Park Lane

Mr. Bloomsbury

Mr. Notting Hill

The Christmas Collection

14 Days of Christmas

The Player Series

International Player

Private Player

Dr. Off Limits

Standalones

Hollywood Scandal

Love Unexpected

Hopeful

The Empire State Series

The Gentleman Series

The Ruthless Gentleman

The Wrong Gentleman

The Royals Series

King of Wall Street

Park Avenue Prince

Duke of Manhattan

The British Knight

The Earl of London

The Nights Series

Indigo Nights

Promised Nights

Parisian Nights

Faithful

What kind of books do you like?

Friends to lovers

Mr. Mayfair

Promised Nights

International Player

Fake relationship (marriage of convenience)

Duke of Manhattan

Mr. Mayfair

Mr. Notting Hill

Enemies to Lovers

King of Wall Street

The British Knight

The Earl of London

Hollywood Scandal

Parisian Nights

14 Days of Christmas

Mr. Bloomsbury

Office Romance/ Workplace romance

Mr. Knightsbridge

King of Wall Street

The British Knight

The Ruthless Gentleman

Mr. Bloomsbury

Second Chance

International Player

Hopeful

Best Friend's Brother

Promised Nights

Vacation/Holiday Romance

The Empire State Series

Indigo Nights

The Ruthless Gentleman

The Wrong Gentleman

Love Unexpected

14 Days of Christmas

Holiday/Christmas Romance

14 Days of Christmas

This Christmas

British Hero

Promised Nights (British heroine)

Indigo Nights (American heroine)

Hopeful (British heroine)

Duke of Manhattan (American heroine)

The British Knight (American heroine)

The Earl of London (British heroine)

The Wrong Gentleman (American heroine)

The Ruthless Gentleman (American heroine)

International Player (British heroine)

Mr. Mayfair (British heroine)

Mr. Knightsbridge (American heroine)

Mr. Smithfield (American heroine)

Private Player (British heroine)

Mr. Bloomsbury (American heroine)

14 Days of Christmas (British heroine)

Mr. Notting Hill (British heroine)

Single Dad

King of Wall Street

Mr. Smithfield

Sign up to the Louise Bay mailing list www.louisebay/newsletter

Read more at www.louisebay.com